SUMMERSET ABBEY

A BLOOM
IN WINTER

SUMMERSET ABBEY

A BLOOM
IN WINTER

A NOVEL

T. J. BROWN

GALLERY BOOKS

NEW YORK   LONDON   TORONTO   SYDNEY   NEW DELHI

G

Gallery Books
A Division of Simon & Schuster, Inc.
1230 Avenue of the Americas
New York, NY 10020

First Gallery Books trade paperback edition March 2013

GALLERY BOOKS and colophon are registered
trademarks of Simon & Schuster, Inc.

For information about special discounts for bulk purchases,
please contact Simon & Schuster Special Sales at
1-866-506-1949 or business@simonandschuster.com.

The Simon & Schuster Speakers Bureau can bring authors to your
live event. For more information or to book an event contact
the Simon & Schuster Speakers Bureau at 1-866-248-3049
or visit our website at www.simonspeakers.com.

Manufactured in the United States of America

1 3 5 7 9 10 8 6 4 2

Library of Congress Cataloging-in-Publication Data is available.

ISBN 978-1-4516-9905-0
ISBN 978-1-4516-9907-4 (ebook)

This book is dedicated with all my love and gratitude to Dr. Colin Cave and Dr. Katie Deming and their teams— amazing doctors and extraordinary people.

ACKNOWLEDGMENTS

It is during a major crisis that you come to realize just how incredibly blessed you are to have a support system, and the health crisis that occurred during the writing of the Summerset Series was no different. Beyond the incredible people in the publishing industry who made this book happen—my agent, Molly Glick, and my editors, Lauren McKenna, and Alexandra Lewis—there were many people in my other life who showed me kindnesses and support, both large and small.

First and foremost, I wish to thank my family, Alan, Ethan, and Megan. You make everything worthwhile.

Next, I give props to my tribe, who fetched and carried and, most importantly, made me laugh. Billy, Vickie, Jeff, Jasmine, Anita, Dave—I love you guys!

More thanks to my bestie, Ann Marie, and her husband, Chris—we can always count on you.

I want to thank Bill and Debbie, neighbors extraordinaire—surely sharing a fence has never been so fun.

Then there were my awesome local writer peeps who propped me up in so many different ways: Amy Pike Danicic, April Henry, Delilah Marvell, Jessie Smith, and Amber Keyser. No one gets writers like writers.

Love you all.

SUMMERSET ABBEY

 BLOOM

IN WINTER

CHAPTER ONE

Victoria paced the length of Summerset Abbey's Great Hall, impatience rippling through her body. In London the mail had come at the same time every day, like clockwork. But at the sprawling country estate that she now called home, the mail's arrival remained frustratingly unpredictable and entirely dependent on her uncle's will. When he was away from Summerset Abbey, it was even more haphazard, unless her ladyship needed something posted or was expecting an important invitation.

When she reached the end of the hall, Victoria doubled back, marching furiously forward, ignoring the light from the circular skylight, which danced and sparkled off the marble columns lining the room. Even the breathtaking frescoes depicting angels floating above battle scenes that covered the domed ceiling, which normally captured her gaze when she entered this hallway, remained hazy on the fringes of her tunnel vision. And all because of an inept mail delivery system that harkened back to the bloody Dark Ages. She'd be waiting outside on the drive if she weren't afraid of the suspicion that would raise, especially after learning that Aunt Charlotte, or Lady Summerset Ambrosia Huxley Buxton, noticed everything that happened at Summerset.

Well, almost everything. Victoria smiled. Her aunt didn't know how often she snuck away to her secret room in the unused portion of the manor to practice her typing and shorthand, study botany, or craft her own articles on plants and plant lore. She didn't know that her own daughter, Elaine, could mix up a mean gin sling, or that Victoria's older sister, Rowena, had gone flying in a plane and had kissed a pilot. So maybe her forbidding aunt Charlotte wasn't so infallible after all.

But Aunt Charlotte had known how to get rid of Prudence. Victoria frowned, a familiar ache twisting in her stomach.

She heard a car in the front drive and she flew to the servants' door behind the stairwell, not caring whether the servants resented her intrusion on their domain. The mail would be taken to Mr. Cairns, who would sort it out in his office, and then presented to Aunt Charlotte, to Uncle Conrad, or to whomever it was addressed. Victoria, however, couldn't stand by and wait for her letter to eventually find its way into her hands. She'd counted the days carefully and knew in her bones she would receive an answer today.

The servants bobbed their heads as she rushed past them. No doubt Aunt Charlotte had already heard of her sudden obsession with the mail. If asked, Victoria would just tell her she was awaiting a letter from a friend and then whine about being bored out here in the country. Aunt Charlotte deplored whining.

She stuck her head around the doorjamb of Cairns's office. "Did I get anything, Cairns?"

The man jumped and Victoria hid a grin. Very little ever surprised this supremely self-contained man, but Victoria had long ago made it her mission to try. She'd spent almost every summer vacation since she was a small child trying to ruffle Cairns, who had no outstanding features except his unflappable composure. She knew he could barely stand her, and the girls used to find it funny.

Now, of course, it would be better if Cairns were on her side, but old habits were hard to break.

His mouth tightened. "I'm just going through it now, Miss Victoria."

She waited, almost screaming with impatience as he deliberately took his time going through the post and sorting it into different piles. She knew he had found her letter by the quivering of his nostrils. He held it out and she snatched it from his hands as if worried he was about to change his mind.

"Thank you, Cairns!" She whisked out of the servants' quarters and up to her room, praying she wouldn't run into her cousin, wanting to break up the boredom by sneaking down to play billiards and smoke cigarettes, or Rowena, wanting to go riding or walking or whatever she could to chase away the guilt she felt over Prudence. Victoria felt bad for both her sister and her cousin, but right now, she had more important things to do.

Once in her room, she put the letter on her white and gold empire dressing table and stared at it, half-afraid to open it. She'd been waiting for it for so long—now that it was actually here, she was terrified it wouldn't contain the news she wanted. Finally she picked it up, crossed the soft Axminster rug, and settled down upon one of the two blue-and-white-striped chaise lounges that sat before a small white fireplace.

Inspired by Nanny Iris, a remarkable herbalist and Victoria's friend and mentor, she'd written an article on the health benefits of *Althea officinalis*, or mallow, and the history of its uses among the healing women who worked with the poor. She had sent it to one of her favorite botany magazines and to her surprise, the editor had written back, telling her he enjoyed the article, and gave her some advice on how to improve the writing. He had asked her to resubmit after she'd revised it. She'd rewritten it ten times, typing it carefully on the brand-new typewriter she had hidden in her secret room. Then she'd sent it back, praying it would be good enough to publish.

Her stomach churned. And here was her answer. Unable to take it any longer, she went to her desk and rifled through the drawers until she found her letter opener. Something fluttered to the ground when she opened it and she stared at the slip of paper, unbelieving. It was a check.

Her eyes widened and she pulled out the slip of paper that came with it. The top of the paper was embossed with the magazine's name in script.

The Botanist's Quarterly, 197 Lexington Place, London. Victoria ran her fingers over it in awe. She and her father used to pore over the magazine every time a new issue came in. A noted botanist, her father had transmitted his love of plants to his daughter and the shared passion brought them close during their last years together. It would always be the one connection she had with him that was solely hers.

He would have been so proud of her.

She wiped away the tears that gathered with an impatient hand.

Dear V. Buxton,

Thank you so much for revising your fine article, "The Many Medical Uses of Althea officinalis *Among the Lower Classes." I am delighted to tell you that we will be using your work in our summer edition of* The Botanist's Quarterly. *I would love to see more articles from you in this vein. Have*

you considered doing a study on the medical uses of plants among the poor and itinerant? At any rate, thank you again for your submission. Please don't hesitate to stop by should you be in London.
Sincerely
Harold L. Herbert
Managing Editor
The Botanist's Quarterly

Victoria read it again before picking up the check. Ten pounds. Not only was she now a published author but she'd been handsomely compensated—and praised!—for her work.

Sighing with happiness, she leaned back against the chaise. Whom could she tell? Who would understand? Not Rowena, who had become so sad and listless that she barely bothered to get dressed anymore. Not her cousin Elaine, either. Even though she and Elaine had grown closer in the months since her father's death, they still weren't to the point of sharing confidences. Kit, certainly, but Kit wouldn't be here until the weekend, if he even came. He usually came with her cousin Colin, when Colin came up from the university. He would understand her excitement— be impressed, even—but then again, he was such a tease.

But the only person she truly wanted to tell had now been gone for over a month. Had it really been that long since she'd last seen Prudence? Her heartache over Pru's abrupt departure felt just as raw as it did the day she fled from Summerset, but as much as Victoria missed her, she understood why Pru could no longer stay. She'd have left, too, had she suddenly been implicated in a Buxton family scandal that Aunt Charlotte had managed to keep buried for years.

Impulsively, she rang the bell and waited for Susie to arrive. She couldn't bear to let her aunt simply replace Pru with a new lady's maid as if Pru were an interchangeable, anonymous servant, so she relied on the scullery maid when she needed help . . . or company. Susie was the only servant who had truly been kind to Prudence, and though she couldn't take Prudence's place, Victoria felt closer to Pru when Susie was around.

Susie rushed in, her cap askew. "Sorry, miss. My hands were deep in the sink when the bell rang and Cook couldn't find my cap fast enough . . ." Her voice trailed off as she eyed Victoria. "Oh, miss, you look as if you'd just received the most wonderful gift!"

Victoria smiled and waved her check in the air. "I have. Well, not a present exactly. But look what I received in the post today!"

Susie squinted as she came closer. "It looks like a check, miss. For ten pounds?"

Victoria nodded and, taking the check, did a little dance around the room. "Yes! Yes! They paid me for an article I wrote on mallow! Can you imagine?"

Susie's eyes widened and she shook her head. "I can't! You mean like for a newspaper?"

"For a magazine!"

"Well, that's just fine, miss! My mother once had a recipe printed in the *Summerset Weekly News*, and we thought that was wonderful. That probably isn't much the same, is it?"

Victoria shook her head and checked a laugh that threatened to burst out. "Not quite, but I bet she was very happy."

"We were all very proud. Did you need anything, miss?"

Victoria shook her head, disappointment sinking her stomach. Of course it wasn't the same as telling Prudence. It wasn't even the same as telling Katie, their kitchen maid back home, who had been her friend and a fellow student at Miss Fister's Secretarial School for Young Ladies. Because she didn't really know Susie. Susie had been Prudence's friend, not hers.

Susie stood to leave. "Wait, Susie." The girl turned and Victoria saw that her cap, which she was required to wear for her duties upstairs, still rested crookedly on her head. "Have you heard anything from Prudence lately?"

A wide smile lit up Susie's plain features. "Yes, miss. I got a letter just the other day. Oh, she sounds as if she's having a wonderful time! She wrote that she and Andrew had the pleasure of staying in a luxurious hotel and dining in fine restaurants while they secured a more permanent place to live. Now they've settled into an elegant apartment near the college where Andrew's studying to be an animal doctor. As soon as he's done, they're planning to move to a big country house. She even has her own small staff!"

Victoria smiled sadly, glad that Prudence seemed to be flourishing the more distance she put between herself and Summerset. But her happiness for Pru was still tainted by guilt and sorrow. "Have you written her back yet?"

Susie shook her head. "I was going to tonight."

"Can I give you a paper to slip into your post? I don't have enough news for a full letter . . ." Her voice trailed off. She didn't want to tell Susie that Prudence hadn't written to her since she'd left, or that she didn't even have Prudence's address.

Susie nodded. "Yes, miss. I will get it tonight on my way to bed."

Victoria hurried to her desk. She pulled out a piece of paper and dipped her ebony fountain pen into her inkwell.

Dear Prudence, she wrote, and then stopped as a giant blot stained the paper. What was she supposed to say? *I'm sorry*? But for what? For discovering that her own despicable grandfather—

the Buxton patriarch—was Prudence's real father? For the insufferable snobbery of her family? For her failure to step in and defend Prudence when she was relegated to the maid's quarters upon their arrival to Summerset in the first place? *But what about the way Prudence is treating me?* Victoria thought stoutly. Prudence hadn't been in touch with her since her wedding to that sweet footman. She wrote to Susie, but coldly ignored the girl who had been like her sister.

Victoria slumped in her chair. She felt overwhelmed by the entire affair, crippled by the gravity of it all. Maybe if she pretended hard enough that it hadn't happened, she could find something to write . . . but no. Rowena had pretended not to see how horrible the situation was until it exploded all around her. Simply *willing* things to change had gotten her nowhere.

Taking a deep breath, she got out a clean piece of paper and started again.

Dearest Prudence,

I hope this letter finds you well and happy. Susie says you are settling into your new home and Andrew is studying for the exams. I wish him the best of luck. I'm sure everything will turn out all right.

Victoria stopped and chewed on her thumb. Did that sound too patronizing? Like she didn't believe he would do well on the examinations? She shook her head.

"Oh, bother."

Dipping her pen, she continued.

I have some good news to share. I wrote an article on mallow, you know, the kind of articles Father and I used to read to each other that bored you and Rowena to tears? Well, I wrote one and sent it to The Botanist's Quarterly *and what do you know, but the editor liked it and bought it! He even sent a check for ten pounds and told me he wanted to see more! So you see, all those lectures Father and I used to attend finally came in handy! Perhaps someday I will become a botanist like Father, for I have decided that is what I would truly like to do. I haven't told anyone else but you, my dear, because no one else could possibly understand . . .*

Here, Victoria stopped and took a deep, shuddering breath as grief over her father threatened to overwhelm her. When she had composed herself, she finished.

> *I miss you more than I can say.*

She paused again, wondering whether she should mention Rowena, but then decided against it. Let Rowena and Prudence sort themselves out. All she knew was that, for her, life without Prudence was growing unbearable.

> *Please write back soon.*
> *Love,*
> *Vic*

Victoria chewed on the end of the pen and then added a stanza from "My Heart and I" by Elizabeth Barrett Browning.

> *You see we're tired, my heart and I.*
> *We dealt with books, we trusted men,*
> *And in our own blood drenched the pen,*

As if such colours could not fly.
We walked too straight for fortune's end,
We loved too true to keep a friend;
At last we're tired, my heart and I.

There. Now it felt complete. Victoria put her pen and ink away and left the letter out to finish drying. She stood and stretched. A part of her longed to rush off to her secret wing of the house and set to work on her next article, but she was too restless for that. Then she remembered that there was someone else who would be delighted over the news. The same person who had given her the idea for her piece in the first place—Nanny Iris!

An hour later, Victoria was sitting at Nanny Iris's table, enjoying a delicious cream scone that even Cook, with all her expertise, could not rival.

Nanny Iris's kitchen was warm and inviting, with printed gingham curtains draped on the tiny windows and a rack of pots hanging over the sink. The scrupulously clean stone floor might have been worn and cracked in spots, but the whole cottage was so charming that Victoria never felt anything but peace here.

"That's wonderful, my dear girl. You know your father would be quite proud," the old woman said from where she stood, smiling, at the stove. She was stirring up a concoction that smelled terrible, but she assured Victoria it would help when she had a breathing episode.

Victoria nodded, unable to speak. Nanny Iris had been her father's nanny and taught him everything she had known about plants and herbs, just as she was teaching Victoria now.

Nanny Iris came over to the table and patted Victoria on her head. Even though Nanny Iris always made Victoria feel like a child rather than the confident young woman she worked so hard to embody, at least the old woman always made her feel warm and genuinely beloved. When Ro and Pru treated her like a child, she always felt patronized, insulted.

The old woman wiped her hands on her starched white apron and picked up the letter again, even though she had read it three times already. Victoria glowed. She'd been right to come here.

But instead of reading it again, Nanny Iris frowned. "Why does it say V. Buxton instead of Victoria?"

Victoria washed her scone down with a sip of tea. "Hmm? Oh, yes. I thought if I used Victoria, someone at the magazine might recognize the name and know me as my father's daughter. I'm very proud of his work, but I wish to be known for my own merits and make my own opportunities."

"Very commendable," Nanny Iris murmured. "Was there any other reason?"

"Well, I thought it sounded more established, more impressive. V. Buxton. Don't you think?"

Victoria grinned, but when she caught sight of Nanny Iris's face, her smile faded. "What? What's wrong?"

"So this editor, Harold L. Herbert, doesn't realize you're a woman?"

"Well, no," Victoria admitted. "But that shouldn't make any difference, should it?"

"No, it shouldn't!" Nanny Iris said firmly, and patted her hand.

But doubt began to creep into Victoria's mind. Just because it *shouldn't* make a difference doesn't mean it *didn't*.

* * *

The leaden winter skies hung over Summerset, as heavy and despondent as Rowena felt. In the weeks since Prudence had left, Rowena had developed a pattern of habits designed to keep her mind as empty as possible. In the last four months, her father had died, she'd let her childhood home slip away, and Prudence had left her. Emptiness of the mind was preferable to endless choruses of *if only*.

She looked up into the sky again. Her fingers fluttered subconsciously over her lips as she remembered the kiss she shared with the pilot on the frozen lake. She hadn't seen him since, and it had been weeks. Even the sky felt empty—and too quiet—without the roar of Jon's plane flying over Summerset Abbey, a once weekly ritual that he'd abandoned without explanation. Rowena wondered whether his brother had put a halt to their budding friendship the moment he had found out at the skating party that she was a Buxton.

She closed her eyes for a moment and breathed his name.

Jon.

She tried to remember how incredibly blue his eyes were and the way his thin, well-formed lips would widen in a smile just for her, but the image was already growing blurry. Instead the memory of her flight in his aeroplane came into her mind. She remembered the thrill of leaving the earth far behind and the soaring freedom of floating above the clouds. She'd felt completely untethered, as if she'd left her problems on the ground. The memory was so sharp and clear, she could almost feel the chill of the wind in her face. Restlessly, she snapped the book she held shut.

Rowena's life had never been as fascinating or exciting as Victoria seemed to find it, but at least it used to be interesting and enjoyable. Now Victoria often buzzed about her like a worried bee, sometimes coaxing and other times accusatory, but nothing Victoria said seemed to reach Rowena at all. It was rather as though Victoria were speaking to her through a wall of jellied aspic. Everything in her life—changing dresses for every meal, entertaining Lady Charlotte's guests, even her occasional trips into the small town of Summerset—suddenly seemed so pointless and exhausting.

So Rowena read voraciously from the ornate library that held thousands of volumes of books. She didn't care what books she read and rarely remembered anything about them when she finished, but while reading them, she had no room in her head to dwell upon anything else. When she wasn't reading, she rode her horse like a fury, taking long runs up through the hills to see into the valley below. Though she rarely admitted it to herself, she was always holding out hope that she'd see an aeroplane soaring through the skies.

"Yes, I think that's about enough."

Rowena jumped upon hearing her aunt's clear voice. She looked up from the window seat in the sitting room to find Aunt Charlotte bearing down upon her with the determination of an angry goose. Aunt Charlotte had been Lady Summerset for twenty-five years and the title had long settled itself in the regal set of her finely shaped head atop a long, definitive neck. Her blue-eyed, dark-haired beauty, which had once awed even the Prince of Wales Marlborough set, was still very much in evidence, even though the tautness of the skin had softened, blurring the exquisite lines of her heart-shaped face.

If her loveliness had once been appealing, Rowena thought as her aunt loomed over her, now it was simply terrifying. Though Aunt Charlotte rarely raised her voice, her temper was known by the frost of her tone and the unrelenting sting of her words.

In spite of her lethargy, Rowena snapped to attention. "Good morning, Aunt Charlotte. What is about enough?"

Aunt Charlotte snatched the book out of her hands. "Enough reading. Enough sulking." Her voice softened just a hair. "Enough grieving."

A lump rose in Rowena's throat, but she only said, "But I like to read."

"Nonsense. Or rather, it doesn't matter if you do like to read, it ruins your eyes and the squinting will give you wrinkles. You'll also get a stooped posture and rounded back. You've met Jane Worth, haven't you?"

Rowena frowned. "You mean the short, little woman with the—" Rowena made a curved movement with her hand, showing a humped back.

Her aunt nodded solemnly. "She always was a bookworm."

Rowena tried to shake her head. Surely that couldn't be true.

Her aunt continued. "And honestly, child, you look a fright. Your forehead is oily, your hair is lank, and I don't know how long it's been since you bathed. You're one of the most beautiful girls I've ever seen, and right now, you wouldn't merit more than even a passing glance. *Enough.*"

Rowena blinked, stunned. Her aunt thought she was beautiful? She'd never told her that before. Had she always thought so?

To Rowena's surprise, her aunt sat close to her on the silk window seat and clasped one of Rowena's hands in her own. Rowena tried to remember another moment when Lady Summerset had touched her affectionately but couldn't recall a single time, even from the many summers that she spent at the abbey during her childhood.

"I understand your loss. I, too, lost my father at a young age.

But you're a young woman, and your father's heart would break if he could see you now."

Something twisted painfully inside Rowena. No matter what her aunt's motives were, there was no doubt in her mind that she was speaking the truth. Her father would hate her moping, her listlessness. Though she had imagined over and over his disappointment at her treatment of Prudence, she had never thought about how saddened he would be at how she was treating herself.

She nodded, defeated. "You're right, I'll go bathe."

Aunt Charlotte squeezed her hand ever so slightly and let her go. "Please do. I've told Elaine she doesn't have to make calls with me this afternoon, as you are coming instead."

Rowena's mouth fell open and her aunt gave her a satisfied smile. "So please wear something appropriate."

Her aunt left her then, her skirts rustling triumphantly.

An hour later, after Rowena had been bathed, Susie was still trying to dry her hair. "If you didn't have so much hair, this would be much easier," she said, toweling a segment, brushing it, and then toweling it again.

Rowena agreed. "If I didn't have long hair or corsets, I would be able to dress myself and in half the time, too."

"Those days are coming," Susie said. "Mark my words."

Rowena smiled slightly, wishing she felt that kind of optimism. She wished she could feel anything besides sadness.

"Her ladyship came in while you were in the tub and chose the outfit you are to wear. It's right lovely, too, miss. You'll look like such a toff in it. Well, not that you aren't . . ." Susie shut her eyes for a moment. "I'm sorry, miss. I think I am just too chatty to be a lady's maid!"

Rowena was too shocked by this information to reassure Susie. "She did? What did she choose?" she asked, rising from the dressing table.

"The navy blue walking suit, miss."

Susie helped her into her chemise, camisole, and corset and waist petticoat, and then brought out the wool walking suit.

Rowena had never seen it before.

She almost said something and then thought better of it. Obviously her aunt had given her a gift and wasn't going to make a fuss about it. The expertly cut wool suit was decorated with black soutache on the lapels and cuffs of the jacket and along the hem of the skirt. The back of the long jacket was gathered together, giving her fullness in the back that softened the silhouette. She marveled at the intricately carved ebony buttons on the front of the jacket and down the side of the skirt. The skirt was a daringly modern four inches above the ground. Either it had been made for someone shorter than Rowena or her aunt was secretly developing modern tastes.

Because Susie had little experience in doing hair, Hortense, Lady Summerset's own lady's maid, busied herself with Rowena's hair, teaching Susie as she did so. Hortense's disdain at having been forced into the task of training a mere kitchen servant was evident in the purse of her mouth. "*Pourquoi dois-je enseigner cette idiote?!*" she muttered under her breath.

"*Soyez prudente, je parle bien le français,*" Rowena snapped.

Susie glared. She wasn't sure what had been said, but she didn't like the tone. Hortense lapsed into a sullen silence, but she was a bit more helpful in teaching Susie how to make the simple chignon Rowena liked best. After she was finished, Hortense handed her the combs and brushes she had used. "Don't forget to wash out your mistress's tools when you're finished." Hortense gave Rowena as small a curtsy as she could manage and left the room.

Susie's face screwed up with dislike after the woman left, but she said nothing. Rowena remembered Vic telling her that Hortense had been especially rude to Prudence, and Rowena fought the urge to make a face, too.

Rowena chose a blue and black pancake hat trimmed with lace, black roses, and an ostrich feather that curled over one ear.

Her aunt nodded approvingly when Rowena joined her in the Great Hall but said nothing. Elaine, dressed in a simple tea gown, gave her a kiss on the cheek. "Thanks for taking my place today, cousin," she whispered. "Good luck."

Rowena smiled at her. She still had a hard time reconciling this pretty, stylish, and vivacious woman with the shy, down-trodden, chubby girl she had known growing up. That Swiss finishing school had done wonders for her. Or more likely it was the simple fact of having a year away from her mother that had given her room to flourish and come into her own.

"I heard that," her mother said as she whisked out the door.

Elaine winked and waved her hand as Rowena followed behind her.

"The motorcar was the best thing to happen to formal calls," her aunt said once they were ensconced in the back of the touring car. "Before I could only make a few calls by carriage; now I get to see so many more people and have to spend less time at each call."

Rowena watched her aunt, roused for the first time in quite a while by curiosity. Who was this formidably stylish and regal woman? "But I thought you liked making calls, Aunt Charlotte?"

The woman snorted. "Goodness no. At least not anymore. I suppose I did enjoy it at one time. But after you hear the week's gossip at the first call, it's just a matter of hearing it repeated at each subsequent call. And you can imagine how dull that becomes."

Rowena gave a surprised laugh. "Is it the same in London?"

"Oh, no. It's much more interesting in London because there's so much more gossip."

Rowena settled back into the fine leather of the motor. "Where to first?"

"We are stopping at the Endicotts' first, because they won't be home. Then we will go to the Kinkaids', because they will be home and I quite like Donald Kinkaid's new wife and it will make her feel honored that I visited. After that we will be going to the Billingslys', which is quite a long drive, but Edith is my friend and we have a few things to discuss."

"I was unaware that Lord Billingsly lived so close."

"They don't, actually. A visit by carriage would have been impossible. It takes us almost two hours by car, but the other calls are on the way there, so it breaks up the drive quite nicely."

Aunt Charlotte didn't miscalculate a single detail. The Endicotts were not home, so they left their card and made their way to the Kinkaids'. The new Mrs. Kinkaid was droll and pretty and properly awed by Lady Summerset. And she was almost twenty years younger than the former Mrs. Kinkaid, who, Aunt Charlotte confided later, had been a bit militant.

Rowena giggled at this last bit and Aunt Charlotte gave her a rare smile. "It's true. This new Mrs. Kinkaid will make Donald a good wife and will be able to give him children." She reached under the seat and brought out a red velvet pillow with gold silken tassels. "I suggest you rest, dear. We have almost an hour before we get to Eddelson Hall."

Rowena laid her head back, puzzling over her aunt's behavior. She had never seen the stately Lady Summerset this engaging or forthright before, especially not with her, and Rowena wondered why her aunt had asked her to come today instead of Elaine. Had she genuinely been worried about her, or—as was often the case with her aunt Charlotte—did her aunt have some hidden motive?

She must have dozed off, because the next time she opened her eyes they were parked in front of a grand mansion that had to be Eddelson Hall. Eddelson wasn't nearly as large as Summerset, but what it lacked in size it made up for in charm. The two circular towers that flanked the front of the home were almost completely covered in ivy and there were so many mullioned windows at the front of the house that it looked as if the walls were made of glass rather than brick.

The butler met them at the front door and took their card. Bidding them to wait, he took the card to where his mistress was apparently waiting in the sitting room. Rowena wanted to ask her aunt whether she found this kind of formality unbearably stupid, but she didn't want to overstep and shatter the sudden warmth that had sprung up between them.

The butler reappeared almost immediately and they followed him through exquisitely charming rooms, decorated and furnished in a French country style, which always appeared far more comfortable than it actually was.

The butler announced them and Rowena found herself involved in a flurry of introductions. Besides Lady Billingsly, four other women were present—society matrons who apparently lived for tea at the Billingslys' on Tuesdays. Rowena had always disliked this kind of superficial social chat and suddenly began to regret taking her aunt up on her invitation. Though in reality, it had been more of a command than an invitation.

"Miss Buxton!"

Rowena turned in relief when she heard Sebastian call her name. "Lord Billingsly, how wonderful to see you again."

He took her outstretched hand and bent over it briefly. "How are your sister and Elaine?" he asked.

"They are doing well, thank you for asking."

Lady Billingsly nodded at them approvingly. "Why don't you young people go for a walk in the winter garden while we catch up on our gossip? It's not raining, is it?" She looked around as if daring anyone to say it was raining. No one did.

Sebastian held his arm out and with relief, Rowena took it. She had endured just about as much small talk as she could handle and felt that if one more pinched-mouthed matron asked how she and her sister were holding up, she would scream.

Eddelson had a mellow quality that Summerset, in all its grandeur, would never achieve. They walked past a pair of open pocket doors that showed a rich, warm library inside with a crackling fire, shelves full of haphazardly placed books, and oversized pieces of leather furniture.

Sebastian caught her gaze as they walked past it. He smiled. "My father spent his summers at his grandfather's lodge in Scotland. I think he copied the library down to the volumes of books and the fireplace poker. It's my favorite room in the house."

She smiled as they walked out the door and into one of the extensive gardens that surrounded the house. Rowena remembered the stolen glances he and Prudence had shared and had often wondered about Sebastian's feelings for Prudence, and hers for him. Of course, when Prudence fled with the footman, all of her conjecture had come to nothing.

While Sebastian still made the occasional call to Summerset, he was not the same lighthearted young man Rowena had met last autumn.

"I miss her, you know," Sebastian said.

Startled, she glanced sideways at him. He nodded his head toward a gravel path that wound its way through a stand of fir trees. She followed his lead, wondering whether he had brought her to this quiet corner of the garden to confide in her. Maybe he needed to talk to someone.

They rounded a corner of slender silver pines that were interspersed with granite obelisks. If he wanted to talk, he seemed in no hurry to begin and waited until they had reached a small frozen fountain before speaking again.

"Do you hear from Prudence quite often, then?"

Rowena's heart gave a little pang. His voice held a note of loneliness that Rowena recognized. "Not very often." Then she gave a harsh little laugh. "Not at all, actually, though Vic has finally heard news of her."

They came to a bench and both sat as if by accord. "She is still angry with you, I take it?"

"I ruined everything when I brought her to Summerset as our lady's maid. I never thought it would last for long, and I never could have imagined that she'd truly be treated as a servant . . . I don't know what I believed, but I know it was all too real for Prudence and she was dreadfully unhappy." Rowena didn't tell him that she hadn't been completely honest with Prudence and Victoria about her uncle letting their London home go, but then, she didn't have to. Sebastian had been present when Prudence had discovered they had no home to return to and that she was trapped at Summerset.

Rowena stared at the ice covering the small fish pond. She

knew how those fish felt, trapped underneath the ice and waiting for the thaw.

"She never said anything to me. I spoke to her after you and
she argued that night. Did you know that?" Sebastian looked
over at her, his dark eyes questioning.

She shook her head. "No."

"Outside. Under the trees. She'd lost her hat." He fell silent
for so long that Rowena wondered whether he was done with
the conversation, but then he continued. "She was going to take
a job as a companion for an acquaintance of mine. I thought—"
He stopped then and looked up at the dead gray sky for a
moment. "I thought I'd found a way to make her happy . . .
I thought we had an understanding. Apparently, we did not."

Rowena sighed, wondering if he knew whether Pru was also
the daughter of the former Earl of Summerset. Not that this
would make a bit of difference. No one of their class would accept a marriage between an earl and the illegitimate daughter of
a maid, regardless of who fathered the child. She glanced sideways at Sebastian, wondering whether she should tell him. No.
She wouldn't betray Prudence further.

"We should be getting back," she said gently.

He nodded absently, and as they started back slowly toward
the house, she offered that Victoria had told her that Prudence
was living in London and seemed to be well and happy.

"Well, that's something," he said.

"I'm hoping she will forgive me someday," Rowena said, with
a catch in her voice.

He squeezed her arm. "You three were like sisters. I'm sure
she won't stay angry for long."

They walked back into the house, where Aunt Charlotte

was gathering her things. "Oh, good. You're back. We were just about to send a maid for you."

"Will you be going back to the university?" Lady Summerset asked Sebastian as she wrapped her wool cape around her shoulders.

"Actually, I'm all finished. I started a term before Colin, so I finished before he did."

"Oh, really?" Lady Summerset placed her hand on his shoulder and smiled up at him in appeal. "You mustn't be a stranger. I'm sure both Elaine and Rowena would love to have you come to dinner sometime, even if Colin can't make it. Wouldn't *you*, Rowena?"

Startled, Rowena nodded. "Of course." She caught an arch look between her aunt and Sebastian's mother and wondered what it meant.

On the long journey home, Rowena puzzled over the conversation she and Sebastian had in the garden. Had he harbored feelings for Pru? Maybe. But now that Prudence had married, it didn't really matter, did it?

CHAPTER
TWO

Prudence looked around their flat, wondering yet again how she was supposed to live in two and a half rooms and a single water closet. Then she berated herself. They were lucky to have the WC and even luckier to be out of the flea-ridden boardinghouse where they had been living since they had arrived in London over a month ago.

She wasn't sure what she'd thought they would do when they'd first stepped off the train from Summerset. She was so used to having someone else in charge that it took her a few moments to realize that her new husband, so confident around motors and animals, was completely out of his element in the teeming mass of people that made up Camden Town, London. It was up to her to collect their luggage and find a boarding-house, up to her to find a flat near the Royal Veterinary College, and to find out what the requirements of attendance were.

Andrew had almost quit right then. "We don't have that much money!" he'd cried out. "That's a bloody fortune."

Quietly, she let him know that *she* had enough money, and if they lived frugally and brought in some extra money here and there, they would be able to make it work.

"I'd be living off my wife," he scoffed, and Prudence couldn't help but agree.

"But then for the rest of our lives, you'll be a veterinarian and I'll be living off *you*," she told him briskly, and he'd relented, seeing her logic. He didn't much like it and Prudence knew it would rankle, but she would be careful not to make an issue of it. Besides, she thought with the new, hard practicality she was developing, they really had very little choice.

Now Mrs. Tannin stood with her hands on her hips and sniffed. "Sir Philip wouldn't like this at all," she said.

Prudence had known bringing the housekeeper here from her old home would be a mistake. This entire flat would fit in Sir Philip's study in the Mayfair mansion, but Prudence was no longer Sir Philip's daughter and mansions were no longer a part of her present. Or her future, for that matter.

"Sir Philip is gone and my husband and I have to live within our means."

"But surely Miss Rowena and Miss Victoria wouldn't want you living in squalor . . ."

"Mrs. Tannin!" Hurt, Prudence drew herself up to her full height. It wasn't much, but she towered over Mrs. Tannin, who was as small as Victoria. "Pray remember that this is my home now, and it isn't squalid or dirty. It's clean and bright and very close to the Royal Veterinary College, where my husband will be attending. It's just small is all." She didn't mention that it was one of four flats situated above a greengrocer. The ever-present earthy scent of potatoes told that tale.

Mrs. Tannin subsided. Had Prudence been able to retrieve all of her things from her old home without help, she would have done so. Carl, the footman, was there to carry some of the heavier items, but she wanted Mrs. Tannin to supervise just to make it plain that Prudence hadn't taken anything that wasn't hers. She didn't want the Earl of Summerset to accuse her of stealing. She had been lucky to get inside and retrieve some of her belongings before the new family took over the house and perhaps denied her access to them.

"My apologies," the older woman finally said. "It's just that I don't understand any of this. Sir Philip dies, the family moves away to the estate, and you return a scant three months later, married to a man who, excuse me, isn't a good match for you, and living in a flat in Camden Town. It's hard for a body to get her arms around, that's all."

Prudence took a deep breath, fighting to keep down her rising temper. She reminded herself how kind this woman had been to her mother.

"Mrs. Tannin, I believe it's your high regard for me that makes you say such things, but remember that my mother was a governess. I have no inheritance, no title, and no blood ties to aristocracy." Prudence's lips tightened for a moment as she remembered that she did indeed have illegitimate ties to the family that had brought her up, but she firmly put that out of her mind. "I was taken to Summerset as a lady's maid and was made to feel as though my presence was a contamination. I have done the very best I can considering the circumstances."

"Not by the girls, surely?" Mrs. Tannin cried, her hand at her heart. Mrs. Tannin looked upon the motherless Buxton girls as beyond reproach, and Prudence decided not to tell her that Rowena was responsible for a good many of her troubles.

"Of course not," she said tersely. "Now can you help me move this table over by the stove? It may fit if we put it crossways."

After Mrs. Tannin had gone, Prudence looked at the trunks and pieces of furniture with dismay. She'd thought she had only brought a few personal items that were given to her especially, but in her small living area, they looked incongruous, not only for their size but for their quality. She had brought a small card table to use as a dining table, but even though it looked tiny at the Mayfair home, it barely fit in the small room that served as the kitchen, dining room, and main living area of the family. The bedroom, oddly enough, was the same size as the kitchen and living area. It was located at the back of the flat, behind the kitchen, and in the front, a small half-room made up the sitting room. Because they lived in a corner flat, the kitchen/living area had two large windows along one wall, and the small sitting room had three windows with a window seat that occupied half the room. There was barely space for her small wing-backed rose-print chair. After spreading a pink and white shawl over a trunk for a table and placing the gaudy standing lamp left by the previous tenant in the corner, almost every available square inch of the sitting room was taken.

She picked up a tablecloth and flicked it over the card table. A piece of paper fluttered from out of the folds. Prudence's heart caught. Victoria's letter. She picked it up and scanned the lines again. At first, she had been undecided as to whether to answer it or not. Clearly, she couldn't tell anyone at Summerset about her present living conditions. In spite of her bravado with Mrs. Tannin, her new home was cramped, confining, and common, and she didn't want either Vic or Ro to know of her exact circumstances. She set the letter on the mantel behind the coal stove. Later. She would figure that out later. She had enough on her mind.

She pushed the other trunks into the back bedroom, trying not to look at her bed as she did so. She and Mrs. Tannin had hired two men off the street to unload it and haul it up the narrow stairs for them. It was large enough for two, but the fine virginal white and blue feather quilts looked strangely out of place in this plain bedroom. Maybe because the quilts had belonged to another life, one that would be ending tonight.

Her husband had been curiously reluctant to start their married life on the narrow bed provided at the boardinghouse. Not that Prudence disagreed with him—indeed, she was grateful for his scruples. To accommodate the crush of people coming in from the country to work in the city, tiny rooms had been further split up by sheets acting as makeshift walls, strung between beds. They were put into a room with two other married couples, one of whom had no qualms about committing the physical act of marriage with other people within spitting distance.

Her face flamed upon remembrance of the unfamiliar noises issuing from the other side of the sheet. She understood from Andrew's stillness next to her that he, too, had heard and interpreted the sounds. She lay beside him for several weeks, disconcertingly conscious of the way his strong form pressed next to hers and how the hair on his arm felt against her cheek as he held her. Her face flushed. She'd only felt that butter melting in the center of her middle once before and as it wasn't with her husband, it shamed her to think of it. It also shamed her that the man in question didn't have to touch her to make her feel that way.

Prudence had always wondered what would come next. She and Rowena had held a few whispered conversations after a trip to a farm to buy a new horse for Sir Philip, but these had always ended in embarrassed giggles. For all Sir Philip's liberal ideas, sex education for his daughters was not one of them.

She pressed her hands against her heated cheeks. Tonight, she would be sharing this bed with Andrew and there would be no one to stop the inevitable. The thought left her both thrilled and anxious. How would she know what to do?

She jumped guiltily when she heard the key in the lock. Was it that time already?

She hurried into the main room just as Andrew stepped through the open door. He filled up the doorway and the room with his height, one of the reasons he had been selected to be a footman at Summerset Abbey. His hazel eyes crinkled into a tired smile when he saw her. They might not have consummated their marriage yet, but she had no doubts about his love for her. She only hoped that in time she would grow to feel the same way.

He caught her with one arm around her waist and pulled her close and she gave him a shy kiss. At first, she'd been taken aback by his easy physical affection with her. She knew the Buxtons loved one another deeply, but it wasn't in them to be that demonstrative. Somehow in that mean little farmhouse where he'd grown up, he'd learned to give and receive love more easily than the aristocrats in their Mayfair mansions. After her initial shock, she grew to rather like it. He never failed to make her feel special.

"Where did you work today?" she asked him. Andrew had found a place that hired workers on a daily basis. He was picking up some extra work a few days a week when he wasn't studying.

"Down at the docks."

She looked in dismay at his dirty clothing. She had learned this morning that the laundry had to be done belowstairs and then hung to dry either out the back window or on a line in the cellar. She didn't want to admit to him that she'd never done washing before and didn't have the first idea of how to go about it. At the boardinghouse, they had just paid to have it done, as there were no facilities. He had been aghast at her insistence upon changing clothes every day, and she soon realized that she would spend all their money on washing if she continued that habit. Reluctantly, she had begun wearing her blouses and skirts for several days at a time and found that it really didn't make much of a difference. She wondered how many other trappings of her former life she'd discover to be completely frivolous.

His eyes swept their small apartment. "You've done a nice job. It looks very different." The neutral sound of his voice stung.

"I know it's a bit crowded, but I just wanted to get as many of my things as I could before the new tenants moved in." Her voice sounded apologetic to her own ears, which was silly. Why wouldn't she want to save her own possessions?

"I thought everything had been taken to Summerset?" He took off his jacket and handed it to her.

She hung it up on a peg next to the door and answered him quietly. "Nothing of mine. I suppose Lord Summerset never intended for me to stay for any length of time." She paused a moment to absorb the hurt and then continued. "I left several trunks of clothing in the attic that I supposed I wouldn't need right away. I can send for them later."

"Righto. It's not like we'll be invited to any balls anytime soon."

His voice was light, but Prudence detected a bitterness underneath. "It's just as well," she answered, trying to keep the hurt out of her voice. "I can't imagine trying to puzzle out how to press an evening jacket anyway. Would you like some tea?"

"Aye." He squeezed her arm lightly as she moved past him,

and she knew he was sorry for his remark. She couldn't help wondering, though, whether this was to be a part of their marriage from here on out, this envious contempt of her old life. Well, she wasn't going to apologize for it.

"I'm famished, too. Did you have a chance to bring in any groceries?"

She put the teakettle on and flushed. "I haven't had a moment. I was busy getting everything packed up and then moved over here and then unpacked again. I thought I could run down to the pub and pick up some cottage pie. Just for tonight," she added quickly at the look on his face. She knew he thought she was a spendthrift, and she really was trying to be thrifty. It was just a whole different way of managing things. Plus, this would buy her one more day before she had to confess to him that she didn't even begin to know how to cook. She cringed as she imagined the disappointment on his face when she eventually revealed her complete lack of skills as a homemaker. A few weeks into their marriage and she was already scrambling to cover up her shortcomings as a wife.

He sat in a small, dainty satin tufted chair that had once sat in front of the fireplace in her bedroom. She had thought it perfect near the stove, but it looked ridiculous now with her husband's long body draped over it.

"Oh, Lord. I forgot how tall you are. I'm sorry. Let's move the old chair out of the bedroom and put it next to the stove."

He glanced down at himself with a wry grin. "It is rather small," he agreed as he carried it through the kitchen to the bedroom to exchange it for the old club chair that had been in the flat when they arrived. "This isn't really good for much of anything but looking pretty."

"Kind of like your wife," Prudence said under her breath.

"What was that?"

"Nothing." Prudence took him his tea as he made himself comfortable in the club chair.

He handed her the money he had made that day and she stared at it blankly. "My ma always kept the money in a cracked cup in the cupboard. Maybe we should do something like that with the money that doesn't go in the bank."

She nodded and stuck the coins into a white glass vase that sat on their dining room table. A fire engine went clanging past them and Andrew jumped. "Not sure if I'll ever get used to that."

"You will." She sat down at the dining room table, tea in hand, and tried hard to think of something to say to him. She'd married him because he was one of the kindest people she'd met during a time when nearly everyone treated her cruelly. She firmed her chin. This would work. Perhaps her marriage had been impetuous, but she hadn't gone into it blindly. She'd chosen him for his thoughtfulness and because he had once fought for her publicly, damning the consequences to himself. "Tomorrow I'm going to go and get some provisions. I set up my dressing table in the corner of the bedroom by the windows. Maybe you could study there? That is, if you don't mind studying at a white and gold desk with pink flowers on it."

She grinned at him and he laughed, dispelling some of the tension in the room. "I think I'll manage. As far as I know, Euclid and Virgil don't care a whit about where they are studied, as long as they are studied."

One of Prudence's biggest surprises was how educated the farm boy turned footman actually was. He'd grown up working the land but had snuck away often to help the local animal doctor, who had mentored him and lent him books. Prudence had a wider knowledge in some things, such as politics, current events, and English literature, but in science, mathematics, and geography, he left her far behind. On Sundays, they had taken to going to a tea shop, reading the newspaper together and dissecting every article, one by one.

Perhaps while she was out tomorrow she might find a cookbook that would rescue her, she thought while waiting for their cottage pie. The pub was just down the street from their flat, and Prudence sat in the back room next to a door discreetly marked *Ladies' Entrance*. The large mirror behind the bar was cracked in several places and the red velvet stools showed tufts of white cotton through the worn spots. She had given her order to the tired-looking woman who worked the ladies' area. Prudence looked around with interest. The male half of the bar bustled with men getting off work, while in the small back room only a few "working" women were in attendance.

A group of young women about Prudence's age pushed through the ladies' door, giggling and chatting. All were dressed in plain dark skirts that came to the ankle, and white blouses under their winter coats, which they soon removed in the heated pub. All wore their hair pinned back neatly, with no-nonsense hats sitting straight on their heads. Prudence tried not to stare at them as they called for ale. The tired servingwoman picked up a bit when they came in. "You'll be the death of me, you gaggle of geese," she teased. "You should all be home taking care of your mas instead of wearing out my feet."

"Ah, you love us, Mary, admit it," a lilting voice teased.

Prudence sat up. She knew that voice. . . . She turned and stared at the table they had taken, trying to see who it was.

"Miss Prudence!"

Suddenly a skinny redheaded girl detached herself from the

group and ran toward Prudence. The girl wrapped her arms around her in a quick hug before jumping back. "Oh, I'm sorry, miss!" she said, her face turning red beneath her freckles. "I was just so surprised to see you."

"Katie! What are you doing here? Mrs. Tannin said you had left and gotten a job in an office."

The girl smiled proudly. "Yes. Thanks to Sir Philip, I was able to get through secretarial school and got a fine office job."

The girls behind her hooted. "Katie still thinks it's a fine job," one of them said, laughing.

"That's because she's still new," another one said.

"Well, it's better than wiping posh arses all day, if you ask me," one of them said, giving Prudence a bold stare.

Prudence flushed, feeling as if she were back in the servants' hall at Summerset, being ridiculed for her high-class upbringing. Bugger that. She'd probably had a happier childhood than most of these women had even dreamed of having. She'd not regret it just because her privileged childhood meant she now fit in nowhere. She straightened her shoulders and looked down her nose at the woman with the black eyes until the busybody looked away. She turned back to Katie. "So you like your job? Do you live near here?" She hugged Katie back, tears stinging her eyes. She had always been friendly with Katie. Unlike at Summerset, servants were treated as beloved and respected employees in Sir Philip's home. Prudence wasn't close with them the way Victoria was, but suddenly she was gladder to see Katie than she could possibly say.

Katie nodded. "I moved here with my mother after I got the new job so I could be closer to work. Mum was finally able to give up working, so now she keeps house for me and my girlfriends who rent rooms from us. It's a good deal all the way around. But what about you? What are you doing in Camden Town, or here for that matter?" Katie suddenly seemed aware of her surroundings and was shocked to find Miss Prudence here, even if she and her friends frequented such a place.

"My husband is going to be attending the Royal Veterinary College as soon as he passes the examinations. We are in Camden because it's close to his school." She didn't add that here her husband could pick up odd jobs when they needed them. It was deeply instilled in her that as a lady she should never talk about money except with her husband.

The server handed Katie a mug of beer on her way to the table behind her and Katie took a drink. "Fancy that! How quickly things change, eh, miss? I'd have never figured you for a Camden Town housewife . . . no offense, miss."

Prudence laughed and wondered why there were tears under the laughter. "None taken, Katie. I actually don't know the first thing about being a housewife in Camden Town or anywhere else for that matter. I can't cook, or sew, or even do laundry."

Katie's eyes widened. "I never thought of that. You're like a babe, aren't you? Tell you what, I'll send you to my mum and she'll take care of you. Teach you all that stuff."

Relief of the load pressing down on her lightened her so much that she felt as if she were going to float away. "Would she, really?"

"Yes, I think she gets bored by herself all day."

The servingwoman handed Prudence the cottage pie in the big bowl Prudence had brought for it.

"Mary, can I get a pencil and paper?" Katie wrote the address down and gave it to her. "You drop by tomorrow and see how happy my mum is to help. I believe she thinks I'm a lost cause."

"Thank you so much, Katie."

As Prudence hurried back to the flat, she wondered how to confess to Andrew about her need for housewifery lessons. Her stomach began to tie in knots as once again she imagined how the conversation would unfold as Andrew realized that his new bride had never even made a simple meat pie, that she was just as uppity as the other servants at Summerset purported her to be. Perhaps she could delay revealing those shortcomings to him for now. . . . After all, he was already fulfilling his promise to her to support them while pursuing his studies, and she couldn't bear the thought of letting him down so early in their marriage.

Andrew had bathed while she was out and wore a soft, loose-fitting white cotton shirt and trousers. His feet were bare and his hair, which he always wore a bit longer than most men, but not as long as an aesthete might, curled damply around his neck. He stood in front of her, his hazel eyes warm and caressing. Word-lessly, she handed him the bowl of cottage pie and moved to take down the dishes. He ate with gusto, seemingly absorbed in his food.

"This is good," she finally remarked, desperate to break the silence.

"Yes." His eyes met hers and then shifted away.

He's as nervous about tonight as I am, she thought in surprise. The realization eased some of her anxiety. "Would you like an-other helping?"

He shook his head and she put the leftover pie in the icebox. Silently, she cleared the table and washed their plates while he added more coal to the stove. They did their nightly chores even though it was too early to go to bed. When there was nothing left to do, Prudence grabbed her nightdress and darted into the water closet. Her face flamed in embarrassment, but she would not, could not, change in the bedroom. What if he came in?

She took her hair down and brushed it until it hung like dark silk down her back. When she could think of no other reason to linger, she opened the door and stepped into her bedroom. Andrew had diffused the gaslight until it cast a soft glow over the room. She blinked and her pulse raced as she saw him standing next to the bed. He had removed his shirt and even in the low lighting she could see the muscles in his chest and arms, deeply etched from a lifetime of labor.

Her mouth went dry.

Then, still silent, Andrew held out his arms. She only hesitated for a moment. More than anything else, Andrew made her feel safe, as if he were a harbor at which she could moor to escape the unexpectedly stormy seas of her life. *I can do this.* He scooped her up into his arms and held her close for a moment before gently laying her on the bed. As he bent over her, Sebastian's face floated to her mind for a fraction of a second before she banished it. She'd made her choice. She ignored the sound of her own heart hammering in her ears and reached up to touch his face. "Andrew," she said softly. "Andrew."

CHAPTER
THREE

ictoria tapped her fingers, waiting for Kit's reply. He stood in front of the fireplace of her secret room. He, too, was tapping his fingers, only on the mantel instead of the desk. Lately, her secret room had begun to feel as though it belonged to Kit, as well. It had become their meeting place when they wanted to gossip or banter or simply have some time to themselves, away from the inane chatter of the other guests.

She sat impatiently, her fingers skittering across the shining top of her lovely round desk, once used by an ancestor who would no doubt be completely scandalized by the plan she had just proposed to Kit.

"Let me get this straight." He frowned at her, his dark red brows furrowing like caterpillars. "You want me to help you to sneak into London for a week?"

She glared at the mocking tone of his voice. "You know, you're usually quite handsome, but right now, you look more like an ogre from a Grimm's fairy tale than a human, so you can stop glowering at me."

His head came up and he looked at her, his eyebrows unfurrowing and shooting up on his forehead in such a comical way, she couldn't help but giggle.

"You think I'm handsome?"

Victoria shrugged. "Yes. Sort of like a fox, with your ginger hair and sharp eyes. But don't let it go to your head; Sebastian and Colin are far better looking than you. Now, back to my plan."

He rolled his eyes at that and got back to the matter at hand. "The only way it would work would be to bring Elaine into it. There is no way your aunt would approve of your traveling to London on your own, and she certainly would never let you drive off alone with me."

Victoria shook her head, frustrated by the fuss. "These people do know I'm of age, right? Why may cousin Colin come and go as he pleases, yet Elaine and I are required to inform everyone where we are at every moment of every day? How is that fair?"

"Do you know you're rather lovable when you act like a suffragette?" he teased.

She threw a fountain pen at him and missed. It exploded on the mantel. "Oh, blast! Now see what you made me do."

He laughed. "*Made* you do? No, leave it," he said when she stood to clean it. "No one comes back here and we'll call it art, much as that crazy art nouveau crowd calls their stuff art."

"Oh!" She stamped her foot. He knew she loved art nouveau.

"Now don't get your petticoats in a bundle, kitten, and let's figure out how to get you to London so you can meet with . . . whom?"

"Harold L. Herbert, the managing editor for *The Botanist's Quarterly*," she said, sitting back down.

"Ah yes, so you can meet with Hairy Herbert. And what do you hope to gain from this meeting?"

For a moment, Victoria drew a blank. "Well, he said he wanted to meet with me. He finds my writing thought provoking. He not only paid me for an article but is also interested in more of my work. So, more assignments, I suppose." She tilted her nose up in the air, waiting for him to make fun of her.

To her surprise, he didn't. "So you've never met Hairy Herbert. Have you spoken to him on the telephone?" He took the seat across from the desk and crossed his long legs. His eyes regarded her gravely.

Victoria shifted uneasily. "No."

"So he doesn't know that the author of the scientific article he paid ten pounds for is, in fact, an eighteen-year-old girl?"

Victoria opened her mouth, but no sound came out.

Kit indicated the letter on the desk between them. "I noticed you didn't use your real name."

She straightened. "I did so."

"No, you used V. Buxton. So you must have known there might be some bias against your sex."

She shrugged a shoulder, refusing to let him goad her. "V. Buxton sounds more serious than Victoria. He likes my work. It won't matter now if I'm a girl or a gorilla. I'm going to meet with him and nothing you say can stop me. If you don't want to help me find a way to get to London without raising Auntie's suspicions, then I will find a way to do it myself."

"Don't be a goose. Of course I'll help you. I wouldn't be much of a friend if I didn't, would I?"

She sat back, relieved. She could have figured something out, of course; it would just be so much easier and more fun if Kit were in on the plot. It was hard to believe they had only known each other for a few months. In many ways he had taken the place of Rowena and Prudence, since Prudence was gone and Rowena had slipped so far away on a sea of sadness that she no longer seemed like her sister. Kit, on the other hand, understood that one could be sad and still wish to have a good time.

"So let's leave the cousins out of this. The more people who know, the more risk that the secret is going to get out. When I return to London tomorrow, I will send a note from someone asking you to visit. Who should it be?"

Victoria frowned, thinking hard. "Priscilla Kingsly. She is still in France, but I don't think anyone here knows that. The Kingsly family is respectable. No one will know."

"What about Rowena?"

Rowena won't even notice I'm gone, Victoria thought with a pang. "I'll tell her that I'm visiting Prudence. They still aren't speaking, so it doesn't matter."

"Where are you actually going to be staying? You can't stay at my house, obviously. Mother would have us married before the week was out. You can't stay in a nice hotel, because you might be recognized. And a boardinghouse is out of the question."

Victoria leaned back in her seat. "Ho! Look at how conventional you are!" she jeered. "I suppose it would be too *unrespectable* for a young woman to stay at a boardinghouse by herself!"

He flushed a mottled red that almost matched his hair. "Blast respectability! It would be *unsafe*. There's a difference. Now do you want my help or not?"

She rolled her eyes. "I'll stay with Katie. She's a friend of mine from Miss Fister's Secretarial School for Young Ladies." Given the way servants were looked upon at Summerset, she didn't add that Katie used to be the family's kitchen maid. "Write the letter. Make it for a week from today and I'll take the railway into town. I'll write to Katie."

A smile tugged at her lips as excitement swelled in her chest. For years she'd been coddled as the invalid little sister. But now she finally had a chance to prove to her family—and, more important, to herself—that she truly was capable of great things.

After posting letters to Katie and Mr. Herbert the next morning, she dressed in her warmest clothing and wrapped a long woolen cloak around her. She wasn't stupid, and going off on an adventure without letting anyone in on her plan was dangerous. Of course, there was only one person she truly needed to tell, and not even nasty weather was going to stop her.

Victoria ran into her cousin on her way out. Elaine held a soft mohair throw in her arms and was already dressed in a flowing pale pink tea gown.

Astonished, Elaine's eyebrows disappeared beneath a fringe of curls on her forehead. "You're not going out in this weather, are you? It's freezing outside and looks as if it might snow. Come curl up with me in the sitting room in front of a fire. We'll read and gossip and lounge like cats."

As inviting as her cousin's invitation was, Victoria wanted to get to Nanny Iris's and back before the weather got any worse. "I'll be back in a bit and we can lounge the rest of the day away. I'll even play you a game of checkers. I'm only going to Nanny Iris's."

Elaine shrugged. "Suit yourself. Don't freeze, poppet."

Victoria began to regret her decision about halfway to her destination. It was a scant two miles and Victoria had walked it many times, but why, oh, why hadn't she had the driver take her? By the time she reached Nanny Iris's she was breathing far harder than the walk would indicate. Nanny Iris quickly took off Victoria's cloak and sat her by the fire in a comfortable rocking chair.

"What in God's name were you thinking, child, coming out in weather such as this?"

Victoria grimaced but couldn't catch her breath enough to

make a scathing retort. Her lungs were tight and cold and her throat felt as if it was closing.

Why could she never remember to carry her nebulizer with her?

"Sit tight. I'll bring you a concoction I made up."

Frustrated, she closed her eyes and began counting slowly as her doctor had taught her. Though now Victoria wondered whether the trick actually helped ward off the attack or whether the counting exercise was simply meant to keep her from panicking and gasping like a strangled fish. *Nine . . . ten . . . eleven . . .* Victoria still struggled to take in air. Sometimes she wondered whether this was the way she was going to die.

Squeezing her eyes shut tighter against that thought, she fought down the panic and counted slowly, taking little breaths every fourth beat.

It seemed only a moment before Nanny Iris was back, holding a hot, steaming cup in front of her nose. "Drink this," she commanded.

The bitterness of the brew hit her nostrils and Victoria jerked her head sideways without meaning to.

"Oh, stop behaving like a baby," the old woman groused.

Surprised, Victoria took an obedient sip, shuddering as the acrid taste hit her tongue. Nanny Iris chuckled.

"I'm sorry I didn't have a chance to sweeten it up a bit with mint and honey, but you're a big girl. Now drink it down."

Victoria did as she was told, sip after little sip, until the cup was all gone and her breathing had returned to normal. Dizziness lurked around her head as it always did after an attack, but she wasn't shaky as she always felt after the nebulizer, which invariably made her ill for the rest of the day.

"What was in that?" Victoria asked when she had recovered enough to speak.

"Licorice, coltsfoot, turmeric, and an herb all the way from the American West, grindelia."

Victoria looked at the muddy leaves in the bottom of her cup with more respect. "How did you know to add that?"

"I've been all over the world, my dear. I know a great many things far beyond the borders of Suffolk and have friends from many a far place. I wrote to one of them concerning your condition and she sent me some of the herb."

Victoria reached out and patted the old woman's cheek. "I can't believe you would do that for me. Thank you."

Nanny Iris cleared her throat and took the cup from Victoria. "That doesn't mean you should go anywhere without your medicine and your nebulizer. You're not a little girl anymore. There will come a time when there is no one to save you with tea."

Suitably chastened, Victoria nodded. Along with Kit, Nanny Iris had made the months since her father's death bearable. She had lived the life Victoria longed to live—independent and adventurous. She had been the Buxton family nanny until Victoria's father's little sister, Halpernia, had drowned. Then she had traveled, teaching English in faraway countries until she finally came home to be with family in her old age. It was a full life that had little to do with catering to a man or children, and Victoria longed to emulate it.

Now that the crisis was over, she longed to tell Nanny Iris about her own upcoming adventure, but for the first time a little doubt niggled. Victoria knew that Nanny Iris cared for her. Would she really be all right with Victoria running off to London by herself? She decided to amend her story a bit, just to be safe.

"Do you remember that article I sold? The one I brought you?" she asked.

"Remember it? Of course I remember it. I told my brother about it just the other day!" Nanny Iris went into the kitchen and came back with some real tea and a plate of biscuits. "Here, this will wash out the nasty taste."

Victoria took a sip of the tea. "Well, I sent him another article." She waited until the old woman settled herself across from her before continuing. "He liked that one, as well. He didn't say he would publish it, but he did repeat his invitation to meet with him, so next week I am going to London to do just that!"

Nanny Iris's eyes widened. "Do you think that's wise?"

Victoria frowned. This was not the reaction she had expected at all. "Of course it's wise! He has asked me twice."

Nanny Iris shook her head. "No, dear. He has asked V. Buxton twice. Not you."

"I am V. Buxton," she told the old woman firmly.

"I know that, but Mr. Harold Herbert doesn't know that. I don't bet often, but I would wager that Mr. Herbert believes V. Buxton to be a young man, possibly a university student or one who has just finished his studies. Not the very bright, self-educated, very young daughter of a brilliant botanist."

Why was everyone determined to ruin this for her? Mr. Herbert was already impressed with her *work*. Surely it wouldn't matter that she was female. She remembered the intellectuals who often frequented her father's dinner parties while she was growing up. Many were women, such as the Italian doctor Maria Montessori and the brilliant physicist Marie Curie, and all were taken seriously no matter their sex. She tilted her chin. "I plan on being a botanist, one way or another. My father taught me how important it is for a scientist to be published.

And Mr. Herbert has already bought one of my articles! It is going to be *fine*."

Victoria swept away any doubts with a wave of her hand. She had to hold firm to the conviction that she was destined for greatness, that she was more than an invalid whose own lungs threatened to fail her at any given moment. Otherwise, she'd still be bedridden, the object of everyone's constant worry and coddling. She was strong. And she would be successful, one way or another. She would show everyone. Including Nanny Iris.

CHAPTER
FOUR

Rowena spurred her horse on to a quicker pace and soon they were galloping across the field. The cold pierced her skin through the carefully arranged netting on her face and she knew Aunt Charlotte would berate her later for chapping her cheeks.

Ever since she and Aunt Charlotte had gone on calls, Aunt Charlotte had taken a strange interest in Rowena, at times treating her as she treated Elaine. Rowena and Elaine puzzled over this, but neither was sure what to make of it, only that her ladyship had something up her sleeve and they should both be on their guard.

But out here, Aunt Charlotte ceased to exist. In fact, everything ceased to exist. It was the closest Rowena had been to happiness since her father died. Except for when she was flying with Jon, or when he kissed her on the frozen pond. But at those moments, she hadn't been close to happy, she had actually been happy. No, happy didn't quite describe it. She'd been euphoric.

But that had been weeks ago. She still searched the sky every day, but the only wings she spotted were those of the crows, whose caws mocked her pain.

So today she was taking matters into her own hands and riding to Wells Manor, which lay just to the southeast of their own home. Long before, a Wells had saved the life of a Buxton heir and had been given a manor home along with a sizable portion of Buxton land. The friendship had been lost over the years until recent history turned the age-old friends into enemies, but surely that had nothing to do with Jon and her, did it?

Rowena slowed her horse to a walk, her mind spinning. Every time she convinced herself that Buxton family history had no bearing on her future, doubt kicked in. Of course it affected them. How could Jon introduce her to his mother? *Mother, I know this is the beloved niece of the man who stole our land and drove your husband, my father, to his grave . . . but I love her.*

Love? Rowena jerked on the reins in surprise and her horse snorted. Where had that come from? Did she *want* him to love her? Her mind answered with speed so blinding she wondered why she had not seen it before. Yes. Of course she wanted his love. The world had felt so cold and gray in the months since her father's death and Prudence's departure, the thought that someone could love her gave her a sense of warmth and comfort. But she couldn't help but wonder whether that meant that she truly loved him?

She thought of the strawberry blond of his hair, the clear blue of his eyes, and the keen way he had of seeing and weighing everything. His bravery and persistence when he was testing airplanes over and over again, even with memories of recent—and nearly fatal—crashes fresh in his mind.

She certainly preferred him to any man she had ever known, but *love*? And why would she want him to love her if she didn't love him back? Perhaps she was far more of a coquette than she'd thought she was. Or maybe she was allowing her fondness for flying, which she loved unabashedly, to influence her feelings for the handsome pilot.

She was used to missing her father—the pain stayed with her day and night—but suddenly an older, softer ache surfaced, and it was her mother she longed for. Someone she could talk to about young men. Someone to help her figure all of this out.

The path turned onto a road with a broken wooden fence and she knew she had arrived at the Wells family manor, left neglected and run-down because of her uncle's greed.

Swallowing, she turned her horse through the fence, wondering again what she had hoped to accomplish in coming here. Perhaps if she could just speak with him. He had asked her to fly with him again and had yet to make good on his offer. Yes. That was what she would say.

Feeling more confident, she nudged her horse into a trot and continued down the frozen track. She rounded a corner and inhaled when she saw the home. It was small compared to what she was used to, and it looked older and mellower than Summerset, though it obviously had been built during the same era, as the basic design and stone were the same. But whereas everything at Summerset Abbey was created to inspire awe, Wells Manor was built to be as comfortable and as useful as possible. The kitchen garden, though fallow this time of year, lay in full view on the side of the house and Rowena could glimpse the family's orchards just beyond it. A worn path from the front door led to a barn on a small copse beyond an old abandoned well house. This was a house where the inhabitants might have had help but were no strangers to working the land themselves, which made good sense to Rowena. If one were to live off the land, one should know how it worked.

No one showed up to help her off her horse, nor to put her horse away. The moment she dismounted, butterflies fluttered in her stomach and her confidence vanished. She shouldn't be here. What if he was angry that she had come? But surely a man didn't kiss a woman and ask her to fly with him if he planned on disappearing soon after.

And, after all, she was a *New Woman*, not a mouse.

Gathering her courage, she tied her horse to a nearby tree. He snorted at such treatment, far preferring to be stabled and rubbed down, especially on such a cold day. She knew she couldn't leave him unattended for long.

She laid her riding crop on the ground and took a moment to wrap her riding skirt around one side, hooking it into place so she would be able to walk comfortably. Then she stepped quietly to the front door. Hesitating only for a moment, she closed her eyes and knocked, knowing she was breaching about a thousand rules of etiquette. She hoped that his mother, a woman who had lost her husband to suicide, wouldn't care about such things.

At the thought of Jon's parents she almost lost her nerve and ran back to her animal. What was she doing here?

The door opened and a young girl of about sixteen appeared in the doorway. Her eyes widened when she took in Rowena's severely cut riding habit of dark Irish linen and the hat tilted just so on Rowena's head.

The girl's brown hair fell untidily down her back and the hem of her ill-fitting dress showed damp stains. "Mother!" the girl yelled. The two of them stared at each other for a moment and Rowena noted the girl had a basket of eggs slung over one arm. Then she slammed the door in Rowena's face.

Moments later an older woman opened the door. Her faded hair must have once been as red as Jon's, and her eyes were the same compelling blue. But whereas Jon's face was made of sharp, intelligent planes, this woman's face had been ravaged by grief, and two permanent wrinkles ran from the corners of her eyes down her cheeks as if worn there by an ocean of tears. The woman, however, wasn't crying; she was smiling a tentative smile.

"I apologize for my daughter. We don't get many visitors back here and she felt she wasn't dressed well enough to receive anyone."

The words were mild but Rowena detected enough of a chastisement to be ashamed. They told her that though this woman wasn't one to stand on ceremony, she knew what was polite, and appearing out of nowhere was just not polite.

"I'm very sorry for not sending word of my visit, but I was just riding by and I thought I would inquire whether Jon was home?"

The woman's eyebrows rose slightly, but the look on her face softened a bit. "No, he hasn't been home for the last few weeks. He's been working in Kent."

Relief washed over her like cleansing rainwater, rinsing away all her self-doubt. He was with Mr. Dirkes. He wasn't intentionally avoiding her, he was just doing his job. Why hadn't she thought of that? "Oh, I am sorry to have bothered you. I just hadn't heard from him and was beginning to worry . . ." Rowena began moving away, her relief making her babble.

But the woman reached out and caught her arm. "I understand. With a job like his, I worry every day. I don't know how he can do what he does."

"Oh, because it's wonderful," Rowena burst out.

"You've been flying?" the woman asked, her voice rising in surprise.

She nodded, shyness suddenly making her look away. She felt her cheeks heating. "He took me up with him once. He's going to take me again."

She heard a little shriek from inside the house and the woman's lips twitched. "Why don't you come in and have a hot cup of tea before you start off again? My name is Margaret, and I am Jon's mother."

"My name is Rowena." She didn't offer her last name, but it wasn't asked for, and she didn't want to give the woman a reason to cast her out. Rowena longed to see where Jon lived, where he had grown up. "Are you sure it wouldn't be too much trouble?" she asked as she was being ushered inside.

"No, of course not. We don't get many visitors, but the day we can't offer a cup of hot tea and some sustenance to a young woman out riding on a day like today is the end of the Wells family."

Rowena detected a slight burr in Margaret's voice and wondered whether she was Scottish. She took off her riding cloak as she was ushered through a wide entryway down a long hall with wide pocket doors on either side. Some were closed while others were open, showing cheery fires roaring inside. The ceilings were low and timbered, giving the home a warm, cozy feeling that seemed to be missing from most of Summerset. But then again, Aunt Charlotte was not exactly the warm and cozy type.

"I hope you don't mind if we have our tea in the kitchen; that is where we live most of the time anyway. With five boys and only one daughter, it just doesn't seem appropriate to make them have tea in the sitting room, where they are apt to spill something or otherwise make a mess."

The kitchen was a huge room with a fireplace on one wall, a wood stove on another, and a cooker against the back wall. The walls were round river stones put together with mortar, and Rowena could tell it was the oldest part of the house. A table made of long wooden planks stood in the middle, while a butcher block the size of a small bed stood to one side.

"Do have a seat at the table. I had just put the tea on when I heard Cristobel's unearthly scream. I am so sorry about that. As I said, we don't have much company and I'm afraid I've let the girl run wild."

Rowena heard an annoyed yelp from the hallway but said nothing. She took a seat at the end of the long table, worried that Margaret would start asking questions about her family that she wouldn't be able to answer truthfully.

In spite of Rowena's assertions that she help, Margaret bade her to stay seated and had a quick tea set on the table in no time. Then she sat firmly next to Rowena and stared at her with her blue eyes.

Rowena squirmed uncomfortably at Jon's eyes peering out of his mother's face.

"How long have you known my son?" she asked.

Rowena ducked her head to hide a smile. That certainly didn't take long. "Not long. Just a couple of months, really."

"How did you two meet? I was under the impression that he had no time for anything except his aeroplanes."

This time Rowena didn't bother to hide her smile. "I think that's true. He was flying, or crashing, actually, when we met."

His mother clapped a hand to her mouth. "So you're the woman on the hill."

Rowena shifted. It hadn't occurred to her that he might have told his family about her. She wondered about his older brother, George, whom she'd met at the skating party and who had been none too happy about her surname. Had he said anything to his mother about her?

"You practically saved Jon's life!" an awed voice said behind her.

She turned to find that the girl at the door had quickly changed her skirt and brushed out her hair. She served herself a cup of tea and joined them at the table.

"I wouldn't go that far," Rowena said weakly.

"So he took you up in his plane to say thank you," Cristobel continued. "He said you were a real trouper. You were hardly afraid at all. I love your riding habit. I outgrew mine and we haven't enough money to replace it yet, but maybe when George comes home from the bank. I, of course, have been up lots of times."

"If lots of times are exactly twice," her mother said, smiling. "Slow down, our guest isn't used to the speed of your tongue."

Cristobel glowered at her mother.

"I have a younger sister, too," Rowena assured them. "I'm used to it."

"Well, that's a mercy. Did you enjoy flying with Jon?" Margaret asked, turning back to Rowena.

"I loved it," Rowena said, trying to find the words. "I felt so free, as if nothing that happened down here mattered at all."

"But it does matter, doesn't it?" a masculine voice said from the hall. Rowena jumped, her heart leaping, but it wasn't Jon who stood in the door, watching her with an unreadable expression across his face. It was his brother, George, who had made it very clear the first time they met that he harbored nothing but disdain for the Buxtons, and thus for her.

"George!" Cristobel leapt up and gave her brother a hug. "I didn't expect you until tomorrow!"

"Business went better than expected."

"Oh, that's a relief," his mother said, getting up to pour her son a cup of tea.

Rowena sat very still, waiting for him to reveal her identity to Margaret and Cristobel, just as Rowena was beginning to like them. He walked into the room and lounged against the butcher block, waiting for his tea. He wasn't as handsome as Jon—the blue of his eyes was darker and he had grim lines sunk on either side of his mouth. This was a man who had known the bitterness of caring for a family before his time.

"Yes, Mother," he said, never taking his eyes off Rowena. "If selling off another part of our land can be termed a relief."

"Not exactly tea talk in front of company," his mother chided, handing him a cup.

"My apologies. I was just surprised to find Miss . . ." He paused, waiting for a name.

"You may call me Rowena. And I thank you so much for the tea, but I really must be leaving."

"But you just got here!" Cristobel wailed. "We haven't gotten to talk about anything yet!"

Margaret smiled as Rowena rose from her chair. "As I said, my daughter has been left alone for far too long. She needs the company of girls her own age, and though I can see you are much older, I would love to have you back here for a real visit. Perhaps you could have supper with us? It's the least we can do, considering how you practically saved Jon's life."

Rowena just wanted to escape George's mocking eyes. She wished she had never come here. What would Jon say when he found out she had ingratiated herself with his family before he had even made clear any intentions toward her? And yet, wasn't a kiss the same as declaring intentions? Or was she being impossibly old-fashioned? "I'd like that very much," she said weakly, reaching for her cloak.

The entire family saw her to the door. Rowena was sure the two holes burning in her back were from George's glaring. The two women said their good-byes at the door, then George walked her to her horse and held the reins as she mounted. He didn't mince words.

"I have a message for you and a message for your uncle, Miss Buxton. Tell your uncle to keep his spy at home. He already has all he is going to get from us."

Rowena's mouth fell open in shock and she snatched the reins out his hands.

"And quit confusing Jon. His loyalty lies with his family." Before she could respond he slapped his hand down on the rump of her horse and her horse leapt away in a gallop.

CHAPTER
FIVE

The rhythmic rocking of the train might have left the other passengers tired and yawning, but Victoria and a toddler in a navy sailor suit were wide awake. One by one the others shut their eyes against the glare of the morning sun streaming in the windows and relaxed, knowing their next stop would be Cambridge and then London.

Victoria and the blue-eyed boy stared at each other for a moment, but each was too preoccupied to pay the other much attention. The little boy had fingers to count and spit bubbles to blow, and Victoria had a whole list of things that could go wrong if she neglected to give each item considerable thought.

Knowing this, she counted off all of the items on her fingers. Her aunt believed she was going to visit the Kingslys and had even sent a note of thanks that had been deftly plucked up by Susie before it made its way down to Cairns. Before leaving, Victoria had warned Susie to be on the alert for other missives.

Rowena, knowing she wouldn't ever stay with Priscilla Kingsly, who was a bit of a pill, thought she was going to visit Prudence and her new husband. The guilt Victoria felt over this lie sat heavy in her stomach. Rowena's beautiful eyes had filled with hurt, but she had only hugged Vic and told her to give Pru her best. She also had given her twenty pounds in case Prudence should need it. Vic had no idea what she would do with the money, because Susie hadn't told her where Prudence lived. To be fair, Victoria hadn't asked, still ashamed that she'd never received a reply to the letter she had added to Susie's.

Kit had insisted on meeting her at the train station, and though Victoria asserted that it wasn't necessary, she was relieved that he would be waiting. He would escort her first to the offices of *The Botanist's Quarterly*, which were located on Lexington Place. She had sent a letter to Hairy Herbert, informing him of her arrival, and arranged to meet with him just before noon. She leaned back against the seat, a pleased sigh escaping her lips. She imagined him being so impressed with her knowledge that he would invite her to lunch, someplace sophisticated, where serious people went to lunch.

But if not, Kit would take her to Coleridge's for lunch and she would treat herself to an enormous napoleon before he escorted her to Katie's house in . . . She frowned and checked her reticule to make sure the paper with Katie's address was still on it. Camden Town. Yes. That was it. He would escort her to Camden Town.

She gnawed on her lower lip. That was the only part of her plan that hadn't checked out. Katie hadn't written back to say whether Victoria could stay with her, but Victoria knew that it would be fine. It had to be. They were friends, after all. And if, for some reason, she couldn't stay, Victoria would just go to their solicitor and request enough money to stay in a hotel for the rest of the week. But she was sure she wouldn't need to do that.

The little boy started gurgling and Victoria furrowed her brows at him for interrupting her thoughts. He quieted for a moment and then began gurgling even louder. She shrugged and looked out the window, watching the fallow fields go by.

She wouldn't let anything depress her now. She could imagine how proud her father would be of her. She would show everyone that she was an adult, an emancipated woman. Let Rowena mope until she wed and let Prudence run off and marry someone the moment things got rough. She, Victoria, was going to be independent. Perhaps after she got a job with *The Botanist's Quarterly* she would move into town and get her own flat. She would live in London until she had enough experience to go do field studies or something exciting like that.

The brakes on the train gave a high-pitched squeal, causing the mother with the baby on her lap to start so violently that the baby almost toppled over. Cambridge, that austere, magical kingdom of spires and castles, looked more forbidding than ever in the cold gray winter's day. Victoria stuck her tongue out at the buildings, condemning the entire place with her childish scorn. As a woman, she knew she wasn't much welcome there.

Seeing the city now emerge from the fog outside the train window, a flood of memories came back. Of playing tag with Prudence and Rowena in the park. Of the good-natured arguing among the many artists, intellectuals, and politicians her father called friends. During one memorable dinner, she, Ro, and Pru had watched wide-eyed as Walter Sickert had drawn an illustration on their dining room wall to prove a point to the other guests. Mrs. Tannin had been aghast, but their father had laughed and laughed and wouldn't let the wall be washed for weeks. She smiled at the memory, forgetting her anxiety.

But her nerves returned by the time the train screeched to a stop in Paddington Station. She had no sooner stepped off the platform than Kit wrapped her into a giant bear hug.

"I thought you would never get here," he told her.

"I told you when I was coming, you twit." She smiled up at

him, noting his suit, impeccable as always. He was almost but not quite a dandy, but as Victoria enjoyed a well-dressed man, she didn't much mind.

They linked arms and dodged throngs of people as he led her to where men were unloading the luggage. He handed a porter some money to carry the two trunks Victoria had brought with her. Then he led her out of the station. "Here now, why don't you skip this boring meeting thing and let me show you the sights?"

She swatted his arm, laughing. "I was born and raised in London. I've seen the sights."

"You haven't seen them with me, though. Think of how much fun we could have at Kensington Gardens or Big Ben. I bet you could get one of the Queen's guardsmen to talk if anyone could."

"I am going to the meeting! Now, where is your car?"

"My driver will meet us out front. How about if we go see if London Bridge is falling down yet, or we could visit Dickens's birthplace, or go to Madame Tussauds, or even go to Harrods and see if we can't find the proverbial looking glass."

He opened the door of a large silver touring car for her and then ran around the other side and hopped in.

"You're being a goose! No, we are going to 197 Lexington Place." She reached forward and gave the driver the address. "Sorry it's so crumpled," she said, her face heating. "I've been hanging on to it for a bit."

"That's all right, miss. I can read what it says."

Victoria gave him a brilliant smile and Kit pulled her back.

"Stop trifling with the driver and pay attention to me," he commanded.

"Oh, pooh, you don't need my attention. You can go to one of your girls for that."

"Who told you about my girls? No, don't tell me. Tell Elaine they are a figment of her imagination. And even if they weren't, I'm with you now, and my best friend is looking quite fetching today."

"Do you think?" she asked, a bit more anxiously than she wanted to. She'd chosen a taupe corduroy gored skirt and matching jacket with an Astrakhan collar and braid trim. On her head she wore a black velvet chapeau, with one simple black feather on the side. On the one hand she didn't want to dress too severely, in case Hairy Herbert (stupid Kit anyway) detested suffragettes, but on the other hand she needed to look serious and not young.

"Yes, you do. And who cares what Hairy Herbert thinks anyway?"

She sniffed. "I do. It's important I make a good first impression. I would like to earn enough money so that I can do what I like."

"Uh-oh, you brought up money. Surely you know that's forbidden among our set?"

"I do think that is silly, don't you? Especially when it's all anyone thinks about."

He threw his head back and laughed. "That's why I love you, Victoria, you say things no one else will."

There was an awkward moment when the word *love* hung between them, but Victoria carried on as if she hadn't noticed. "For instance, I'm not supposed to talk about the way my uncle basically controls all our money until I'm twenty-five or until I get married—"

Kit sat up straight. "He what?" he interrupted. "That's not possible. Especially not with Rowena—she's twenty-two, isn't she? She could actually protest that in court."

Victoria shook her head. "I don't know all the legalities of it. We're certainly well-off, but our uncle is to be our money manager until we are age twenty-five or married to a suitable young man. I believe my father was afraid we would become the victims of treasure hunters."

"So that's why you and Rowena moved out to Summerset."

Victoria nodded. "It's not as if we don't love it there, but we were hardly accustomed to that sort of life."

The car stopped in front of a tall brick building and Victoria felt a wash of cold pour over her. It was now or never. She found herself gripping Kit's hand, desperately wishing he could go in with her. But no. How would she ever stand on her own if she kept relying on other people to help her? The driver had come around and opened the door. Suddenly she felt a slight tightening in her chest and her heart almost stopped.

Oh, dear God. Please not now. She willed herself to remain calm. For once, Kit had no funny jokes or sarcastic remarks to make; he merely held her hand until the tightness eased. She gave him a bright smile as a reward and stepped out of the car. "I'm not sure how long I'll be," she told Kit. "Perhaps an hour?"

"Are you sure you don't want me to go in with you?"

She shook her head. "Of course not. I'll be fine."

A little bell on the door rang as she opened it and stepped into the dark offices of *The Botanist's Quarterly*. Victoria had expected the headquarters of such a serious and scientific journal to represent how important the journal was to the scientific community. Instead, they seemed rather small and dreary, and the glass cases on the walls enshrining dried plant specimens from all over the world could have used a good dusting. An older woman with iron-gray hair and a severely cut black dress looked up when she entered. If she was surprised to see Victoria, she didn't show it, but then, Victoria suspected that the watery blue eyes underneath the wire spectacles rarely showed any emotion whatsoever.

Victoria took a deep breath and marched up to the desk. "I'm here to see Harold L. Herbert, please."

The woman didn't even bother to look down at the ledger in front of her. "I'm sorry. Mr. Herbert is in a meeting. If you are here about the transcriptionist position, please leave your references . . ."

Victoria drew herself up to her full height, which admittedly wasn't very tall, and tried to look as old and self-possessed as possible. "I'm sorry. Perhaps I wasn't clear. I actually have an appointment with Mr. Herbert. My name is V. Buxton, and I'm a . . . a botanist," she told the woman, wishing she hadn't stumbled on the word *botanist.*

The woman shot her a look that told Victoria she'd been found out, but the woman looked at the ledger, made a notation, and excused herself. "I will be right back." She disappeared down a narrow hall and Victoria heard the clicking of a door opening and shutting.

Victoria stood at a standstill, half afraid to breathe. Her eyes took in a dozen dark filing cabinets standing against one wall and the dozen or so issues of *The Botanist's Quarterly* arranged across the desk in front of her. The woman came back and ushered Victoria silently down a narrow hallway into an equally narrow office.

Victoria barely had time to take in a small wooden desk with a chipped top before being attacked by a short, balding man in a long black coat. It crossed her mind that Hairy Herbert wasn't hairy at all.

"What is the meaning of this, young lady?" The gravel of his low voice grated on her ear. "What kind of joke are you playing?"

Though he was only a bit taller than she, his anger made him seem larger and more intimidating. She stepped back. "I don't understand. I am V. Buxton and I have an appointment to discuss my writing with the managing editor. Are you Harold Herbert?"

"Of course I am, but you are not V. Buxton!"

The trembling began in her toes and spread throughout her body. No one in her entire life had ever shouted at her. Prudence and Rowena would occasionally get into terrible rows and scream at each other like banshees, but no one had ever, ever raised his voice at her. "I most certainly am. If you would care to sit down, we could look at some other articles I have penned—"

"I'm not looking at anything. If you are indeed V. Buxton, then you have committed a terrible fraud."

"How can I have committed a fraud by being who I say I am?"

"I expected V. Buxton to be a man. I wanted to buy articles from a man, not from a chit of a girl!"

"But you did accept and pay me for an article. You can't denounce the quality of my work and the thoroughness of my research—you thought it was good enough to put in the magazine! I came here today to discuss writing more articles for you, as you yourself requested!"

"That was when I thought you were a man. And your article will not be appearing in *The Botanist's Quarterly*. You can keep the money rendered to you."

Her mouth fell open and tears gathered behind her eyes.

Mr. Herbert cleared his throat. "I will speak plainly, Miss Buxton, if that is indeed your name, so there will be no further doubt. There is no room for women in the sciences, my dear young lady, except perhaps as a help to their husbands. Women just are not suited for such work. Their brains are not made for it. And quite frankly, it will be a cold day before *The Botanist's Quarterly* accepts the contributions of a woman over those of a man who may be a husband and a father needing to earn money to take care of his family. I don't wish to be cruel, but that is the truth."

At some point during this speech, the tears she'd tried so hard to hold back overran her efforts and fell down her cheeks. The urge to stomp her feet or throw something was strong, but the days when she could get her way by throwing a fit were long over, and she would just be feeding this man's low opinion of women if she did so.

"Do you have any daughters, Mr. Herbert?" she asked him suddenly.

He looked surprised. "I have one. She is a good girl who stays at home and helps her mother and will do so until she is married."

Impatient with herself, she scrubbed at her cheeks with her hands so she could face that despicable man dry-eyed. "I wonder if she would be proud of you today. The way you wouldn't even discuss a young woman's writing because she was not the man you expected her to be." He started to bluster, but she quieted him with a hand. "I was extremely proud of my father, Mr. Herbert. My father would have never done what you did today; he understood that women could be just as passionate about science as a man could be."

"Maybe that's because your father wasn't a scientist, Miss Buxton. Now, I bid you good day."

He turned and Victoria reached for the door. "Oh, but he was a scientist, Mr. Herbert. His name was Sir Philip Buxton and he was not only a noted botanist, but was recognized and knighted for his scientific work. Now I bid *you* a good day."

She swept out of the office with her head high, but that composure only lasted as long as it took for her to pass the receptionist and out the front door. What a fool she was. Had she really believed that just because she had been raised in an atmosphere where women were valued that everyone would feel the same way? Hadn't Madame Curie herself once discussed the lofty attitude of some of her fellow scientists? But she hadn't listened. Instead of just writing incognito, she wanted to be acknowledged for her work. What silly pride she had shown. She saw Kit's car waiting for her and she burst into fresh tears, knowing she would have to share her humiliation and stupidity. She passed the car and heard the door slam moments later.

"Victoria, what happened? Did he hurt you? Do you want me to challenge him to a duel?"

"No! Why don't you just say I told you so? You knew this was going to happen, didn't you?"

"I don't even know what happened. How could I possibly when you haven't told me?"

"I was ordered to leave unless I was interested in the transcription position! They aren't even going to publish the article he'd already accepted."

"Oh, my dear, I'm so sorry."

The sorrow in his voice made her want to hit something. Hit *him*. She slammed her valise into his chest and he grabbed it.

"But you knew it was going to happen like this, didn't you? You knew! How did you know?"

"I didn't know. I just guessed. Most men aren't ready for women like you and Rowena."

She turned to face him, her fists clenched by her side. "But that isn't . . ." It was on the tip of her tongue to say "fair," but that sounded so childish, as if she expected life to be fair, when it most assuredly was not and never would be. "Right," she said, not meeting Kit's eyes. He knew what she'd been about to say, she was sure of it, and it embarrassed her to be so spoiled and childish that she would expect the world to play fair with her when it didn't with anyone else. "It isn't right," she asserted.

She turned and started walking again.

"Victoria? Where are you going?"

"I don't know!"

Out of the corner of her eye she saw him motion to the driver and the motor pulled out and began following them. She felt silly and cosseted, as if she were a bomb about to go off, and that only made her angrier. How could she expect anyone to take her seriously if she kept acting like a child?

CHAPTER
SIX

Katie's mother was a tall, thin woman with faded brown hair and snapping black eyes who radiated warmth. She looked barely older than her daughter, but arthritis had swollen her joints, making her hands look like a crone's. After years as a scrubwoman, she happily kept house for her surprisingly successful daughter and three of her equally successful friends. Muriel Dixon made no bones about either her daughter's illegitimacy or the fulsome pride she felt about her daughter working as an office girl. Sir Philip Buxton, the man who had made it all possible, was no less than a god.

"And if he's not a god himself, he was put on earth special by the Almighty, that's for certain."

Prudence, who had been coming to see Muriel for housekeeping lessons twice a week for the past two weeks, would always agree.

"I still can't believe you've never even baked a scone before." Muriel shook her head as she thrust her stiff hands into a bowl of dough. Prudence tried the best she could to imitate Muriel's movements. Last week, she'd learned to make scones and iron sheets. She had washed and dried the sheets at home and brought them to Muriel's to iron. She had only burned them once, and Muriel said that if she kept the burnt spot at the bottom of the bed, Andrew would never notice.

Today, Muriel was teaching Prudence to make a meat pie. It was just in time, too. If Andrew thought it strange that he had three straight meals of scones, he'd kept his mouth shut, but Prudence guessed that it wouldn't be for long. Prudence picked up the carefully listed ingredients from the greengrocer and the butcher on the way to Katie's house. She bought enough for two as payment for the lessons, even though Muriel told her she didn't have to, that she needed to learn how to live frugally.

It was a difficult lesson for Prudence, who had never had to budget before.

"It's the first time I've made a meat pie, too. Fancy that," Prudence said, in her new brisk way. The only way she kept herself going was to accept each moment as it came. Some were good, some were bad, but all had to be gotten through somehow.

She and Andrew had fallen into a routine that seemed to be working. Three days a week, he left early in the morning and picked up odd jobs for the day. Those were the days she came to Muriel's house for housekeeping lessons, or, as Muriel called them, "lessons in slavery and servitude." The rest of the week he stayed home and studied, except for Tuesdays, when he went to study chemistry, mathematics, and French with a tutor, and on Sunday mornings, when he treated Prudence to their customary breakfast out.

The entrance examinations were held four times a year, and the next round of tests would be held in Glasgow in the spring. They would be given in London next fall, but Andrew and Prudence agreed they did not want to wait if that could be time spent in school. They didn't discuss what might happen if he didn't pass.

"So tell me again what Sir Philip was like," Muriel said once they had gotten the pies in the oven.

"I thought you were going to teach me how to clean out the icebox?" Prudence asked, smiling.

Muriel waved a hand. "We can do that later. It will keep. Here, have a cuppa. Even slaves get a break now and again."

"Why do you call us slaves?"

Muriel smiled, showing her crooked teeth. "Oh, it's just a pet name. Actually, I've never had it so good in my whole life as I do keeping house for the young ladies. Precious gems, all of them, especially my own Katie. I knew she was too smart to be a scrubwoman, but what did I know about getting her into school? That's why Sir Philip and that little girl of his, Victoria, are saints, that's all. But you wives, that is practically slavery, right there. Those suffragettes have it right. Now tell me about Sir Philip."

Muriel and Katie's flat was larger than Prudence's and the kitchen was separate from the living room. It was a long, narrow room with only one window, but Muriel kept it scrupulously clean. Because there were five women in the house and one or the other always had a date, the ironing board was always set up next to the stove. They sat at a long wooden table and Muriel handed her a cup of tea.

Prudence had no idea that Sir Philip had paid for Katie's education. Her throat tightened. It was so very like him. She racked her brain for a good story. "Well, you know, Sir Philip always had these odd notions about education. He would read a book about a new educational technique and soon we would be trying some completely different method of learning, like the

Charlotte Mason method or something like that. My mother was the governess and sometimes she would just throw her hands up in the air and let him have his way with us." Prudence sipped at her tea, remembering. "Between him and my mother, I'm surprised we got an education at all."

"What do you mean?"

Prudence jumped a little and her cheeks colored. "Oh." She stared at her nails while Muriel waited next to her. Finally, she looked up at the older woman and smiled.

"My mother wasn't always a governess. She started as a parlor maid. My family were poor townsfolk and probably Buxton serfs at one time. But Sir Philip felt sorry for my mother, and he hired her to help take care of his baby daughter and his expectant wife. He employed a woman with a baby of her own, that's how kind he was." A lump rose in her throat. She knew of course that Sir Philip was only making amends for his father's abhorrent behavior toward her mother, behavior that left her pregnant with an illegitimate Buxton child. She didn't tell Muriel that; she wanted to forget it herself.

"And then, Sir Philip's wife died in childbirth and he retained my mother as the nanny and later just kept her on as the governess. He knew she didn't have an education, but she was an avid reader and he trusted her to help him educate us. It was a rather odd partnership. After I grew older and lost her, I used to wonder how she'd managed it." Prudence paused thoughtfully. "But I remember that, as a little girl, I would lie awake for hours, waiting for her to turn down the lantern and come to bed. I realize now that she was studying to stay ahead of her students."

There was a moment of silence before Muriel reached over and patted her hand. "She sounds as if she was a very determined woman."

Prudence took a deep, shuddering breath. "She was. I just wish . . ." She hesitated.

"What do you wish, child?"

"I just wish she had told me about my own birth, my lineage. Like you told Katie."

Muriel shrugged. "Oh, that wasn't my doing. I had to stay at home with my own mother or else we would have been out on the streets. My mother called Katie 'the little bastard,' so I started right off letting her know what it meant and that she was still loved no matter what her grandmother said. If I would have had a choice like your mum did? I don't know if I would have said anything either."

Prudence thought about that after she walked the ten blocks back to her flat. Would she have told her daughter in similar circumstances? She wasn't sure. She only knew how hurtful it was on the other side of a lifetime of lies.

Once home, she put the pie, covered with a clean cloth, on a shelf in the kitchen. She would heat it up just before suppertime, when Andrew would be home. At least she knew it would be good, and she was fairly certain she could imitate the results in her own home. At least she hoped she could. The flat was clean and there was little she could do here but read, so she slipped her warm woolen coat back on and headed out.

Camden Town teemed with life at all times of the day, so unlike her old neighborhood in Mayfair. Here men and women of all ages and classes jostled together on the sidewalks and the streetcars. There were blocks of factories interspersed with blocks of neighborhoods. Some of the neighborhoods, like hers, had started out as rows of stately old houses that had been chopped up into flats. She often took long walks in the afternoon to alleviate her boredom. She wondered whether taking care of

Andrew would be all that she would ever do. Even after he became a veterinarian and they moved to some rural town where he'd set up shop, she would still be looking after him, only in a different place. Her days would still consist of cooking and cleaning and doing laundry. If they had children, it would be the same work, only more difficult. Was that what her mother and Sir Philip had prepared her for?

She turned down Crowndale Road toward the park. If they knew this was to be her fate, why bother to educate her at all? What good did Chaucer or Shakespeare do for those stuck in "slavery and servitude," as Muriel put it? But then, maybe how she felt about her life depended solely on her attitude. Perhaps if she were truly in love with Andrew, ironing sheets wouldn't seem like such a chore?

Guilt gnawed at Prudence's insides. It was only on her walks, when she was alone, that she could entertain her true feelings. Somehow it seemed less of a betrayal when she was away from the little home she was trying so hard to create for them. She cared for her husband deeply, and their lovemaking grew more loving every night as they both learned what they were doing, but her heart didn't flutter when he smiled at her and his laugh didn't make her legs go weak. Not like they did when she saw Sebastian. Her cheeks flamed and for a moment she allowed herself to recall his face. The way his mouth moved into an easy smile, or the way his eyes warmed when he looked at her.

Then, as if she conjured him out of thin air, she heard his laughter.

She froze, looking around her. Regent's Park was full of ladies and gentlemen on their afternoon walks and nannies taking small children out for an airing. Her heart thudded in her throat. How could she have possibly heard Sebastian? He was away at university, wasn't he? But she knew that laugh. She would know it anywhere. She heard it again, but it was farther away and she wondered for a moment whether she was going mad. The sound transported her back to the last moment she'd seen him on the night before she'd left Summerset. He'd assured her that everything would be fine—he knew of the perfect employment opportunity. She closed her eyes and could almost hear the words he'd uttered that night.

"There's another thing that makes it perfect." He'd stopped walking and turned to her. His eyes had shone mysterious in the darkness. "It means you won't disappear and I will get to see you again."

Her heart thudded in her chest and for a moment she thought that perhaps he was going to kiss her, but then he turned away and began walking again. It was as if he sensed that she was too fragile for even one more emotional incident. She swallowed.

Now she wished fiercely that he had kissed her, even if she had never seen him again; she wished she had the memory of his kiss to sustain her. She turned away and hurried out of the park, her pulse racing. She almost felt as though she had been unfaithful to her husband. Her face burned as she hurried through the waning afternoon sun, back to the home she shared with Andrew.

* * *

"Oh, bloody hell, Billingsly. You don't mean to say that the Labor Party has valid points?" Kit clapped his friend on the back. "You're getting worse than an old man, worrying about this and that. If I didn't know better, I'd say you were in love."

Sebastian started and Kit's eyes narrowed. Though most of

the men in the Cunning Coterie played at love, they had all been successful at dodging marriage. Apparently, Kit would have to keep an eye on Sebastian.

"You're trying to change the subject because you haven't a clue as to what I'm talking about," Sebastian said. "You're woefully out of touch with current events."

"Current events are as dull as university was. Eventually, you'll see that I'm right. Now what do you say we get out of this cold and go to the club, eh?"

Sebastian shrugged. "You're the one who wanted to take a turn in the park."

"I thought it would liven you up a bit."

"How can a turn in the park liven me up when we have so many pressing things to think about?"

"Ah." Kit nodded sagely. "Are we talking about the Irish question again? Or the teacher strikes? See, I do know about current events. But do you realize that it's all you talk about? You've always been more serious than the rest of us, but you used to like a bit of fun, as well. Now you mope about like a lovesick puppy."

A swift punch to the arm told Kit his dig had found its mark. "Now, now. No fighting in the gentlemen's club. They may think we're not gentlemen," Kit said as they entered the dark club room.

"They'd be right in your case, you conceited upstart," Sebastian muttered.

The Turf Club was one of the most exclusive clubs in a city full of exclusive clubs. Both Kit and Sebastian had been inducted because their fathers had been members. The drinks were the best money could buy and the food delicious, though not as fancy as at Brooks's. Nor was the atmosphere as convivial as that of White's, but they were happy at the Turf Club, where most of the male members of the Coterie spent their free time. The female members were, of course, not allowed.

"So what is the story with the enchanting Victoria?" Sebastian asked once they were seated in the dining room. "Is she a contender for the Kittredge family crest, or are you just toying with the girl?"

Kit snorted. "She is not one to toy with, let me tell you. She's too smart for that. No, actually, I am trying something completely different. I've offered true friendship and have received it in return. We're buddies, chums, pals, and I rather like it."

Sebastian's brows rose up his forehead. "Why hasn't your mother made the classic bride's ploy yet?"

Kit laughed. Whenever his mother thought he might be paying special attention to a girl, she invited her to the Kittredge family estate. Kit usually ended the relationship soon after. "I actually think she is playing her cards differently this time. Either that or she doesn't know how much time Vic and I spend together."

Sebastian laughed. "You're fooling yourself if you think she doesn't know, my friend. Not with Colin's mother sniffing around for her like a trained hunting dog."

"I think I'm more afraid of Lady Charlotte than I am of my own mother," Kit told him. "And that's saying something."

"Aren't we all," Colin said, joining them.

Kit stood and clapped Colin on the shoulder. "How we all managed to have dragon ladies as mothers is what I'd like to know. Not a single dove amongst the lot of them. It's like Jolly Old England bred an entire generation of harpies."

"So what are you doing here, old chap? Aren't you supposed

to be at the university, finishing your studies?" Sebastian asked Colin.

Kit glanced at his watch while the others talked. Victoria expected him to take her to the opera this evening. Of course, he hadn't expected to run into Sebastian and Colin. If he ate quickly, he would have just enough time to extricate himself from a night of debauchery and pick her up. He took up the thread of conversation just as they started in on the Irish question. "Oh, bloody hell, hasn't this been talked to death? If words were weaponry, they would all be dead by now and there would be no question."

"But don't you think—" Sebastian started.

"No, I don't," Kit interrupted. "Or as little as possible. And that is something I'll drink to."

"Hear, hear!" Colin said, signaling for another round. "Now, what were you discussing before I showed up?"

"Women," Kit said.

"Your cousin, to be specific," Sebastian said.

"Which one? The lovely, tormented Rowena, or the minx?" Kit laughed. "The minx is far more to my taste."

"You'd better be careful of that one," Colin told him.

"I'd never do anything to hurt her," Kit said, stung.

"No, I meant, *you'd* best be careful. Let me share this and you will get a fair understanding of what I mean." He leaned in and the others followed suit. "Even my mother handles her with kid gloves."

Kit leaned back and Sebastian raised his brows. He nodded toward Kit. "You're welcome to her," he said.

"I already told you we're just friends. Neither of us wishes to get married. And she means that," he added, remembering how she had once called him on the carpet when he expressed his doubt at her sincerity. As he recalled, she'd actually hit him. Or pinched him, or otherwise threatened violence. Oh, she was serious all right.

"You'd better hope she never changes her mind." Colin grinned.

Kit raised his glass. "I'll drink to that."

"I met the lovely Rowena not too long ago. Your mother had coerced her into doing calls," Sebastian said. Their meal arrived and they fell silent for a moment as they appreciated the simplicity of stew, steak and kidney pie, and fish and chips.

"Mother's taken Rowena under her wing. The poor girl can't seem to get over losing her maid or whoever it was."

"Prudence wasn't their maid," Sebastian flared. "That was a ridiculous ruse Rowena made up to pacify your father."

Colin shrugged and Sebastian fell silent. "Well, whoever she was, Rowena is as desolate about losing her as she is her father. Lainey's just happy that Rowena is taking some of the heat off her, now that Mother has a new cause." He looked at Sebastian. "You had best be careful. If you won't marry Elaine, I think our mothers would be just as happy if you married Rowena."

Sebastian shook his head. "Maybe I'll drop by and take her for a drive. Get her out of the line of fire. If we give them something to talk about, maybe they'll lay off for a bit."

Colin looked dubious. "It's worth a try."

Kit sat back and checked his watch again. "Well, I'm sorry to cut the evening short, but I have another appointment I must get to."

"What? You're leaving your friends and a night of decadence and dissipation? It can only be a woman," Colin said.

Kit smiled but didn't share which woman it was. Everyone

else believed Victoria was off visiting friends and it was Kit and Victoria's intent to keep it that way. There was enough gossip circulating about them without adding fuel to the fire. She had promised that no one would recognize her tonight. Kit couldn't wait to find out what that meant.

"I can't believe you're leaving us for a woman," Colin said. "She must really have you on a short chain."

"She doesn't! I just promised her I would take her somewhere."

"But surely that doesn't mean you can't have at least one more drink?" Colin tempted.

Kit checked his watch yet again. "Well, perhaps one more." He would have his driver go full speed all the way there. They would only be a few minutes late and surely that wouldn't make her too angry. And it would do her good to be a little angry, prima donna that she was.

* * *

He was far more than just a little late, he realized sometime later as the driver pulled the car up to a building in Camden Town. And too late, he remembered what a terrible day she'd had and just why he had promised to take her to the opera in the first place.

He frowned at the paper in his hand, unable to make out the words. He'd had much too much to drink. His driver pointed at the door.

"I think it's upstairs, sir."

"I knew that," he muttered.

He opened the door and made his way up the narrow staircase. When he reached the top he realized there were doors on either side of the landing. "Oh, bloody hell." He looked down the stairway for guidance, but the door had shut behind him and the driver was no longer there.

By the dim gaslight he saw that one was door number one and the other was door number two. He squinted at the paper in his hand but couldn't see either number on it. How like her to keep him guessing. He smiled. She was a minx. A soft, lovable minx.

Who was going to be very, very angry that he was so late. He frowned at the doors. Well, he had a fifty-fifty chance of getting it right. Of course, he had a fifty-fifty chance of getting it wrong, too.

He didn't much like being wrong.

So he called her name instead of knocking. "Victoria," he whispered. "Victoria?"

Nothing.

"Victoria!" he bellowed. Whoops. A bit loud, that.

A door opened to his right, but it wasn't Victoria; it was a tall, thin woman with furious black eyes. She was wearing a pink wrapper that was much too short for her.

"I'm looking for Victoria," he told her with as much dignity as he could muster.

"I know that, you big oaf. Everyone on the bloody block knows that," she snapped. "You're too late, she's gone to bed."

But they were supposed to go to the opera. "She hasn't!" he said. "We were going somewhere."

"You *were* going somewhere three hours ago! Now you're just going back down those stairs and you're going home!"

Kit leaned up against the doorjamb, suddenly dizzy. "Three hours ago? Are you sure? Oh, that's bad," he told the woman. "She'd had a terrible day. I was going to make her happy so she'd forget."

"Too late for that now," the woman said, her voice a bit softer. "Now go on home before you're sick in my hallway."

"I bet she's really angry with me, isn't she?"

The woman snorted. "You have no idea."

She shut the door, and for a moment Kit thought about kicking it, just to show that he didn't care whether she was angry with him. It wasn't as though they were . . . anything. He turned toward the stairs, which suddenly seemed like a climb down Mount Everest. Silly women. Who needed them anyway? They weren't anything. Just friends. Best friends.

"Silly women," he repeated out loud. He found that by leaning against one wall and clinging to the railing, he could get down the steps one by one. His driver jumped out as soon as Kit opened the door.

"Now you're here," he said as the driver led him to the car.

"Pardon me, sir?"

"Never mind." Kit looked up at the windows on the top of the building. For a moment he thought he saw someone looking out the window, but it was just his imagination. "I don't care!" he yelled as he fell into the backseat of his car. "I bloody well don't care," he muttered again, but he had a terrible feeling that in the morning, he would care very much.

CHAPTER
SEVEN

After a sleepless night, during which she found herself imagining different ways of humiliating Kit in return, Victoria sat at the Dixons' kitchen table and seethed.

When Victoria had appeared on Katie's doorstep the previous afternoon, Muriel hadn't even been expecting a visitor, but after one look at the girl's swollen, red-rimmed eyes, she gathered her and her trunks up in one fell swoop. She set out fresh crumpets and hot tea and listened to Victoria's story, clucking in all the appropriate places. When Katie and the other girls arrived, Muriel had told and retold the story, her black eyes snapping, while Victoria sighed dramatically and looked aggrieved. They planned all sorts of delicious revenges until all agreed that Victoria's stunning success would be the best revenge she could get.

Plotting how to make Victoria a stunning success was much less enticing than revenge, and she found herself alone there. But that was all right. She knew that she and Kit could figure it all out.

Then Kit failed to appear.

Victoria clenched her fists. A month ago, she wouldn't have believed it could happen. She wouldn't have believed that he'd have gone out drinking with his friends when he had *promised* to take her to the opera. She hadn't even asked to go, he had *offered, to help her feel better*. Then not only did he fail to show up at their agreed-upon time, he had appeared hours later, making a horrid scene in the hallway like a common dockworker.

The girls assured her before they left for their jobs that they had all had beaus who had done all that and worse. They didn't believe her when she told them that Kit wasn't her beau, he was her best friend, which made it so much worse.

Lottie, the one woman who hadn't gone to work, poured herself a cup of tea and sat across the table from Victoria, curiosity etching her sharp features.

"You know, moping around all day won't bring him back. You're much better off without him. Men are bad news all the way around. They exist solely to propagate the species and keep women in subjugation."

Victoria studied Lottie. She looked older than the other girls, with a face like an ax. Her hair was pulled back in an unbecoming bun and her mouth was straight and flat and looked as if it didn't smile very often.

"How come you're not at work?" Victoria asked.

"I have the day off." Lottie tilted her head and observed Victoria. "I'm meeting a friend for lunch. She's the leader of an organization I belong to, the Suffragettes for Female Equality. You're welcome to join me. Are you a suffragette?"

Victoria nodded. "Oh, yes. My sister and I are members of the National Union of Women's Suffrage Societies."

Lottie snorted.

"What?" Victoria asked.

"Nothing. It's a good organization for ladies who don't want to get their hands dirty."

Lottie gave what Victoria could only term a challenging look.

"Oh, I'm not afraid of getting my hands dirty," she told Lottie. "You'll find that I'm afraid of very little."

"Good, then you'll come?"

Victoria smiled her assent, even though part of her really wanted to wait for Kit's apology note. She knew it was only a matter of time. Of course, it would do him some good if the driver reported that Miss Victoria had been out when it was delivered. Yes, it would serve him right. "That sounds wonderful. Where are we going to lunch? Am I properly dressed?"

Lottie's mouth twitched, and Victoria detected a hint of mockery in her expression. She hoped her friend was kinder than Lottie was. Or at least didn't have a face that could curdle milk.

Sometime later, she was sitting in Frascati's Winter Garden and feeling as if she, in a plain dark walking suit, and Lottie, in a black skirt and white blouse, were woefully underdressed for such a venue. The gold and silver décor and large palms seemed to have stunned Lottie into silence. Victoria didn't much like silence and hoped Lottie's friend would be more engaging. If Kit were here, he would be whispering snide remarks about the other stuffy patrons and making her laugh. She gave a sharp sigh and turned to Lottie. "Tell me about your friend."

To her surprise Lottie looked away and shifted in her seat. "Her name is Martha," she finally said, somewhat reluctantly.

"What does your organization do?"

"We fight oppression," Lottie said.

"How?"

"At the moment, we're concentrating on our newspaper."

Victoria leaned forward. "Oh, really? Who are your readers?"

"Wait until you talk to Martha. She will answer all your

questions and then tell you what you can do to help. If you want to, that is."

That last line was uttered derisively and Victoria burned. Lottie clearly thought her a wilting violet.

Just then a slight, dark-haired woman in a wine-colored velvet and lace dress put her hand on Lottie's shoulder.

"I am so sorry I'm late. I hope you haven't been waiting long."

Lottie actually smiled. "Not long at all," she said. "Martha, this is Victoria Buxton. The Honorable Victoria Buxton, if you will, and she has quite the story to tell. Victoria, this is Martha Long, founder of the Suffragettes for Female Equality."

Victoria stared wide-eyed at the elegant woman who stood before her. "Pleased to meet you."

Martha gave her a charming smile as she took a seat at the small, linen-covered table. "We don't do titles in our organization, but I am still pleased to meet you. Tell me your story and I'll judge whether it's front page or not. Lottie tends to exaggerate everything." She gave Lottie a quick smile as if to take the sting out of her words.

Victoria cocked her head at the pleasing, cultured tones of Martha's speech. They might not do titles here, but Martha was as wellborn as Victoria was, she'd stake her life on it. As Victoria told her about *The Botanist's Quarterly*, Martha pulled a pencil and a tattered yellow tablet out of her reticule, jotting down notes as she spoke.

They fell silent as a waiter approached with silver salvers full of delicate tea sandwiches and a heaping platter of miniature scones. Lottie took up the task of serving as Martha regarded Victoria, her dark eyes ablaze.

"So your last name is Buxton? And you say your father was a respected botanist?"

Victoria nodded. "He was knighted for his work." Victoria shifted uneasily. "I'm not sure if we should use my full name." She hadn't known Lottie had brought her here for an interview, and while the prospect of a newspaper article sounded exciting, she had a feeling her aunt and uncle would be much less enthusiastic.

Martha read her mind. "I can't imagine the Buxtons would be too pleased with this type of exposure."

Victoria frowned. "You know of my family?"

"Mm-hmm." Martha jotted something on her pad. "This is definitely worth a story, but I'm not sure whether it should go on the front page or on the editorial."

"I take it you run the newspaper?"

Martha nodded. "Among other things. There is so much we need to do to further the cause. It's just impossible to do everything ourselves."

Victoria nodded, recalling the few suffragette meetings she'd attended in the past. She was no stranger to crusading. Her father and his friends were always championing a cause such as labor rights, and listening to their discussions and arguments had taught her a thing or two. She began ticking off items on her fingers. "Fund-raising, education, delegation, a moderator to smooth relations between the different suffragette groups, an entire committee of people to do fieldwork . . . people can't work or vote if their children are starving to death."

Martha's dark eyes lit up. "You have more than a passing knowledge of our challenges, Victoria. May I call you Victoria?" When Victoria nodded, Martha continued. "It is difficult to do everything, but there is such *need*!"

Martha's voice quivered with passion and Victoria was fascinated by this charismatic woman who clearly had a deep desire to make a change in the world. "How did you become involved in the movement?" Victoria asked.

"I suggest we eat our tea," Martha said.

Obediently, Victoria took a small bite of the watercress sandwich Lottie had placed on her plate. "That's hardly fair. I told you my story." Victoria swallowed, remembering the last time she almost used the word *fair*. Briefly she wondered what Kit was doing, but then she squared her shoulders and turned back to Martha.

Martha's brows shot up in amusement. "So fairness is important to you, is it? How old are you?"

Victoria hesitated and then shrugged. She had no reason to be ashamed of who she was. "I'll be nineteen next month."

Martha smiled. "And that also answers my question about why you still think things should be fair. So, what exactly would you like to know?"

Victoria flushed and then cleared her throat. "What is your real name and your father's title?"

Caught off guard, Martha startled, then narrowed her eyes. "Oh, you're a cagey one, you are. I can hide my identity from almost everyone except my own kind. Which is why I generally avoid you all like the plague."

Martha pushed away her plate and flicked open a gold and ivory compact. She took out a cigarette and lit one up to the dismay of the other patrons, but Martha's commanding and confident presence seemed to dare anyone to protest her desire to smoke. She looked up. "I'm sorry, do you want one?"

Lottie and Victoria both shook their heads. Then, not wanting to seem like a prude, Victoria explained. "I have asthma and the smoke seems to worsen it." She almost choked on the word *asthma*.

"I mostly love the way they smell," Martha said, blowing a smoke ring over her head. "Back to your original question. My real name is Beatrice Martha Longstreet and my father is a count."

Victoria raised an eyebrow. The Longstreets were definitely peers but didn't travel in the same circles as the Buxtons. "How did a Longstreet end up running a subversive suffragette organization?"

"How did a Buxton end up applying for a job at a botany magazine?" Martha countered, and Lottie laughed.

After a startled moment, Victoria joined her. "Touché!"

Victoria tried to help pay for their tea, but Martha waved her off. "You gave me a wonderful story for the newspaper and I owe you for it. Now, let me escort you and Lottie home."

To her surprise, Martha led them to a small, plain Saxon Motor Car. More surprising, Martha worked the crank and then climbed in.

She looked across at Victoria and grinned. "Well, get in! My apologies for the snug fit. I have found that a small motorcar is much more convenient."

Expertly navigating the narrow roads, clogged with people and horses, Martha pressed the gas pedal and drove east. "This is one of the few luxuries I decided to keep when I started the organization," she yelled over the sound of the engine. "I can get about faster and can relocate women in need more quickly than if we were taking the Tube or a cabbie. It just made sense. Besides, I love to drive!"

She swerved around a corner, barely missing a woman pulling a cart of chickens. Victoria clutched the handle and laughed. Martha glanced sideways at her and then, after a moment, joined her.

Victoria clung to Lottie as Martha navigated London's narrow streets at breakneck speeds. Lottie seemed unperturbed. Perhaps she was used to this. Victoria felt a pang of jealousy. What would it be like to speed about London, an independent woman, effecting real change in the world? When they stopped in front of Katie's flat, Victoria reluctantly climbed out of the motorcar, wishing the afternoon didn't have to end.

Martha stretched out a hand. "Please come to headquarters, poppet. Lottie will bring you. I would love to give you a tour and show you our work there. It's so very important."

Victoria clasped Martha's hand. "I'd like that very much."

Martha's smile lit up her pretty face, making Victoria feel, for the first time since arriving in London, that she was indeed someone special, someone of worth. "Wonderful. I have a feeling you could be very important to the cause, Victoria. I am delighted to have met you."

Victoria stared after Martha's motorcar as she sped off down the street. Excitement shivered through her. She felt as if she were on the edge of a great adventure, perhaps the adventure she had been looking for her entire life.

CHAPTER EIGHT

owena pulled her scarf tighter around her neck. "Thanks so much for taking me out. Summerset gets a little close at times."

Sebastian smiled sideways at her. "I just wish it had been a better day for a drive. Hard to appreciate anything when the windows keep freezing over. What do you say we give up the drive and head into town for some hot tea?"

She nodded and within minutes they were parked in front of the Freemont Inn. "Oh," she said so quietly that Sebastian didn't hear her.

This was where she'd met Jon just before he took her up in the sky. He still hadn't written to her, and she wondered whether his family had told him about her visit. Sometimes she wondered whether he had forgotten all about her.

Sebastian opened the door for her and they hurried into the inn, trying to escape the chilling north wind that had blown up.

"It's freezing out there." She laughed, unwinding her scarf. Suddenly she stopped cold, her heart almost leaping out of her chest.

Jonathon.

Well, not Jonathon exactly, but Mr. Dirkes, and where

Mr. Dirkes was, Jonathon was nearby. So it was no surprise when she spotted him coming around the corner from the salon part of the inn. He spotted her about the same time and his face lit up with pleasure. Next to her Sebastian said something, but she missed it, her entire attention focused on Jonathon's face. As always, everything around her seemed to go from a dull gray to living, breathing color the moment his gaze met hers.

Jon hurried toward them, his eyes focused on her. She felt Sebastian take her arm, but she pulled away and ran the last few steps to meet him. They both stopped just short of being in each other's arms. For a moment they stood awkwardly, unsure what to do next, until Jon snatched up both her hands and kissed them. She shivered and flushed at the heat from his lips. They stared into each other's eyes, transfixed.

"I say, this would be a bit awkward if I weren't pining for someone else," Sebastian said, coming up next to her.

Jon appraised him, reluctantly dropping Rowena's hands. "Yes, it would, mate. But as you have eyes for someone else, I would be happy to make your acquaintance. My name is Jonathon Wells. This is my friend and employer, Douglas Dirkes."

Mr. Dirkes had joined them and shook Rowena's hand.

"And this is my friend Lord Sebastian Billingsly. Have you eaten lunch yet?" She couldn't take her eyes off Jonathon.

"No, we were just seated. Please join us," Mr. Dirkes said, leading them to their table. "Two more, sir," he called to the waiter. "Now before you get angry with our young man, Miss Rowena, it's my fault that he has been so long away. We received an order for a large shipment of aeroplanes and we haven't been able to get away."

"I suppose you wouldn't let him write me either," Rowena

said tartly. Jon had captured her hand under the table the moment they were seated and for that he gave her a hard squeeze.

"And let your aunt and uncle know that we're such *good friends*?"

Rowena glowed. So they were *good friends*, were they? He squeezed her hand again, more gently this time. Rowena thrilled at her boldness, holding a man's hand under the table. "I guess you couldn't do that."

"I take it your family wouldn't approve?" Sebastian asked curiously.

Rowena flushed. "About as much as yours would have approved of Prudence," Rowena snapped, and then immediately felt sorry for the look in his eyes. "I do apologize, Sebastian. I shouldn't have said anything."

"That's quite all right," he said, his jaw tight. "And I see your point. My family would not have approved, but I would have done it anyway, had she given me the chance."

There was a moment of discomfort at the table before Sebastian turned to Mr. Dirkes. "So you build aeroplanes?"

With relief the topic turned to business and Rowena focused her attention once more on Jon, whose thumb was running lightly across her knuckles and making it difficult for her to think. "How long will you be home?" she asked underneath the conversation.

"Only a week. Are you ready to go up again?"

She leaned closer. "I have done nothing but think about it since the first time you took me up."

"Is flying all you have been thinking about?"

"No. And you know it, too."

He gave a low laugh and she turned her attention back to

the conversation. "You should really go up in one of their aeroplanes, Sebastian. I know you would love it."

He nodded. "I'd like that very much, actually."

Rowena squeezed Jon's hand and gave him a meaningful look. Catching her glance, he leaned forward. "Well, how about tomorrow then? You could fetch Rowena, and she could show you the way."

Sebastian caught their plan immediately. "So I'm to be an accessory, eh? I can do that. But I do expect to be taken up in an aeroplane as part of my payment."

Jon grinned and held out his hand. "It's a deal!"

The food arrived and the talk moved on to other things, but Rowena hardly followed the conversation. All she knew was that Jon was next to her, holding her hand, and that was all that mattered.

"So a little bird told me you made a surprise visit to the Wells Manor a while ago."

Rowena looked down at her meal, the sponge cake turning to dust in her mouth. "And what little bird was that?" She could just imagine the things his brother would say.

"Cristobird." He laughed. "She said you didn't stay nearly long enough but you did promise to come back and sup with us. Can we arrange that for this week?"

"Perhaps." She finally raised her eyes to look at him. Her breath caught and she wondered whether she would ever stop being surprised at how very blue his eyes were. "I'm sorry I rode over there. I was just so confused, and I hadn't heard anything from you . . ."

His hand squeezed hers under the table and he leaned close to her ear so that only she would hear his words. "You don't need to doubt my intentions toward you again, all right? Even if I can't get in touch with you, just remember that I will always make my way back to you."

The words were stark in their intent and sounded more like a vow than any wedding pledge Rowena had ever heard.

The meal ended far too soon for Rowena, but she could part with him knowing they would see each other tomorrow. She could bear anything if she could go to bed each night knowing she would see him again. He held her arm possessively as they walked to the car. Discreetly, Sebastian and Mr. Dirkes went to the front of the motorcar. Sebastian cranked the starter and the sound of the motor drowned out their conversation.

Jon's eyes searched Rowena's face. Even though the pale winter sun was far in the west, she could see the blaze of his blue eyes. Her body leaned toward his, as if the distance between them was just too great. Without warning, he bent his head, pressing his lips against hers. Just like the first time he'd kissed her, they were in public, but this time, Rowena didn't hesitate. She kissed him back and the moment spun out between them like an eternity. Then Jon broke away and laughed softly. "I'll see you tomorrow."

"Tomorrow," she murmured.

* * *

The next morning, her aunt was at the breakfast table when Rowena finally appeared downstairs. Elaine shot her a look of warning, and Rowena's heart stilled.

"Good morning," she called to both her aunt and her cousin. She gave Elaine a look in return and mouthed "What?" behind her aunt's back.

Elaine shrugged.

No help there.

Breakfast was served buffet style on a large ornate side table so that the family could eat whenever they arose. Her uncle usually ate first, as he woke up earliest to get a good start on his daily work, and Aunt Charlotte rarely came downstairs for breakfast, preferring to eat in the comfort of her own room. She usually only appeared when there were visitors, so today her presence was highly unusual and highly suspect.

Rowena had come downstairs famished, and even the advent of her aunt couldn't stay her hunger. She served herself a bowl of strawberries with a dab of fresh cream and a few poached kippers on a thick slice of bread and butter. Kippers were her father's favorites and though a lump rose in her throat at the thought of him, the feelings of anguish had abated. He wouldn't want her to be unhappy. Ever.

She sat down at the table and began eating with enjoyment. "I don't believe it's going to be nearly as cold today as it was yesterday," she said to her cousin and her aunt. Her aunt smiled politely and continued reading her newspaper.

Elaine shook her head. "No. And the wind has stopped, too, thank God. I thought the roof was going to blow right off last night," she said, her eyes darting between her mother and her cousin. Years of experience with her mother made her anxious and Rowena could feel the misery coming off her in waves. In her mother's presence, the mischievous and fun-loving Elaine disappeared, leaving behind the intimidated, gauche little girl she used to be.

Rowena gave Elaine a smile she hoped was bolstering and met the problem head-on. "So what has led you to grace us with your presence this morning, Aunt Charlotte?" she asked, sounding almost as impudent as Victoria.

Her ladyship put down her newspaper and leveled a stern look at Rowena, who remembered suddenly why she detested confrontation so much. It terrified her, as did her aunt. She stared down at her kippers, her appetite waning.

"I thought it was time we had a chat, my dear. When you and your sister came to us, I realized how many years we had lost because your dear father chose to take you and your sister abroad so much instead of spending more time here."

"But we spent every summer—"

Aunt Charlotte raised her hand to stop her. "Yes, I know you spent your summers here, but so much time was spent entertaining that we did not have time to become as close as I had hoped. Now, of course, you are a young woman and the time for me to step in as a mother to you is long past."

Rowena risked a glance up at her aunt, but her aunt wasn't looking at her. She stared off in the distance, over the top of her teacup, a slight frown marking her lips as if she was pondering chances lost. Rowena glanced at Elaine, who looked as baffled as Rowena felt. Where was this leading? She had a sinking feeling.

"So when I hear a report concerning your behavior such as the one I received yesterday, why, I'm almost at a loss as to how to proceed . . ."

Elaine's eyes went wide and Rowena slumped in her seat.

"Auntie—"

But her aunt continued as if she hadn't spoken. "And while I am, of course, appalled at such public behavior, and *certain* that it will never happen again, I think I am far more hurt that you didn't tell me that you and Sebastian were engaged."

Rowena froze. *Sebastian?* Public behavior? What on earth was her aunt accusing her of? Her face flamed as realization suddenly struck. Her aunt must assume that because Sebastian had picked her up, it was Sebastian she had kissed outside the inn. But who had reported her? "Oh, no, Auntie, we're not, I mean . . ."

Her aunt set her cup down with such force that the tea sloshed over the sides. "What do you mean you're not? Don't tell me he took such liberties in public without any kind of understanding?"

Rowena held up her hand. "No, of course not."

"I should hope not. You were both raised better than that and the gossip is all over town. And at an *inn*."

Her aunt didn't say "where there are bedrooms," but Rowena imagined she was thinking it. She looked at Elaine for help, but Elaine's mouth hung open and she looked as if she was going to burst into laughter or tears. Rowena shut her eyes for a moment. God forgive her for lying. "It's just that we haven't made it public yet because, of course, Sebastian would want to talk to Uncle first. He just asked me and . . ." She let her eyes fall to the table demurely. "I guess we got carried away."

There was a moment's pause, as if her aunt was judging her sincerity, which Rowena had no doubt that she was. She only hoped she had given a good enough performance.

"Well, I can see how that could happen, my dear. But it puts us in a bit of a bind as we will have to make the announcement as quickly as possible before the talk gets out of hand. Right now, I'm sure it's just Summerset gossip, but we will want to announce it before anyone outside the town hears about it." Aunt Charlotte reached out and covered Rowena's hand with her own. "I can't tell you how very pleased I am. For a while I had hoped Elaine and Sebastian would make a match, but you will be so much more fitting of a wife for him than Elaine."

Rowena smiled weakly while her cousin rolled her eyes. Oh, God. What had she gotten herself into? And Sebastian. What would she tell Sebastian?

Just then Cairns came into the room. "Lady Summerset, Lord Billingsly has arrived."

Sebastian breezed into the room. "My apologies for arriving so early, but I wanted to get a good start on the day, and don't tell Mother, but your breakfasts are the best."

Rowena wanted to die.

Elaine took one look at Rowena's face and leapt from her chair. "Let me be the first to welcome you into the family," she cried. "Of course, you've always been a part of the family, but this just clinches it!"

Elaine kissed Sebastian's cheek, and from where Rowena was sitting, she could see her whispering fiercely into his ear.

"My dear boy," Aunt Charlotte said, rising from her chair. "What a surprise you both have handed us. I had no idea."

He embraced her awkwardly while shooting Rowena a look of panic over her ladyship's shoulders.

Rowena shrugged helplessly. She felt as if she were aboard a runaway train with no discernible way to get off.

"This does leave us in a bit of a dilemma, though. His lordship has gone out early this morning and won't be back until this afternoon. You can speak to him them. Does your mother know yet? No? Oh, no! I did so want to start planning the engagement party with her over the telephone. Well, this will have to do. You can tell her tonight and I will come to Eddelson tomorrow. Planning will be much more delightful in person. Now, what are your plans for today?"

If Rowena felt dizzy at her aunt's barrage, Sebastian looked positively sick, so Rowena took matters into her own hands. "We're going for a drive. We thought we might drive to Norwich for the afternoon. We'll be back in time for Sebastian to talk to Uncle."

"You must take Elaine. After yesterday's little display, you must not be seen alone together again."

Sebastian gave Aunt Charlotte a weak smile.

"I'd be delighted to chaperone them. Just give me a moment to change," Elaine said.

Elaine left and Aunt Charlotte patted Rowena's arm. "Again, I am simply delighted about this turn of events. I am going to go begin planning your trousseau." She exited the room and for the first time since they'd become an engaged couple, Rowena and Sebastian were left alone. He took her by the arm and propelled her from the room and into the sitting room, where they could talk undisturbed.

"What the hell was that?" he asked as soon as he closed the door behind them.

She sank into an ugly rose-patterned wing-backed chair and slapped a hand to her forehead. "I am so sorry. I had no idea what I was walking into this morning. It felt like an ambush."

"I'm familiar with the feeling," he said, his voice carefully neutral.

He sat across from her and crossed his long legs. "I think you had better start at the beginning."

"That was the beginning," she said. "Word of Jon's kissing me had reached my aunt by this morning and she mistook him for you."

He nodded. "And the part where you didn't enlighten her but instead led her to believe we were engaged came after?"

"No, she just assumed that if you had kissed me in public that we must be engaged, unless you were a cad and wished to die by firing squad with her and your mother at the trigger."

He nodded again. "That also makes sense. The only part now that doesn't make sense is the bit where you allowed her to believe it was me and that we are, indeed, going to be married."

His voice held a trace of humor now and Rowena sighed with relief. "Well, that part is a bit more complicated. You see, the Wellses and the Buxtons don't speak. In fact, his family hates my family with a passion and for good reason. I'm fairly sure my uncle believes the Wells family to be little more than ants that invaded his picnic. My aunt, on the other hand, will be upset because the Wellses aren't exactly society, and as Jon is the younger brother, he won't even inherit."

"Ah. So not only does he come from the wrong family, but he's not even rich. A double sin, so to speak."

"Exactly." Rowena sighed.

"So just how far are we supposed to take this little charade? To the engagement party? The wedding itself? And will you protect me from Jon? Because once he hears about our engagement he may come after me with blood in his eyes. The man is obviously in love with you."

Her cheeks heated and she couldn't help the delighted smile that played about her lips. "I promise we can break off our engagement soon. But it would work out perfectly if we let the rumor go on for at least a week. He's heading back to Kent then."

He stood and regarded her intently. "And what do I get out of this?"

Rowena shook her head. "I don't know. Amusement?"

"Well, there is that, but you do know this is going to cost me a great deal of trouble with my mother, don't you?"

She nodded, holding her breath.

He sighed and shook his head. "I'm either the world's leading dolt or just a fool for true love. That's fine. We both know there's no reason for me not to go along with a phony engagement, but we'd best inform Jon before he hears of it on his own."

"Thank you, Sebastian. You're a very nice man, do you know that? I think Prudence was a fool."

His jaw tightened for a moment. Then he nodded and held out his arm. "Shall we be going, my dear?"

Rowena linked her own arm through his. "Anything you like, my dear."

CHAPTER NINE

"Are you ready yet?"

Victoria resisted a childish urge to stick her tongue out. Something about Lottie just grated on her nerves.

She checked her hair again in the looking glass. She was wearing the same suit she had worn to her disastrous interview with Hairy Herbert. She wanted Martha to take her seriously and resolved to be sober and solemn when they met again.

"I'm ready," she said, giving her reflection a stern nod.

After Victoria had slipped into her dark coat, she and Lottie hopped aboard the Tube to the east side of London.

The scent of raw sewage and garbage assaulted her nose when she stepped out of the station. Children hunched in the wide doorways of dilapidated brick buildings. They watched her pass with huge eyes in starving faces, their feet covered in cloth or newspapers. Down one alleyway, she spotted rats fighting over the body of a dead cat next to a stinking pile of refuse. Overly rouged women with babies in their arms slipped furtively past as they peddled their daytime wares of rags or soap and waited for the sun to set.

This wasn't just a different part of town; it was an entirely new world for Victoria, who had spent most of her life in the protected oases of Mayfair, Belgravia, and St. James, though she didn't tell Lottie that. There was something smug about Lottie that made Victoria contrary, so she was careful not to show her shock at the filth and poverty that surrounded them almost the moment they emerged from the Tube.

Victoria pressed her lips together and followed Lottie, who kept watching her out of the corner of one eye. She felt judged for her title, her background, and most of all her naïveté. But maybe she should be judged. How could she have so much when these people had nothing?

Sobs gathered in her throat, making it hard to breathe, and finally she made a motion to Lottie to slow down.

Lottie turned toward her, her brows knit together. "This isn't a safe place to loiter," she said, but then she took a look at Victoria and her face softened. "I cried for hours the first time I came here," she said quietly

"I'm not crying," Victoria gasped out, only to discover that she was. Lottie waited for her to wipe her eyes. Victoria finally said, "I can't walk very fast without triggering an attack."

"Why didn't you say something?" Lottie asked, exasperated. "My little cousin has asthma." Victoria winced at the word. "Do you have your nebulizer with you?" Lottie asked.

Victoria held up the large reticule she carried. She was learning. As much as she didn't want to admit she had a problem, her last attack at Nanny Iris's had scared her.

"Well, that's something," Lottie went on. "Anna forgets hers all the time. We'll try to get a ride back to the Tube on the way home."

Victoria felt herself warming to the woman a bit. "So why is the headquarters all the way out here?" she asked.

"No money," Lottie said shortly. "We use our money to fight tyranny."

"How?"

"However we can." Lottie turned to open the door of a stone building that might have once been a barn.

Victoria firmed her chin and followed Lottie up the narrow stairs. The smell of horses permeating the stairwell confirmed its not-so-long-ago use as a barn, but as the scent was so much nicer than the garbage and decay out on the street, Victoria didn't mind.

There was another door at the top of the staircase and Lottie rapped three times before unlocking it.

"Why all the secrecy?" Victoria asked, and Lottie rolled her eyes. Victoria resolved to hold her tongue.

The room spanned the entire upper floor of the building and had two windows in the front, one on the side, and two in the back. Whether much light came through them was hard to say, because all had the shutters locked tight. There was a large machine on one side of the building and a large rack of what looked like iron tools.

A small, completely inadequate stove sat in one corner of the room with several desks clustered around it, cutting off heat to the rest of the room. Three women were gathered around one desk, reading something, when Lottie and Victoria walked in. Martha broke away from the group and greeted Lottie and Victoria with warm hugs.

"What's the latest catastrophe?" Lottie asked.

"We only have about three more hours of coal left for the stove. The police are throwing Salma out of jail and telling her to go get a good meal, our rent is due, and our coffers are empty."

"Just the usual, eh?" Lottie smiled.

"Thank you so much for coming to our humble headquarters," Martha said to Victoria. "That machine over there is called Gerta and she is both my pride and joy and the bane of my existence."

"She's always breaking down," Lottie explained.

"What is it?" Victoria asked.

"Our printing press," Martha said, waving a hand. "Come, I'll show you."

Martha explained the press, the newspaper, and their work. Her face grew animated as she spoke and her lilting voice filled with fire as she recounted stories of injustice.

Listening, Victoria remembered the humiliation she felt at the hands of Mr. Herbert, and how ostracized she felt solely due to her sex. Her chest tightened as reality dawned.

She would never be a botanist if women weren't ever taken seriously, and they would never be taken seriously unless they could participate fully in the political process.

"I'd love to help out," she burst out earnestly. "In any way that I can."

Martha's dark eyes lit up. "I've never believed in divine intervention, but for the first time, I think we just got an answer to our prayers."

Victoria laughed. "I've been called many things in my life, but never an answer to prayers."

Martha led her to a quiet corner away from the others. "I have a great many workers and I have many workers who are great, but for quite some time now, I have noticed the need for someone who could grasp the whole picture. Someone who could be my second." She laid a finger over her lips while her dark eyes considered Victoria. Victoria straightened, knowing she was being judged. Then, after a moment, Martha nodded as if she'd made a decision. "If you will excuse me for a moment."

Martha went over to Lottie and had a quiet conference with her. Lottie stared at Victoria several times and shook her head. Then she finally shrugged.

Martha turned and addressed the others. "Victoria and I are going out to dinner. Lottie, I will make sure Victoria gets home safely. The rest of you work until the coal runs out and then call it a day. I'm sure something will turn up in the morning. It always does."

Victoria waved at Lottie, who ignored her, perhaps sulky at being left behind. Victoria didn't care. She found Martha fascinating, and Victoria couldn't believe that a woman like this was impressed by *her*.

Martha drove as if rushing to a fire, expertly dodging pedestrians, horses, and other cars. Instead of arriving at a restaurant, she parked the car near a shabby tea shop, ignoring a man with a pushcart who screamed at her for parking in front of his cart. "This place has wonderful meat pies that will sustain you all day. I always come here when money is tight," Martha said with a smile.

The two ladies were seated and a pot of tea put between them. Martha ordered steak and kidney pies.

She lit a cigarette and smiled. "I brought you here to learn about you. This is a job interview of sorts, you know."

Victoria straightened. "No, I didn't know exactly, though I suspected it, but isn't it as important that I want to work for you as it is that you want me to work for you?"

Martha blinked and then laughed. "I hope you write more eloquently than you speak."

"You understood me perfectly well." Victoria laughed. "Why don't I answer a question about myself and you answer a question about yourself?"

Martha looked amused. "Oh, that's right. You like things to be fair. I'll start. Why are you even interested in helping our Suffragettes for Female Equality? You could be working with the Women's Social and Political Union or the NUWSS. Those organizations are far larger than ours are."

"And why is that?" Victoria wanted to know.

Martha shook her head. "No, you first."

Victoria thought about it for a moment. She had a feeling the question carried a great deal of weight, and she truly wanted Martha to like her. "All my life I have been not only pampered but coddled because of my illness. No one thought I was capable of anything and they always underestimated me, even my father, who adored me. I took a secretarial course to prepare myself for whatever I would end up doing, though I always thought it would have something to do with botany. But I see now that, at this moment in time, this is more important. Not only should women have the ability to vote, but there should be laws that make what happened to me impossible. Someone shouldn't be able to deny me employment for something I am qualified for simply because I am a woman. We may never get there, but I'm realizing I want to work with an organization that at least feels it's possible. And one that doesn't stop with the right to vote."

There was more that Victoria wanted to say, but she could see in Martha's expression that she didn't need to go on.

Martha gave her a wide smile and again Victoria was struck by how pretty she was. "I think that is a fine answer. Now let me tell you a bit more about us, and you can decide whether you want to join us or not. We walk a fine line between legal and illegal. Some of the women who have gone on hunger strikes belong to my organization. Even though I don't necessarily agree with that tactic, I admire their tenacity and commitment. I don't agree with anything that puts a woman in harm's way, though my partner in crime believes that there are things worth dying for."

"Partner in crime?" Victoria asked, curious.

"Oh, yes. Didn't Lottie tell you that she and I are joint publishers?" She paused. "Where was I? Oh, hunger strikes. We don't do that, but we do help women escape men who are beating them if we can, and that takes quite a bit of our resources, not to mention that it's quite dangerous. The law doesn't side with us at all and oftentimes we have to sneak them out in the dead of night. I know that is a bit of a stretch for a women's rights organization, but Lottie believes that unless we save women from brutality and educate them, the vote isn't worth much."

The meat pies arrived and Victoria cut into the flaky crust, freeing the fragrant gravy trapped inside. Tender pieces of steak and vegetables spilled out, and both women tucked into the food as if they had been starving for days. For several minutes they said nothing until Victoria took a sip of her tea. "Does that weaken the organization, though? It seems to be spread rather thinly. Don't the most successful organizations focus their efforts?"

Martha grimaced. "I suppose, but it's difficult to stop helping when you see a need."

Victoria leaned forward, excited. "So do you have a list of other organizations that help with specific needs that you can't fulfill? For instance, food charities, nurseries that mind young children while their mothers work, or organizations that help women who are being beaten? There must be some."

"There are, but most have less funding than we do," Martha said.

"It seems like you need someone who can connect women with the organization that would best help them. That way we could focus our efforts a bit more."

"That's brilliant!" Martha exclaimed, and Victoria warmed under her praise. "The first thing I want you to do is to create a master list of all the organizations that help women, what they do, and what their weaknesses and strengths are. That way we're not wasting time emulating the work of other charity organizations and we can move our focus back to furthering women's right to vote and education."

A flush of excitement rushed over Victoria. "I'll start it first thing tomorrow, right after I buy coal and pay rent on the building a month or two."

Martha lit a cigarette and tilted her head. "The Suffragettes for Female Equality and the Women's Equality League will gladly accept your gift of a week's worth of coal and one month's rent, but no more than that." Martha raised a hand at Victoria's protests. "You think I don't have more money than I give to the organization? I will not allow anyone to impoverish herself for a cause. Lottie doesn't agree with me on that point, but what good would it do to have one more impoverished woman on the street? Money, my dear girl, is the great equalizer. It is one of the only things that will protect a woman when times get rough. So while I give the organization a monthly stipend, I refuse to give it everything. You would be surprised at how quickly money gets eaten up. Men wouldn't impoverish themselves for a cause;

why should women? Because we are more compassionate?" Martha shook her head, causing a riot among the curls dangling around her face. She'd obviously had this argument before. "Besides, you're only eighteen. Who has control of your money?"

Victoria looked down at the tablecloth. "My uncle actually takes care of all of my expenses, but he's never objected or even questioned any of the bills sent to him."

Martha lit another cigarette and curled a lip. "You'd be surprised just how quickly he'd throw a fit at your giving money to the Suffragettes for Female Equality. If I were you, I would go to the bank myself and withdraw cash. That way it isn't linked to us at all. If he questions you about it, you can always say it was for underthings. That always shuts them up."

Victoria giggled. "Is that what you do?"

A shadow fell over Martha's face. "I'm much older than eighteen and I no longer have any family to watch over me."

"Oh, I'm sorry," Victoria said with a pang of sympathy. "I know . . ."

Martha's mouth turned down and she put out her cigarette with an aggressive jab. "That's not what I meant. There's just no one in my family who cares what I do."

"Oh." She didn't know what to say to that.

Martha waved away Victoria's attempt to pay the bill. "Don't fret. I have plenty of people who love me and I have my work with the Suffragettes for Female Equality and the Women's Equality League."

Something struck Victoria and she frowned. "Why does your organization have two names?"

Martha tilted her head sideways and regarded Victoria. "We have two organizations because many women are afraid to do the real work of the cause. The Suffragettes for Female Equality is the main organization. The Women's Equality League is the more exclusive, lesser-known group. It's for those workers who have proven their loyalty and bravery. I suppose if you're to work for us, you're going to have to know."

Victoria sat up straight, trying to look worthy.

Martha made up her mind. "Emily Davison? The woman who tried to disrupt the Derby by stepping out in front of the King's horse at the Derby and was killed? She belonged to the League."

Victoria's heart stalled for a moment. "I thought she was WSPU?"

Martha nodded. "Yes, but she was also one of my most fearless leaders."

"She's not anymore," Victoria said shortly.

"No, now she's a martyr for the cause. Some of the women who disrupted Parliament last month were ours. Others are in prison, as we speak. We are very, very serious about the right to vote."

Victoria drew in her breath and looked down at the pastry she was eating. Then she tried to be nonchalant. "I am, too," she said. She drained the last bit of her tea and then bit her lip. "There's something else I have to tell you."

Martha smiled. "Don't look so glum. And please don't tell me that you're betrothed or something."

"Oh, no, nothing like that! I just don't actually live in London right now. I will be moving back after Easter, but for right now . . ."

"Don't tell me, the uncle who looks after your money insists that you live on the family estate, am I right?"

Victoria nodded. "But I do have the ability to come and go as I please and I can do a lot of work from Summerset." She paused before adding, "I have my own office."

"That will be fine for now, but eventually, you will need to move to town. We can only pay you fifty-five pounds yearly, but it's what we have." Martha raised her eyebrows, waiting for Victoria's reaction.

The amount would barely pay for Victoria's yearly expenditure on books, but she was just thrilled to be compensated for her work. She clapped her hands together. "I had no idea we were talking about a paid position!"

They stood and walked out to Martha's car. The rain had begun and it took a few minutes for Martha's car to start. The light had waned and Victoria wondered how long they had sat talking in the tea shop.

"There are six of us who are actually paid, though there are times we have to wait for our money. One of the things you will be doing is canvassing rich women for donations, though most of them are already involved in the National Union of Women's Suffrage Societies. Funding is essential. And don't let on that you're getting paid. Some of the volunteers may think veterans would be better suited to the position than a newcomer. They don't understand that they lack your qualifications."

As they drove, Martha told her that her work had taken her all over Europe to lecture at meetings. Victoria found herself utterly entranced. This was a woman who had true adventures and worked for the good of womankind. As she hugged Martha good-bye, it briefly occurred to her to wonder what kind of qualifications she had that the others did not.

* * *

Rowena and Elaine both shaded their eyes with their hands, waiting for Jon to bring the plane down. Sebastian was in the barn, talking to Mr. Dirkes. It had been several days since the engagement debacle and Sebastian had been a good sport, bringing Rowena out every day to see Jon and fly in the plane.

"I don't know which you like better," Elaine said, still staring into the sky. "Jon or flying."

Elaine had so far successfully resisted going up, though Sebastian and Rowena had both been up twice. "Both," Rowena said, smiling. "I love both."

She couldn't explain to Elaine how intertwined her love for Jon and her love for flying were. To her, they both meant color, freedom, life. Today Jon had promised to give Rowena her first flying lesson. He told her it would all be on the ground, which disappointed her to no end, but she was just happy that he had finally relented.

It was one of those rare February days when the clouds melted away, leaving the thin winter's sun shining in the sky. So far the wind had stayed away, which made it more comfortable, but it was still bitterly cold. It nipped at her cheeks and toes and for a brief moment she thought of fireplaces and hot chocolate, but she realized she would rather be in this field, watching that plane and that man come closer and closer to the earth, than do anything else.

Besides, after her lesson, they would be having dinner at Jon's home with his family. Elaine and Sebastian would be heading to Thetford for dinner and then meeting them in Summerset afterward. It was a little complicated, but Rowena was grateful for the time it bought her and Jon.

The aeroplane bumped across the field toward them and then did an ungraceful loop so it was ready to be rolled into the barn.

She stepped toward the plane after it had come to a complete stop and ran her hands across the fuselage.

"I'm not sure if you're happier to see me or the aeroplane," Jon said, taking off his leather helmet.

It was so similar to what Elaine had just said that Rowena laughed. "Why? Are you jealous of Lucy?"

He smiled down on her from the pilot's seat. "You named her Lucy?"

"All aeroplanes should have names," she told him. "They might like you better if they had names, and maybe you wouldn't crash so often."

He swung down, laughing, and grabbed her by the arms. "Is that so?"

"Hey, you two, we're off," Elaine called from the car. Sebastian cranked the car starter and waved a hand. "We'll meet you outside the Freemont Inn."

"Well, do you want your lesson or don't you?"

"Yes, please."

He grabbed a ladder and leaned it against the plane. Rowena climbed up and settled herself into the cockpit. Her heart thumped with excitement even though she knew she wouldn't be flying today. He explained the instrument panel and made her repeat the name and function of every device until she had committed everything to memory. Then he made her get out of the aeroplane and they repeated the exercise on the exterior.

"You learn fast," he complimented, and she glowed. "I've trained grown men who didn't pick up those terms as quickly as you did."

"That's because I was meant to be a pilot," she told him.

He slipped his arms about her waist. "You were, were you?"

She nodded. "Yes, I was."

"Let's put Lucy to bed so that we can let the rest of the crew go home," Mr. Dirkes called from the barn.

Jon grinned. "Lucy?"

"Well, we have to call it something," Mr. Dirkes said, his tone sheepish, and Jon laughed.

"See, you're getting under everyone's skin," he whispered, before pulling away to help roll the plane into the barn.

Jon had borrowed Mr. Dirkes's Silver Ghost for the evening while Mr. Dirkes got a ride back to the inn from one of their hired men.

"Does your brother know I'm coming?" she asked as they headed out toward Wells Manor.

Jon nodded. "He's not happy about it, but I told him that you were coming and that would be that."

He reached out and squeezed her hand. She tried to smile, but her nerves got the better of her and it turned into a grimace. "Do your mother and sister know who I am?"

Jon was silent for a moment. "I told my mum, but she told me not to tell Cristobel until she had gotten to know you. She was our father's pet and still cries at night for him."

Rowena stared straight ahead, guilt over her family's actions settling in the center of her stomach, even though realistically she knew she had nothing to do with it. But how could she use logic to eradicate a feeling as potent as guilt? She felt responsible for the Wells family trouble in some way that couldn't be undone by rationale. She was a Buxton, and a Buxton had systematically stripped the Wells family of a portion of their land and their wealth. "How does your mom feel?" she asked in a small voice.

Jon twined his fingers round and round hers and stared straight ahead. "My mother is a strong woman. Her ma was a Scotswoman, which is where we get the red hair and the stubbornness. So she was shocked. She also knows that I have never before felt strongly enough about a woman to bring one home with me, and for my mother, that speaks louder than anything your surname could imply. She will head off any trouble with George."

They rounded the corner and again, Rowena was struck by the difference between Wells Manor and Summerset. Whereas every aspect of Summerset was planned and well thought out to be as grand as possible, Wells Manor looked as if everything had grown from a sense of practicality. The only whimsical touch was the ivy that had been allowed to grow up one side of the house and onto the roof, tickling several of the chimneys.

"I love your house," Rowena said truthfully.

"It was actually here before most of Summerset. Turns out the first Wells, or whatever their name was then, was a smith who didn't want the protection of the local ruling family, an ancestor of the Buxtons, and refused to build near the castle. So you see, except for a brief period of affability, the Wellses and the Buxtons have always been at odds."

He stopped the motorcar in front of the house and leapt out to open her door. Not wanting to look as if she were putting on airs, she had taken care to wear a sensible tweed suit, with a fine linen blouse underneath. Her hair had been dressed in a simple chignon, low on her neck, which was draped with a strand of pearls. She didn't want them to think she wouldn't bother dressing well for them, but neither did she wish to play the dame of the castle, either.

Rowena's hands were slick with nerves by the time she and Jon entered the house. Jon's mother stuck her head out of the kitchen door. "Take her into the sitting room, Jon. We're having a slight problem here."

"We are not!" Cristobel cried out, and then there was silence.
Jon winked at Rowena and ushered her into the sitting
room. Low beams crisscrossed the ceiling every few feet, and
the gleaming dark oak was answered in the wide planks on the
floor. Comfortable, worn sofas and chairs dotted the room,
and there were several tables stacked with leather-bound books
and decorated with vases of evergreens, perhaps placed there by
Cristobel, excited to have a guest. Dark paneling lined the walls,
and the room was only saved from dimness by the five leaded
windows lining one wall, each with its own window seat. The
most decorative item in the room was the fireplace, a beautiful white, highly molded piece that glowed with simple beauty.
Rowena could have curled up with a book for hours on one of
the window seats.

"I love this," she said, walking over to one of the windows.

He joined her. The window looked out onto the kitchen garden, though Rowena also spotted a cutting garden on one side.
In the summer, the household would have both fresh vegetables
and fresh flowers. "Cristobel loves this room, too. My brothers
and I preferred the kitchen. That's where the food was. Though
when Dad was alive and well, we spent lots of time in here on a
winter's evening after the work was done."

A lump rose in Rowena's throat, not only for the Wells family, who had lost their father, but for her little family, who had
also lost a father. "We usually gathered in Father's study. Victoria
and Prudence and I used to take turns reading French novels so
Father could correct our pronunciation. Sometimes Prudence
would play the piano, or Victoria would recite poetry." She
looked down at the ground. "I miss those times often."

He squeezed her hand in sympathy. "Who is Prudence?
I don't think you ever mentioned her before."

"She is . . ." Rowena faltered. To say "governess's daughter" wouldn't come close to explaining what Prudence was to their family. She was family. "She was like a sister to Victoria and me," Rowena finally said. "We loved her."

"Oh, wasn't Prudence the little maid you got rid of?" George asked from behind them. "A friend of mine who works in the house told me all about it. She came to Summerset as your lady's maid because your uncle wouldn't allow her in the house, because her mother was a maid. The next thing everyone knew, she was married to the footman and sent off to London. You Buxtons certainly know how to take care of unsavory messes."

George tried to sound casual, but bitterness leached out, filling the peaceful room with spite. Jon rushed forward, his fists clenched.

Rowena hurried to Jon's side and put a placating hand on his arm. Her stomach burned at the thought that her private life should be dissected and judged.

She looked George in the eyes and was struck by how dissimilar they were from Jon's. For while Jon's blue eyes glowed with the richness of summer, George's blue eyes held the chill of winter sky. "You certainly listened well to rumors and half-truths, but your sources couldn't possibly know what really happened. Prudence was someone Victoria and I loved like a sister. I'm surprised you would take gossip for fact."

"I would not," Jon said shortly, still staring at his brother. Though they were of similar height, Jon was more slender, with lean hips and long legs. His shoulders were wide and strong, but George's powerful frame looked as if he had wrestled with one-hundred-pound fleeces and bales of hay his entire life.

"You told me what happened with her uncle had nothing to do with her, little brother, so I inquired a bit and discovered this dirty little tale. The whole family is full of bad apples. This is what I get for my thanks?"

"You'll get worse than this if you don't back down," Jon said, his voice tight.

"I'm glad to know nothing has changed since I went away," a voice called through the door. "George and Jon are always ready to fight over something, though I don't remember it ever being over a woman before. And especially not such a beautiful one as this."

For a moment neither man moved, as if breaking eye contact was a form of surrender. Rowena slipped her arm through Jon's and leaned close. She could feel his muscles relax with her proximity.

"My name is Rowena." She turned to give the new guest her widest smile. Then with a narrowed look at George she added, "Buxton, my name is Rowena Buxton." The man's brown eyes widened in comprehension, but Rowena continued. "My father was Sir Philip Buxton and though he was born at Summerset, he moved away long ago and my sister and I were brought up in London."

She held out her hand, her heart pounding. She could tell from the red hair that this was a Wells, and she couldn't stand to have another brother against her.

The man looked at her hand for a moment and then he smiled. "It is very nice to make your acquaintance, Miss Buxton. Since both of my brothers are behaving like philistines, I shall introduce myself. I am the second-oldest brother, Samuel. And don't worry, Miss Buxton, there will be no judgments here."

It was then that she noticed he was wearing the plain black suit and white collar of a vicar. She almost laughed out loud.

"Please call me Rowena. Cristobel doesn't yet know who

I am, and I would much rather tell her myself." She glanced at George, who had the grace to look away.

"That sounds like a good plan to me."

"What sounds like a good plan?" Margaret Wells asked, coming in the door. "Please don't be making plans before the girl has a chance to get used to us. She'll be thinking us stark raving mad."

Again, Rowena detected the slight burr of Margaret's voice. Jon's mother came to her immediately and kissed her in greeting. "A handshake or a bow seems much too formal to greet the girl who has brought such happiness into my son's life. I never thought anything but those silly aeroplanes could give him that silly smile on his face, but all he has to do is mention your name—"

"Mother!" Jon protested, while Rowena glowed. "Slow down a tetch, next thing I know you'll be showing her the family Chantilly lace."

"Don't give her any ideas," Samuel said, kissing his mother and wrapping her in a bear hug.

George stood stiffly to one side, apparently irate that his plan to put a wedge between her and Jon hadn't worked. Rowena watched him under her eyelashes, wondering what his next move would be. He didn't seem the type who gave up that easily, and Rowena knew that even though Jon would stand by her, it would be best to give him an accounting of exactly who Prudence was and what had happened. Her stomach stirred uneasily. She would tell him the truth without sparing herself. If they were to have any kind of future, they must be honest with each other.

Just then his mother offered everyone a glass of Scotch whisky. "I've heard the Americans have started a new tradition called predinner cocktails, and though I rarely think of the word *civilized* in conjunction with the Americans, I think that a very civilized idea, indeed."

The boys agreed as Cristobel made her entrance into the room. She looked neat in a white wool dress with antique blue silk piping. Rowena could tell the dress had been made over to fit and had been done very well. She knew better than to mention the dress, though, as the girl might be self-conscious of it, and instead complimented her hair as they greeted each other. "However did you get your hair to roll so smoothly?" she asked. "I could never get mine to look so lovely when I did my hair that way."

The girl flushed pink with pleasure. "You'll have to ask Mother. I'm afraid I'm a bit of a klutz with a hairbrush."

"I was so happy to finally get a girl that nothing could stop me from playing with her hair." Margaret laughed, pouring out drinks. Jon took two glasses and led Rowena to a sofa. Cristobel took a chair close to them. Rowena sipped a bit of whisky and coughed.

"Take it easy," Jon cautioned. "Relatives make and bottle this stuff in Edinburgh. They send us a case every year because they claim our English blood will turn us to pansies without the right Scotch."

Rowena smiled. "The glasses are lovely, Mrs. Wells."

"Please call me Margaret. Yes, my aunt gave them to me when I married. They're Waterford crystal called the Star of Edinburgh."

Rowena took another careful sip and gave everyone a weak smile. She couldn't possibly finish this and yet was afraid to hurt their feelings. It almost felt like a test, especially with George on one side of the room, staring at her with such disdain. Cristobel was a blessing, as she spoke nonstop of horses and riding.

"I desperately want to be asked to go on a hunt next season. I'm a good enough rider to."

"You're still a bit young to be in society yet," Margaret said.

Rowena smiled. "I'm always invited to several during the season. If you like, and your mother doesn't mind, I would love to have you come with me the next time I go."

There was a moment of silence and Cristobel blushed up to where her forehead met the chestnut brown of her hair. She looked down at the ground.

Rowena looked from Jon to Margaret, unsure as to what her mistake had been.

"I'm not sure if her new riding habit will be done by that time," Margaret said, and Cristobel looked up with relief.

"Oh, but the hunts aren't for months yet," Rowena said. "And if her habit isn't done, she can borrow one of Victoria's. My little sister is about the same size."

Cristobel brightened. "Oh, that would be wonderful! I've been working with Grenadine, my big hunter, and I know he'd be up to the challenge, though not as well trained as some of the horses . . ."

George threw his glass against the wall, where it shattered. Everyone fell silent.

"We don't need a damned Buxton giving us charity."

Cristobel gasped and her blue eyes turned to Rowena.

Margaret stood. "You just broke a valuable glass that meant the world to me, not to mention ruined the set."

"Father meant the world to me, Mother. Did he mean the world to you? Because you have a funny way of showing it, inviting a Buxton to dine with us."

Rowena watched as Margaret paled and her fingers tightened

around the glass she held as if she, too, wanted to throw it. "I am not even going to dignify that with an answer. Not one of you loved your father as I did, and if I thought for one moment this girl had anything to do with his death, I would not be welcoming her into my home. But she did not. The only one responsible for your father's death was your father. Not the barristers or the judges or the Buxtons. I'm sorry if you can't accept that."

Margaret threw the rest of her Scotch back. "I'm sorry, Rowena, for this confrontation. George can be as headstrong as a child. When a man takes his own life, it is difficult to understand why and we often try blaming everyone but who was responsible for it."

An elderly servant appeared through the door. "Dinner is served, madam."

Margaret gave a grim smile. "I hope you boys have all washed up and remember your manners. We do have a guest tonight for dinner. Rowena, you will still be joining us? Please don't let this turn you away. Any family with this many boys is bound to have a few rows."

Rowena stood, her legs shaking. "We had three girls in our family and there were plenty of conflicts among us, as well. Though of a different sort."

Jon took her arm and led her to the table in the kitchen.

"I hope you don't mind eating in the kitchen. As I told you when you visited, this is where we spend most of our time."

Rowena heard a door slam and understood with relief that George decided not to join the rest of the family for dinner. Judging from the relaxation of Margaret's posture, it appeared his mother was relieved as well.

Cristobel, on the other hand, hadn't said a word about the argument. Rowena tried to draw her out but had little success, so she turned her attention to the other three diners, trying to learn as much about Jon's family as she could. William, the fourth son, was two years older than Cristobel and was working with family in Scotland in the whiskey business. Samuel had a church in a little town outside of Theton and was engaged to a parishioner. She also learned that Mr. Dirkes was an old friend of Jon's mother.

The food was simple, good, and plentiful, and by the time they finished the sour cherry pudding and cream, Rowena was sated.

"Are you sure you won't have another wee bowl?" Jon's mother pressed, but Rowena shook her head.

"What I would really like is to see the stables," she said, squeezing Jon's knee under the table before he could volunteer.

"Cristobel, why don't you show me Grenadine?" The look on the girl's face showed that she knew she was being led, but Rowena had judged that her pride and love of her horse would move her.

The stable was every bit as clean as those at Summerset, though Rowena imagined that the Wellses had limited help. The tack hanging on the wall was worn but well cared for, and the horses appeared fit and healthy. The nicker from the last box in the barn told Rowena exactly which stall Grenadine was in.

Cristobel withdrew a lump of sugar from a box on a nearby shelf and held her hand out to a large bay.

"He's gorgeous," Rowena told Cristobel. "He looks intelligent."

Cristobel nodded and her shoulders relaxed for the first time since dinner. "Oh, he is. He knows what I want, often before I even let him know. He's very responsive."

Rowena mentioned her own horse and added that she often rode the acres of Summerset for hours when things were troubling her.

Cristobel ran her hand up Grenadine's face and scratched under his forelock. "What kind of troubles would *you* have?"

The emphasis on "you" hinted to Rowena that she hadn't been forgiven for who she was. With the loss of her own father so fresh, Rowena ached to reach out to this girl whose suffering was so similar. "My father died five months ago. It was completely unexpected, as he had always been healthy. I miss him so much it hurts to breathe sometimes."

Cristobel climbed up the gate to get better access to her horse, no doubt forgetting about her newly remade dress. She didn't look at Rowena, but she could tell that the girl was listening intently.

"I let myself be paralyzed by grief, and someone I love ended up being hurt because of it . . ." Her voice trailed off and she swallowed hard.

"Why are you telling me this?" Cristobel asked, her voice low.

Rowena walked over to the stall next to Grenadine's where a pretty chestnut mare stood quietly. "I don't know. Maybe to let you know that other people have suffered and felt the whole world shift, too."

"It's different," Cristobel whispered fiercely. "Your father didn't want to leave you. Mine killed himself."

She kept her face away from Rowena, and Rowena knew the girl was crying.

"I know what it's like to be angry with him for leaving," Rowena said.

Cristobel wiped the tears from her face and turned back to Rowena. "Will you really take me hunting this summer?"

Rowena smiled and held out her hand. "Of course. When I'm not flying, that is."

Cristobel picked up the lantern and they exited the barn. The chill darkness hit Rowena and she shivered. Cristobel latched the barn door behind them.

"Is Jon really teaching you how to fly an aeroplane?"

Rowena tilted her head back and looked at the stars in the winter sky. "Yes. Soon I'll be able to fly in the sky all by myself." She smiled. "I can't wait for that day."

CHAPTER
TEN

Prudence hung her husband's shirt up to dry on a line strung from one end of the cellar to the other. She shared the cellar with the four other families who rented rooms above the greengrocer and the hardware shop. Only on Tuesdays was Prudence able to come down here and do her washing.

A large basin split into two separate sinks sat in the back of the cellar under the one dingy window. Attached to the rim of the divider was a hand-turned wringer that in theory was supposed to wring the soap and dirt out of the clothing, but in reality did neither very well. Prudence had developed a rash after wearing underthings washed in the cheap laundry soap she had bought, and now she had to do all her finer clothes in the bathroom basin upstairs.

The cellar itself was a place from hell where Prudence imagined rats made their home, though she hadn't seen evidence of them. One of the tenants kept the basement, the stairs, and the hallway clean in exchange for a rent deduction, and whoever it was seemed to be fairly conscientious about it. It wasn't the filth that sent shivers up her spine, it was the lack of light and having only one way in and out. If there were a fire . . . Prudence shuddered and picked up her pace. Because of the boiler that heated the entire building, the cellar was warm enough, and in the winter the clothing dried fairly quickly. In the summer, she would no doubt join the rest of the East End and use the ropes and pulleys that ran out her bedroom window to a wall on the other side of the street. If she weren't so conscious of every penny she spent, she would splurge and buy herself one of those new electric machines that emptied in the sink.

She wasn't the only one conscious of their money. It had become an obsession with Andrew to see how little of her money they actually had to use. She put her foot down when he wanted to work an extra day a week. "You need the time to study," she told him firmly, and he had to concede that she was right.

Prudence filled the right sink with water and then carefully measured out the bluing Muriel had given her to whiten their whites. She sprinkled it into the water and then added their sheets and Andrew's undershirts. Because of the cheap laundry soap, the sheets had taken on a dingy, yellow cast. She would let them soak for a bit to get them really white. Rubbing her lower back, she carried the load she'd just wrung to the line and hung it up. Then she took the basket upstairs with her. She had lost her first basket after leaving it down here, and though no one admitted to taking it, she knew it had to be someone who had a key. By unwritten rule, the clothing was never touched, but anything else was fair game.

Prudence let herself into her flat, ready for a cup of tea. Andrew was home today, working in the front room, where she had made him a makeshift desk. The little desk in the bedroom was too close to the bed, he told her. It was too tempting to set down his books and crawl in for a cozy nap. This afternoon, he would go work for an hour with Professor Gilcrest, a retired professor from Cambridge, who now made extra money tutoring people in his King's Cross flat. Prudence put the water on for tea and checked her supplies. They had leftover ginger biscuits from her last attempt at baking and some bread that she had bought down the street, having decided that her skills weren't up to bread yet. Muriel, as encouraging as she had been, agreed. So bread and butter and biscuits for tea would be good.

She poked her head through the sitting room doorway. Andrew was sitting in his chair with his stocking feet propped up on the window seat, reading a book on animal husbandry. After spending so much of his time in livery, he loved having his own home, where he could dress as he pleased, and usually padded around in trousers, stockings, and an undershirt. He could still be dressed nicely at a moment's notice, but he was like a big child about being informal. Prudence, having rarely seen Sir Philip in anything more casual than a smoking jacket and then only on special occasions like Christmas morning, thought it one of the most endearing things about her rather shy husband. "Would you like your tea now?"

He glanced up, his reading spectacles low on his nose. "That would be lovely, thank you."

She pulled out the bread and then paused at a knock on the door. She wondered whether she'd imagined the sound. Katie had only been over once and they had yet to make any friends in London.

When she answered the door after a second knock, she froze, unsure of whether to cry out or just cry. Victoria stood in front of her, wearing a beautiful black Diane coat and small toque with almost an entire bird's worth of black feathers. Her hands were pressed in front of her and her blue eyes were filled with both joy and trepidation, as if she were deeply unsure of how she would be received. Katie stood behind her, grinning.

"Miss Victoria wasn't sure you would want to see her, but I saw how the three of you doted on one another and knew you wouldn't be able to resist, no matter what sort of water has gone under the bridge."

And Katie was right. Prudence's heart surrendered moments before her arms opened wide to receive her friend. Victoria rushed into them and Prudence gathered her close. How could she have thought that she could live without Victoria? Even though a scant two years separated them, Victoria had been almost a child to Prudence, who watched over Victoria's flights of fancy when she was young with a certain sense of awe.

Prudence remembered too late all the stories she had told Susie concerning her home and way of living. She just couldn't imagine letting anyone at Summerset know how different her new life was. Did Victoria expect a glamorous flat? Servants? Prudence hid her laundry-reddened hands behind her back. "Welcome to my home," she said in as dignified a manner as she could manage. Perhaps Susie hadn't mentioned her foolish stories to Victoria. And if she had, there was nothing she could do about it now.

"What are you doing in town?" Prudence asked as Victoria and Katie entered the flat.

"Oh, there's so much to tell you! I came here to be a writer for a botanist magazine and instead have secured a position as a clerk and spokeswoman for the Suffragettes for Female Equality!"

Prudence took Victoria and Katie's coats. She couldn't take her eyes off the young woman standing in front of her, looking very adult in a zebra-striped street dress hemmed just above the ankles and leaving the bottom of the skirt split for six inches up the front. When did Victoria grow up so? "But how did this all come about? Does Rowena know what you're doing, because I know your aunt Charlotte can't approve . . ."

Victoria waved her hand. "Oh, pooh! I want to know about you. There's plenty of time for me later."

Prudence noticed Victoria looking around the flat, with wide curious eyes and flushed. Her home suddenly looked so small and shabby. "I'm just making tea," she told them. "Please join us."

"Oh, we wouldn't want to be an imposition," Victoria said, taking a seat at the table. "Oh, look! You're using our old gaming table as a dining table. How clever!"

Prudence's cheeks heated further. If only she hadn't spent the last two months lying, she could enjoy having Victoria here instead of wondering how much Susie had told her.

Katie handed her a box she'd been holding. "Mum sent us over with sponge cake." She smiled. "I don't think she thought you would have anything to feed us, though she does say you're making progress."

Prudence frowned and made a motion with her head toward the front room. "Andrew's here and he doesn't know I'm taking lessons on how to run a house," she whispered.

"You're what?" Victoria asked, her voice rising in astonishment. "Whatever for? Why don't you just hire a servant or two for goodness' sake?"

Prudence bit her lip and, without answering, opened the box and took out a perfectly baked cake swirled with pink French cream frosting.

Victoria groaned. "That looks delicious!"

"I'll never be able to bake like this." Prudence shook her head, relieved that Victoria had been sidetracked. "Just when

I think I'm making progress, I see this and realize I've got so much to learn."

Prudence fetched plates and called Andrew in to tea. His eyes widened. "I was so lost in my book, I didn't even hear the door," he said. "Oh, look at that cake!"

"Katie brought it for us," Prudence said. "This is Katie, a dear friend of mine, and of course you know Victoria." To Prudence's surprise, Victoria and Andrew greeted each other coolly, almost formally. She wondered whether the sense of class was so strong that they would never become friends, or whether it was something else. Victoria was anything but class-conscious.

A quiet settled over the table where there had been chatter before. Prudence cut the cake and handed a plate to everyone. There weren't enough chairs at the table, so Andrew moved to the oversized, ugly plaid chair near the stove. "This is my favorite seat anyway," he said, giving Prudence a grin. She blushed, remembering their first night here alone.

"I simply can't believe you don't have any help, Prudence," Victoria said, after taking a bite of her cake.

"Oh, pooh," Prudence said, embarrassed by Victoria's blunt way of speaking. "I'm perfectly capable of looking after Andrew and myself."

"Wouldn't you rather be teaching French or piano than trying to learn how to do laundry and roast a goose or whatever things you have never known how to do?"

"Victoria!" Prudence groaned, and put her hands over her face.

"You don't know how to do laundry?" Andrew asked, his expression shocked. Prudence froze, realizing that she had been caught in her lie. She slowly shook her head.

"Why on earth would you hide that from me? I could have taught you." The betrayal and hurt in his voice pierced her heart and she wished Victoria would just hold her tongue. But then, Victoria wasn't known for her discretion.

Prudence gave Andrew a weak smile. "It was nothing, really. And Victoria, I don't want to teach lessons to other people's children. I love what I'm doing."

Victoria's face fell. "All right then." She brightened. "Oh, I have a better idea! Why don't you ask Susie to visit? She could at least help you settle in!"

This was a disaster. Victoria had created a disaster. Prudence didn't know whether to laugh or cry. But Victoria had one thing right. She would love for Susie to come visit. With Andrew gone so frequently, the thought of having company made her smile with relief. She needed to start Victoria on another subject to allow Andrew enough time to ponder the notion of a houseguest. He wasn't one to make rash decisions. Marrying her was probably the hastiest move he had ever made.

"You still haven't told me about the job!" Prudence said.

Victoria grinned and Prudence knew Victoria well enough to know that trouble was coming. "Well, as I said, I'm working for the Suffragettes for Female Equality. For the moment, they want me to compile a list of women's emergency services so we don't get too scattered. For instance, right now, we're not only trying to gain women the vote and educate women so we know how to fight for our own rights, but we are trying to help women who need jobs find safe nurseries for their babies, and help abused women get away from the men who hurt them. Trying to find money to pay for rent so people don't end up in the workhouses is a constant battle. But all of these things take time and resources away from our original intention, so I'm compiling a list of groups that help women besides us, so we can narrow our focus to the vote for now."

Victoria finished her speech with a flashing smile and dug back into her cake as if she had said nothing astonishing. Prudence had always been amazed by Victoria's ability to speak her mind without holding anything back, but this was the first time Prudence was left without a response.

She glanced at Katie, who smiled as if this were all very normal, and then at her husband, who kept eating his cake, a surprised smile playing about his lips.

"Well, that's nice," she finally said.

"Nice?" Victoria waved her cup in the air. "It's more than nice, it's stupendous! I think I will be wonderful at it and I am finally doing more than changing my clothes for tea. I've been longing to do something important my whole life, and this may be it, this may be my chance."

Katie giggled at that and Prudence gave a tentative smile. "How long have you been dissatisfied with your life? You've never said anything before."

Katie and Victoria both laughed this time. "I was taking a secretarial course before Father died. Katie and I both were."

Prudence's brows rose. "I had no idea."

"Well, back then, I was doing it in order to help Father with his work. I always thought I would be a botanist like Father. Or maybe write like one." Victoria chewed on her thumb and a shadow crossed her pretty face. "But I can't be a botanist until women have the right to work in any field they choose. Then I met a friend of a friend, Martha Long, who is the head of this small organization, and suddenly I found not only a job but a mission, a real purpose."

Victoria picked up her cake and began eating again, but her enthusiasm had dimmed considerably. Prudence's heart constricted. Whatever had hurt Victoria had gone deep, and

Prudence hadn't been there to help her at all. But then, maybe it was better that way? Look how grown-up Victoria had become.

Andrew stood abruptly and put his plate and cup in the sink. "I'm sorry I can't stay and chat, ladies, but I have an appointment."

"He works with a maths tutor twice a week," Prudence explained, pride in her voice. "He is studying to take the Royal Veterinary College examinations this spring."

Andrew gave her a grateful look as he went back into the bedroom to finish dressing. He nodded to everyone as he left and Prudence turned to Victoria.

"You still haven't told me what your aunt Charlotte or Rowena have said about this new venture."

"Well, they don't know yet," Victoria explained patiently, as if talking to a child. "I just got the position. I've only worked at it for a couple of days. Martha knows I don't live in London, but I can work from Summerset until I move back to London."

Something struck Prudence. "You've been staying with Katie?"

"The last few days, yes," Victoria said.

Katie caught Prudence's thought immediately. "Now don't be angry with Ma for not telling you. Victoria said she wanted to surprise you and see you face-to-face. Surely this was better, right?"

Prudence's eyes filled with tears and Victoria was next to her in a moment.

"Don't cry, darling Prudence. I missed you, too. Let's not worry about the past anymore, all right?"

Prudence sniffled. "That's easy for you to say," she said, thinking of Rowena.

Katie produced a handkerchief for Prudence. Prudence blew

her nose and then rested her head against Victoria's shoulder. For the first time Victoria's arms felt strong and comforting around her, as if she could lean into them. There was so much she wanted to tell her, but it was all tangled up inside.

"So what do you think about my idea?"

"I think it's wonderful," Prudence said. "Do you think your aunt will actually let Susie come?"

Victoria wiped her eyes and resumed her seat. "I will work on her. I'm pretty persistent."

Prudence narrowed her eyes suspiciously. "So when and what are you going to tell Rowena and your aunt?"

Victoria shifted in her seat as if she were suddenly sitting on a cushion of rocks. "I'm not sure I am," she said. "I'm fairly certain it will be far more trouble than it's worth. So I think I will keep it my little secret. I've been told we are all coming here for Easter anyway. I will simply visit all of my friends until then."

Prudence looked away. Rowena had kept telling her that if she could just hang on until Easter, life would go back to normal. And then she'd discovered that Rowena had been lying the entire time. Tears rose up again, but Prudence blinked them back fiercely. She had cried enough over Rowena's betrayal. She would waste no more tears on her.

"When are you going home?" she asked.

"Tomorrow." Once again, a shadow crossed her face, but Prudence didn't ask about it. Somehow this new Victoria was much more intimidating than the old one had been, and Prudence guessed it would be a bit until they fell into their old patterns. If they ever did. Perhaps Victoria had grown beyond them.

They spoke for a few more minutes before Victoria stood to leave. In spite of all the embarrassment Victoria had caused, Prudence's heart ached to see her go. Being with Victoria reminded her of everything that was brilliant about her old life and about everything that was missing from her new one. She held her close.

"Come back soon," she whispered in Victoria's ear. "I've missed you so."

"I will, I promise. And we will get Susie to help you with the scrubbing until you are all settled." She gave Prudence a final hug before heading down the stairs. She turned and waved as she left. To Prudence's eyes it looked as if Victoria gave off a glowing light wherever she went, and when she left, everything diminished a bit.

After her company had left, Prudence did up the dishes and wondered what Andrew thought of her now that he knew she hadn't even known how to do laundry. In his world, even men knew how to do laundry, even if they never had to. Would he even have married her had he known how useless she actually was? *Laundry!*

Drying her hands quickly, she ran down the stairs two at a time and let herself into the cellar. After flicking the light on, she hurried over to where her sheets and Andrew's undershirts were still soaking. Snatching up the laundry stick, she pulled up the washing and deposited it into the rinse water. Frantically, Prudence stirred the wash to try to rinse out the bluing but it was no good—both of their sheets and all of Andrew's undershirts were freckled with deep blue spots. She let the water out and rinsed the clothes twice more before she gave up. She still wore the apron she'd donned when she washed the dishes and she wiped her hands carefully before covering her face and sinking to the ground in defeat.

Well, if Andrew had been surprised before to find out she couldn't do laundry, he certainly wouldn't be anymore.

* * *

Victoria stood in Katie's doorway, unsure whether to slam the door in Kit's face or enjoy the spectacle of watching him grovel.

She chose the groveling.

"You didn't answer my note," he said.

She crossed her arms and kept her mouth closed. Her things were all packed and ready near the door, but she still hadn't decided whether she would accept a ride to the train with him or let Martha take her. Martha would be more than happy to drive; all Victoria had to do was call.

But this might be more entertaining.

"I apologized for my behavior in my note. I met Sebastian and your cousin at the club and I lost track of time. I tried to come here and explain, but you wouldn't open the door." He looked at her, accusing.

"You showed up completely blotto, after everyone had gone to bed. Hardly the time for an apology."

Kit shuffled his feet. "I sent a note." Sulkiness had crept back into his voice and Victoria had trouble suppressing a triumphant smile.

She reached down and grabbed one of her bags and shoved it at him. He stumbled, nearly falling.

"Hey! What was that for?" he asked.

"I thought you were driving me to the train station?"

His face brightened. "So you forgive me?"

"I didn't say that." She shoved a second bag at him. "Go put those in the car. I'll be right down."

She gave Katie and Muriel each a hug. Lottie had gone out earlier, saying she would see her soon. She didn't seem elated about Victoria's new position in the organization, but she was resigned to it. Of course, Lottie worked another job and put most of the money into the organization, so she had a reason to be sour.

"Look, Vic, I said I was sorry, what else am I supposed to do?" Kit asked once they were in the car.

His voice sounded peevish, not at all repentant, and he glared at the road in front of him instead of looking at her with remorse. Of course, he was driving, but those old French novels she liked to read were very clear about how apologies were supposed to be handled. This was not the way. Of course, those were always between men and women who were in love, and that was not the case between her and Kit. Not at all. So maybe apologies were different, too? She settled back into the fine leather of his motorcar and let him sweat a bit. No reason to give in too quickly. She had been humiliated. Twice. Once when he stood her up, and then again when he was howling and drunk outside Katie's door.

His shoulders were bunched under his fine jacket by the time they reached the station. "Do you have your ticket?" he asked tersely.

She nodded and he hopped out of the car. Instead of coming around to let her out, he opened the back door and pulled out her bags and gave them to a porter. Uncertainly, she climbed out of the car and approached as he tipped the porter.

"I forgive you," she said in a rather small voice.

"What's that?" he barked as the porter left.

She tilted her head back to get a better look at him. "I said I forgive you."

"Oh, you forgive me, do you? How nice. How entirely big of you. Who do you think you are? A princess? Should I be grateful for your forgiveness now?"

She stepped back, alarmed by the sarcasm in his voice. Then anger burned through her again. "You're quite lucky I forgive you, as you behaved like a beast! You humiliated me in front of my friends—"

"Oh, now we've come to the real problem, haven't we? You were embarrassed in front of your friends."

Victoria looked around the sidewalk, her cheeks heating with humiliation. "Stop it. You're making a spectacle of yourself."

"Well, maybe I should just leave, then?"

"Maybe you should. It's not as though I can't find my way to the proper platform," Victoria said, her voice clogged with tears. This was not the way it was supposed to be going at all. How did it get so far out of hand? Kit was supposed to be her *friend*.

"Good day, then." Kit's cheeks were mottled, but he tipped his hat and turned to go.

"You're behaving like such a baby!" she yelled after him, and though he paused for a fraction of a second, he didn't turn around.

Fine, she thought, wiping her tears with her gloved fingers. If he wanted to be a bore, he could just be a bore. Her breath caught in her lungs, but it wasn't the tightness that preceded an attack, it was a sense of loss nearly as acute as the one she'd felt when she lost Prudence or even her father. Which didn't make any sense at all, she thought as she resolutely found her platform. Kit wasn't family, he had just been a friend and a rather poor friend at that, if she thought about all the ways he'd teased her or completely misunderstood her.

She boarded the train, remembering all the ways in which Kit had disappointed her. And after all, they had been friends for only a few months. Maybe they weren't compatible after all.

Let him have his silly friends and their drinking all night and their Cunning Coterie. She had *real* things to do. She had real things to do for Martha, who was not only her boss but a friend.

Victoria entered her train compartment feeling better. Not completely better—it was still sad to lose a friend, after all—but still much improved. She had work to do.

* * *

Victoria's mouth fell open when she spotted Rowena waving her hat and umbrella as the train pulled into Theton Station. What a departure from the sad, listless girl she had left just a little over a week ago.

Rowena caught her up into a tight hug the moment she stepped off the train.

"Lord, I've missed you. So much has happened."

Rowena's complexion had always been fair, but she had taken on a sickly pallor the past few months. For the first time in ages, a healthy pink stained her cheeks, and her eyes sparkled. "I don't believe it!" Victoria breathed. "You're in love!"

Rowena pulled away from Victoria, her eyes wide. "How on earth did you guess?"

Just then Sebastian appeared behind Rowena, smiling from under his black umbrella.

Victoria looked from one to the other, confused. "Sebastian?"

"Congratulate us, sister dear, for I am engaged to your sister!"

Victoria felt her mouth open. "What did you say?"

Rowena laughed. "It's a very long story, little sister. Just let me say that quite a bit has occurred since you left."

"I'll get your bags while Rowena fills you in," Sebastian said.

The rain poured down as the girls raced to Sebastian's car.

"I can't believe how quickly the weather changed. It wasn't anything like this in London," Victoria said, once they put down their umbrella and climbed into the car.

"This just started yesterday. Before that it was perfect. Sunshine, no clouds or wind. Perfect flying weather." Rowena gave her a sideways look and Victoria pounced on her.

"You had better tell me what's going on. It's about the pilot and not Sebastian at all, isn't it?"

Victoria kept quiet until Rowena had completely finished her story.

"But what are you going to do about Aunt Charlotte? She is going to be devastated when you tell her you're not marrying Sebastian, and that instead you are marrying a pilot from an impoverished family."

Rowena avoided her eyes and Victoria burst out, "Wait. He hasn't asked you to marry him?"

"No. We're not even thinking about that yet," Rowena said. "I'm learning to fly! I'm going to be a pilot and I'm in love. Isn't that enough for a week?"

Victoria narrowed her eyes. "Well, yes, I just don't understand. If he loves you, why hasn't he asked?"

Sebastian opened the back of the motorcar and set Victoria's bags inside before coming around to the driver's side.

Victoria fell silent, the muscles in her back bunched in a disgruntled knot. Part of her wanted to tell Rowena about her own exciting adventures, but her news couldn't compete with a sham engagement. She wasn't used to being upstaged. Plus, her argument with Kit still rankled.

"Well, when are you going to tell Auntie that you have broken off the engagement? You had better do it before people start sending engagement gifts."

"Jon leaves for Kent in a few days," Rowena managed, suddenly crestfallen.

Victoria shifted, uncomfortable. She'd never seen her sister in love before and Victoria knew nothing about her beloved, other than the fact that he hurtled himself and her sister recklessly through the skies.

After they reached Summerset, Victoria bided her time until she could slip away to her secret office. She chatted with Elaine and her aunt and told them about London, as if she had spent the entire time with society. She had a hard time inventing people who were in society whom her aunt didn't know. At last, she admitted that though she'd seen most of those people at the opera and such, she had spent most of her time at the Kingslys', and with some friends of her father's. Though Aunt Charlotte's mouth had puckered at that, there hadn't been much she could say.

Once she had spent as much time as she decently had to discussing fake wedding parties, she dashed up to her bedroom, gathered the leather folders Martha had given her, and secreted herself in her hidden office. After building a roaring fire to help fight off the ever-present chill, she settled herself down with her work. A moment of disappointment transpired when she thought about what she had originally planned to tackle upon her return to Summerset—more articles for *The Botanist's Quarterly*—but that evaporated when she thought about how worthy the work was that she now committed herself to.

One of the folders Martha had given her contained information on how to perform her new duties. Martha wanted her to be a spokeswoman for the organization, as well as help with clerical duties. The other folder was filled with papers Victoria had put together herself on various services for women. She pulled out the first packet and went through it. First, she discovered a small packet of cards, with *The Suffragettes for Female Equality* printed on them, with a post office box address in a lovely, feminine script. Then she looked over a packet of papers containing a list of names separated into groups. Victoria frowned, wondering by what criteria they were grouped. Then her brows rose as she caught the differences. The first group included her aunt's name and was a list of twenty women who could be considered first-tier society. These were the women who set the standards that all others lived up to. Like Aunt Charlotte, most were titled, wealthy, and in their forties.

The next group was more of a puzzle, but Victoria soon figured it out. These women were fashionable and stylish. They were also wealthy, but they were younger, not necessarily titled but definitely society. The third group was easy. They were all Jewish women who were tolerated by society because of their wealth and their attention to detail. The fourth packet contained the most names, but Victoria recognized only a few of the names on the list. It took her several minutes before she realized they were all newly rich, social-climbing wives of self-made men or they were Americans. After this list there was a note from Martha.

So glad to have you with us! I know you are going to be such an asset. Because my name has been besmirched among society, I no longer have any clout with these women. But you, my darling, are the perfect person to incite in these women sympathy for our cause. I think you should emphasize how we help poor mothers and downplay our suffragette activities, as many of these poor women have been deluded by their husbands into believing that not having any rights is for our own good. Can you believe this? It makes me so angry!

So it is best working among these women to use our main name, the Suffragettes for Female Equality, which might be less inflammatory. You wondered why I wanted you to use discretion when discussing your work with others and this was one of the very main reasons. Of course, my darling, I am not asking you to lie about our activities; just be careful about which truth you share!

So about this list. I am sure you will be able to persuade your aunt to introduce you to these women if you do not already know them. The season is approaching and there will be many opportunities for you to speak about our worthy cause. We will of course have several training sessions before sending you soliciting into the wild, so to speak, so I need you to come back to London as soon as you are able. Besides, I will miss you dreadfully.

So for now, your assignment is to memorize this list, make sure your aunt knows how eager you are to take your place in society, and plan a trip back as soon as possible! I trust in your ability to do all those things, enterprising creature that you are.

Best,

Martha Long

Victoria frowned. Take her place in society? She hated society. Their father had raised them to detest such snobbery and now she was going to have to court it?

She shuddered. Martha had no idea what she was asking. But then again, she could see the wisdom of having someone on good footing not only with the people who had the money to keep their organization running, but with those whose husbands made parliamentary policy. She just wished she didn't have to be the one to win these women over. She had thought she would be working more on the front lines rather than in the sitting rooms and parlors of the wealthy.

She wondered what Nanny Iris would say about her new position. She should be happy for Victoria, who had long wanted to find an outlet for her energies and talents. But Victoria had a feeling in her stomach that Nanny Iris wouldn't be thrilled with her new employment at all.

* * *

The world was coming to an end. Kit had long suspected it was going to happen before he had truly had the time to enjoy himself, and now here was the proof, right in front of his own eyes.

The Lady Edith Billingsly of Eddelson Hall is delighted to announce the betrothal of her son, Lord Sebastian Billingsly, to the Honorable Miss Rowena Buxton, niece of the Lord and Lady of Summerset, Lord Conrad Buxton and Lady Charlotte Buxton, and the daughter of Sir Philip Buxton, deceased.

There was more, but Kit couldn't bear to read any of it. He felt like Benedick in *Much Ado About Nothing*, when he lamented, "Is't come to this? Shall I never see a bachelor of three score again?"

He was heading to the Billingslys' tomorrow to stay for a couple of days. He would have to try to talk some sense into the young man. A favor, as it were.

Kit threw the paper down onto the table in disgust. He sat in a tea shop, waiting to meet a friend of his. They planned to walk to the club together and play a game or two of tennis before it was time to go home and dress for dinner. Soon, he wouldn't have any friends who were still available to do such things. They would all be married to spoiled little snits like Victoria, God save them. At least her sister had a better temperament.

Oh, but of course, Victoria wasn't going to be married. Ever.

Kit poured himself a bit more tea and picked up the paper again, making sure to turn the page. Good Lord. She'd get married, of course, to some stuffy fellow who wouldn't mind the way she just burst into recitations at the oddest moments, or recited bits of fairy tales at the most inopportune times. Though the incident where she quoted the big, bad wolf when the Lady Billingsly entered the room for tea was hysterical, even if her aunt did nearly have an apoplectic fit.

Certainly, she could be witty and sometimes downright funny, like the time they found the dead bird in her secret room and she had insisted having a ceremonial cremation for it until she realized, to her horror, that it smelled just like roast chicken and made their mouths water.

But she was so infernally grumpy. You never knew what would set her off. Sebastian would have a much easier time with Rowena, who was more even-tempered, and she was undeniably lovely, if you liked the black-haired, pale Madonna type with the sea-green eyes. Everyone considered her to be the far lovelier of the two, though Kit didn't. He found Rowena to be rather apathetic and her coloring common when compared to her sister, whose blue eyes snapped with intelligence and personality. Victoria might be small, but her fairylike looks made everyone else seem big and bumbling by comparison.

Not that it mattered to him. Not a jot nor a farthing did any of it matter. Little Miss Victoria had made it abundantly clear what she thought of him and then again when she "accepted" his apology. She was lucky he hadn't wrung her spindly little neck.

An errant fly buzzed around him and he rolled up the newspaper and swatted at it. So what if he rather missed her? Having a woman best friend had been an experiment that had not worked out, that's all. He hadn't expected it to, really.

He swatted at the fly again. Women were too bothersome, and Victoria was the worst of the lot, the way she was always going on about wanting some kind of accomplishments. Ladies didn't work. They were decorative. Hell, gentlemen didn't work, either. They hired solicitors to manage their money and give them enough to live on every year.

It wasn't his fault that Victoria made him feel rather . . . idle. He was doing what he was supposed to do. What his parents, who were "new rich" by anyone's standards, had brought him up to do. He lunched. He attended all the right functions, had his clothes made at Peel's, and flattered the right people. He'd even had the right affairs with the right women, women unattainable enough to make him seem rather the rake. He was an important man in their world. Young, yes, untried, yes, but up-and-coming.

He swatted again at the fly and almost upset his tea. Stupid thing. Where was Peter, for God's sake?

Except Victoria judged him through different eyes. Lovely, critical blue eyes that wondered about a man who didn't wake up excited about his work. It was her father's fault. A highly successful man who'd studied plants, of all the bloody things. He'd ruined her, the way he'd brought her up among intellectuals, artists, and captains of industry. Incited her to believe that everyone had a talent and a passion and a God-given edict to find it and nurture it. He'd produced a daughter who looked like a goddess, with the mind of an intellectual, the imagination of a sprite, and the temperament of a harpy. She'd been brought up to have absolutely no respect for men at all.

He found himself hating Sir Philip Buxton and he hadn't even known him.

The fly bombed him again and Kit stood, swatting wildly. Bloody pest. What kind of place was this anyway?

"Is this some kind of new modern dance?" a voice asked from behind him.

"Where the hell have you been?" Kit asked. "I've been waiting for hours."

A dark-haired gentleman raised an eyebrow. "That's not my fault, pal. I'm only five minutes late."

"Felt like forever." Kit tossed a coin on the table.

"Someone's in a bad mood. A few games of tennis and supper at the club will knock that right out of you. Are you saving that for later, for our match perhaps?" He looked meaningfully at the rolled-up paper still in Kit's hand.

Kit threw it onto the table. "No," he said rather more viciously than was warranted. "I'm damn well finished with it."

CHAPTER
ELEVEN

Rowena closed her eyes as Jonathon planed downward. She savored the sensation of weightlessness and the cold wind whipping about her cheeks. Droplets of mist stuck to her goggles and she wiped them away impatiently. They were flying low, beneath the cloud cover, and Rowena watched the fallow patchwork of fields as they moved lazily past.

They were testing a new aeroplane. Usually, Jon didn't let her up in anything except a tried-and-true model, but she had insisted and he had given in, a tribute to her increasing knowledge and bravery. The new aeroplane seemed slower than Lucy, the plane he usually took her up in, but steadier, moving through the air smoothly, like a ship cutting through water. Jonathon dipped to the right and her stomach hit her ribs in that free-floating feeling she knew so well. Then he banked deeply back to the left and Rowena leaned with the aeroplane as she would a horse.

Then the nose tilted up in the air as Jon took the aeroplane steeply upward. Soon the cloud cover obscured everything, but Rowena could sense the aeroplane straining as it gained altitude. Within no time, they broke through the clouds and the world sparkled blue and white.

He leveled it out and Rowena wanted to scream in exultation. Tears came to her eyes, steaming up the corners of her goggles.

The change that flying had made in her life was irrevocable.

She would never return to the depressing grayness that had consumed her for too many months. Flying might not be considered a ladylike activity, but she would fight anyone who tried to ground her, because she had finally found something that completed her.

There must be other women like her. She would meet them, emulate them. Learn from them. She would stop Jonathon's and Mr. Dirkes's lollygagging around about her flying solo. It was time for her to find a way to break off the engagement with Sebastian and stand up for what she believed in: her future as a pilot. Her future with Jon.

She flung her arms out to embrace the sky, not caring whether Jon thought her gesture silly or foolish.

She would make her father proud.

* * *

"How did you say you broke your arm again?"

Kit glared at Sebastian. "Do I detect amusement in your voice? What kind of person would laugh at a friend with a broken limb?"

"No laughter here. What you're hearing is disbelief and curiosity. How does the club tennis champ not only lose to Peter Tremain but break his arm while doing so?"

The two men were eating breakfast in the formal dining room of Eddelson Hall. The buffet had been set up to one side and a footman stood next to it in case they needed anything. Kit stared at the clumsy cast on his right arm. The only thing he truly needed was to learn how to eat with his left hand, and that was something the servant couldn't provide.

"I was distracted," he snapped. He didn't tell Sebastian that he had seen a fair-haired woman walking by the lawn and for a moment thought it was Victoria. Before he knew it, he had pitched headlong over the net, busting his arm in the process.

It shouldn't surprise him. They weren't even on speaking terms and she was still ruining his life.

Kit had driven down late last night, unable to stand his mother's meddling. Besides, he needed a distraction from his constant thoughts of Victoria. "If we wish to talk about something amusing, let's move on to the topic of your engagement to Rowena. I turn my back for a moment and suddenly you are engaged? Are you out of your mind?" Kit's arm ached and he knew he was being grumpy, but he couldn't help it. Besides, Sebastian deserved it. Who got engaged without first telling his best friend?

Sebastian stared at him. "Good God, man, settle yourself. You're worse than an old woman."

Kit shrugged. "I thought I would be the first to know if you had fallen head over heels, that's all. I could have saved you from yourself. What happened to our agreement?"

Sebastian suddenly looked tired. He leaned closer to Kit and said under his breath, "I'm not in love with her. It's a fake. A sham. She's in love with someone else. It seems as if a scandal would have broken concerning her and her young man and, through a very opportune misunderstanding, I saved the day." He looked distantly out the window. "It's all rather comical, really."

Kit blinked. Sebastian didn't look amused but rather sad. Kit lowered his voice. "So you're not in love?"

"Not anymore," Sebastian said so quietly that Kit barely heard him.

He was confused. "Had you been in love with Rowena?"

Startled, Sebastian glanced up and smiled. "No. Of course not. Though the more I get to know her, the more I respect her."

"You're pretending to be engaged because you respect her?" Kit felt as though he was missing something elemental, but he couldn't put his finger on it.

Kit studied his friend as Sebastian busied himself with his breakfast. "Of course not. I just wanted someone to have a chance at love. Call me an old-fashioned romantic."

This wasn't his forte. Kit's specialty was witty repartee, not serious discussion concerning matters of the heart, but the quiet desperation in Sebastian's eyes moved him. "What happened with the woman you were in love with?"

"Her name was Prudence and she married someone else."

Kit sat back in his seat. "Victoria's Prudence?"

Sebastian nodded, then cleared his throat. "How is Victoria anyway? I haven't seen her since she got back from visiting her friends in London."

Kit's mind still reeled from Sebastian's confession, but he could tell his friend no longer wished to discuss it. And no wonder. "I suppose Victoria is fine. She's like a cat, always lands on her feet. I haven't seen her since then either."

Sebastian looked at him, curiosity evident in his eyes. "I thought you two were thick as thieves. What happened?"

Kit's mind blanked. What had happened? Nothing, except he had been a cad and she'd called him out on it. Of course, if she had been like most girls, she would have forgiven him sweetly the moment he had apologized. But then, most girls bored him to death.

And Victoria did not. Ever.

He drummed the fingers of his left hand and then finally glanced up at Sebastian. "Difference of opinion."

Sebastian whistled. "She got to you."

Kit slammed his hands down on the table and then groaned as the pain shot up his broken arm. "She did not get to me," he said through gritted teeth. "She's a friend. That's all."

Sebastian raised his eyebrows. "Are you sure? Because you were a much nicer person when she was around."

Kit bristled. "I resent that remark."

"All right. All right. She didn't get to you. If she walked in the house right now, you would be unaffected. I get it."

"Good," Kit said shortly. "I would hate to beat you up with my cast."

Sebastian pushed his plate away and the servant jumped into action, clearing it. "I suggest you make yourself scarce today. Mother's taking calls all afternoon and I will no doubt have to pay my respects to her guests. You can convalesce in the library if you like. I'll have a maid check up on you periodically to keep you in hot tea."

Kit gave a shudder that was only partially put on. The thought of spending the afternoon with Sebastian's mother and her cronies was chilling. He'd cozy up to the fire like an old man and read. His arm throbbed with pain and Kit hated taking the laudanum the doctor prescribed. He'd seen too many people become dependent on it.

But Kit couldn't concentrate on the book once ensconced in the library. He had a crackling fire, all the fine literature he could read, and a hot cup of tea, but thoughts of that spoiled minx Victoria kept creeping into his mind. When had that argumentative, spoiled, selfish little chit of a woman gotten under his skin?

And more important, how could he get her out of his mind?

* * *

If Lady Summerset was surprised to find that all three of her young charges wished to go on calls with her that day, she didn't show it, but then, Rowena reflected, her aunt wouldn't stoop so low as to show her surprise.

Rowena was going because she desperately needed to confer with Sebastian about how they were going to break off their engagement. Elaine was along for moral support and because she didn't want to miss anything that might be scandalous or exciting, and Victoria was going . . . Rowena frowned at the back of her little sister's head. Why was Victoria going?

As if summoned, Victoria turned around in her seat. Because so many of them were going in the motorcar, one of them had to sit up with the driver, and Victoria had been the first to volunteer. "Who all are we going to see today, Auntie?"

Aunt Charlotte took a list out of the handbag she had tucked next to her. "The Kinkaids, the Honeywells, the Winthrops, and, of course, the Billingslys. We will go there last and stay for supper. It's just going to be a few friends and family. We have so many wedding plans to discuss."

She smiled at Rowena and Rowena smiled back weakly.

Wedding plans.

"Well, I think this is going to be such fun," Elaine gushed from the seat next to her. "Everyone will make such a fuss over you."

Rowena jabbed her surreptitiously in the ribs. Sometimes Elaine's teasing got to be a bit much.

"Oh, don't start nattering on, Elaine, or this drive will take forever," Aunt Charlotte snapped.

Rowena could feel Elaine's hurt and she wished she hadn't poked her. She laid her head back against the leather seat. The slight throbbing in her temples told her it was going to be a very long afternoon, indeed.

She let the talk flow around her and concentrated instead on Jon. She remembered how he had kissed her before he had left, his lips seeking an answer to something unasked. Let Victoria worry about an engagement if she wanted to. Rowena knew Jon loved her. Things were more complicated than Victoria knew. It would all work out eventually.

She heard Victoria's voice, talking to her aunt in an animated way. What was she speaking of? She opened her eyes.

"You know, Auntie, I am so excited about this season and not just because of the extra fun of Rowena's engagement festivities. I've never done a full proper season before, did you know that? Do you think I have enough dresses? I know I should wear dark dresses for most of it, but Father wouldn't want me to stay in mourning forever. Do you think I should order some new clothes?"

Rowena's mouth fell open. Her sister hated the season and thought it a complete and utter waste of time. She tried to catch Victoria's eye, but her sister was staring fixedly at her aunt.

Aunt Charlotte greeted this barrage in the same even manner with which she greeted everything. "Why don't you and I go through your dresses tomorrow? Surely you will want at least four new ball gowns if you are going to do a proper season. Elaine ordered two more last fall and all her new accessories, so she is ready, and of course Rowena will need an entire trousseau."

She frowned. "I can't believe I didn't think of this before.

They will charge a fortune to have everything made up so quickly, but you will both need new gowns for the season."

Victoria smiled as if excited by the prospect of endless fittings, but Rowena knew better. Though they both loved pretty things, fittings were their special pet hate, to be avoided at all costs, and now her sister was practically begging for them. Rowena narrowed her eyes. Something was going on. First Victoria's excitement about coming to do calls and now this? She would corner her to ask the first moment they were alone, Rowena decided. Find out exactly what was going on in her sister's head.

That moment was more difficult to find than she'd anticipated. Everyone wanted to see the antique family engagement ring Sebastian had given her. She'd balked at wearing it at first, but Sebastian had insisted, to keep up the ruse. "You might be the first Billingsly woman to wear it who was actually in love," he'd joked. The thought depressed her.

While Rowena was swept away into a sea of wedding conversations at the first call, Victoria mingled with an intent that puzzled her sister. Before Rowena could get a chance to corner Victoria, Aunt Charlotte hurried them all back into the car for the next visit, where the sequence were repeated. She might have to wait until she got to the Billingslys'. Perhaps she could ask for some time to rest before supper and take her suddenly social sister with her.

Sebastian met them at the door and kissed her hand warmly. "And how is my beautiful fiancée today?" he asked with a teasing smile.

She wanted to hit him. He was enjoying this. But then, remembering how sad he had been the first time she'd come to Eddelson, she decided she'd much rather see him smiling.

As before, Rowena was rushed off into a whirl of wedding discourse, but because the groom's mother was involved, everything seemed to take on a greater importance. Her every opinion, no matter how thoughtlessly given, was taken as gospel and commented on by either her aunt or Sebastian. After Rowena had been told, in no uncertain terms, that orange sherbet was absolutely not the same color as orange blossom, Elaine took matters into her own hands.

"I'm sure Rowena is getting a bit tired, as am I. Could we rest and freshen up before dinner?"

"That would be wonderful." Rowena tried to look pathetic and wan.

"Of course. Larson will show you both to one of the bedrooms."

"Victoria, would you join me?" Rowena asked over her shoulder as she turned to follow the butler.

Victoria, who'd been chatting up one Lady Worthington, raised her eyebrows. "But I'm not really tired, Ro, and I'm having such a lovely chat." She flashed the woman in the lavender tea gown next to her a beatific smile.

The woman patted her knee. "Go ahead, my dear. Your sister probably wants to talk about the wedding."

Victoria gave way reluctantly but not before she surreptitiously passed the woman a card. The trio followed the butler to a large bedroom overlooking the same sculpture garden she and Sebastian had walked through the first time she was here. A large ornate bed decorated the middle and there were several comfortable sofas and chaise lounges in front of a cheerful fire.

Elaine lay down on a striped chaise and waved her hand at the others. "Relax, for God's sake. It's not even my wedding and I feel like I'm being hounded to death. Everyone thinks I know

more than I'm telling. Of course, I do, but I can't tell them that.
Can you imagine?"

Rowena reclined on a sofa and pulled a throw over herself.
"It's not even a real wedding and I feel the same way."

Victoria glared at her and then plopped down into the chair
closest to Rowena. "I don't understand why *I* had to come. I was
having a perfectly fine time."

Rowena flipped over on her stomach and eyed her sister.
Victoria's health had improved since she'd moved to Summerset,
but she had become quieter and more thoughtful. Now she had
a secret, which wasn't that unusual. Victoria had always harbored secrets like they were pearls to be treasured, but this one
was different. She suddenly seemed self-assured, almost adult.

"And that is exactly why I wanted to see you. Where is all
this love for polite society coming from? If anything, you've
hated doing your social duty even more than I have, and now
you're going on calls and asking Aunt Charlotte to introduce
you around? Ball gowns and fittings? The season? Really?"

Victoria's eyes shifted away from hers. "We all have to have
something, Rowena. You have your flyboy and a fake engagement and I have a newfound love of gaiety. The Coterie will be at
most of those functions, right?" She looked at Elaine, who nodded in confirmation. "See, my new set is going to be going. Why
wouldn't I want to spend as much time with them as possible?"

"Does that include Kit?" Rowena asked.

For a moment a look of hurt so profound crossed Victoria's
face that Rowena had an urge to gather Vic up into her arms
and tell her that everything was going to be all right, but then
she regained the impudent expression that made Rowena want
to shake her. Prudence had always been much better with Vic in
this kind of mood than she was.

"Of course that includes Kit. What do you think? And why does everything have to be about a man?"

Rowena's eyes widened. "It doesn't. I just thought you and Kit were special friends." She raised her hands to show that she didn't mean anything by it.

"Just because you fancy yourself in love doesn't mean that everyone needs to be. I'm never going to get married, you know that. And Kit has absolutely nothing to do with anything!"

Rowena shook her head. They were getting way off topic now. Swinging her feet around to sit up, Rowena reached across and captured one of Victoria's arms. Vic tried to yank it back, but Rowena held firm and, slipping her fingers under the lace cuff, pulled out several cream-colored cards.

Rowena read the fancy script: *The Suffragettes for Female Equality.* Underneath was an address.

"What are these?" she asked curiously.

To her surprise, Victoria flew at her in a fury that she hadn't shown since she was a child throwing a tantrum. Rowena found herself being shoved back down into the sofa while the card was snatched out from her fingertips.

"That, my dear, prying sister, is none of your business."

"Is that what you have been giving out and why you are suddenly so eager to meet people?" Rowena couldn't understand. Why was her sister being so mysterious about a suffragette society? They all belonged to one or another anyway.

A mottled red stained Victoria's pale face and her mouth tightened. "I don't understand why my business always has to be your business. Now, if you will excuse me."

Tilting her chin, she marched out of the room. Rowena expected a slam of the door but it never came.

Elaine sat straight up on the lounge, her blue eyes wide. "What on earth was that all about? I haven't seen her like that since she was a child."

Rowena snorted. "That's because you haven't been around her much."

But Rowena pondered that question the rest of the evening.

* * *

Victoria wondered the same thing as she hurried down the hall. Why had she gotten so angry? It was perfectly fine if Rowena knew about her involvement with the Suffragettes for Female Equality. Her stomach twisted uneasily. It just seemed so confusing. But still, she could have told Rowena about her job and instead she felt violated, as if Rowena had been picking away at a festering sore that just couldn't seem to heal.

Wait. Shouldn't she be in the salon by now? She looked around; nothing looked familiar. Even though Eddelson Hall wasn't near the size of Summerset, it was obvious that one could still get confused. The walls were much lighter than anything at Summerset, a pretty pale blue, dotted with portraits of dead Billingslys and their equally dead hunting dogs.

Ornately carved pocket doors opened on either side of the hall, and Victoria found herself less eager to make it back to the gossip of the salon when she could possibly find a quiet nook to relax in. It turned out that being social was infernally hard work.

Victoria wanted to blame her behavior on anything but the truth. It was because Rowena had brought up Kit, and Victoria missed him terribly, in spite of everything. She missed him so much it hurt to think about it.

She shook her head as if to shake the thought of him loose.

He had made his choice—to act like a selfish bore and cast their friendship aside as if it were nothing. Now she just wanted to find a place to be left alone. At least for a while.

She tiptoed down the hall, peering into various rooms. When she finally poked her head around the corner, she knew she had the perfect place. The space was both rich and mellow, with hundreds of books lining the walls and comfortable leather furniture. Leaded windows covered one wall and let in splashes of natural light, and a fire burned happily in the hearth.

Slipping inside, she noiselessly slid the pocket door shut, hoping for at least an hour of quiet before she had to make an appearance for dinner.

And what a lovely place to escape to, she thought, meandering over to a giant bookshelf that covered one wall. Whoever designed it had done so for comfort alone and perhaps a love and respect for Scotland, she thought, eyeing the green-and-cream plaid throws on the furniture. She had just turned to the books, hoping to find a volume of poetry among the impressive historical tomes that lined the shelf, when she heard a noise. Something between a snort and a snuff. She froze, her heart pounding in her chest. Suddenly she knew with certainty that she wasn't alone in the library. As she turned soundlessly around, her eyes darted to every corner of the room, searching for the interloper. Of course, in reality, she was the interloper, but Victoria had come to think of this delightful room as hers. At least for the next hour.

There was nothing. Her eyes swept the room again and then caught on the corner of the armchair facing the fire. The back of the chair was so high that she couldn't see a head, but that definitely looked like a man's sleeve.

Sebastian was down in the sitting room, being bombarded

with wedding talk, and his father was dead, so who . . . Then her heart stopped beating. This had probably been Sebastian's father's library. A room that he had loved. She stared fixedly at the black fabric barely showing around the side of the chair. It looked real enough. Suddenly a ghostly white chunk of a hand fell off the arm of the chair and dangled there as though it weren't attached to anything.

Victoria tried to scream but instead only squawked. Loudly.

The person belonging to the sleeve leapt to his feet and whirled around. "Good God, woman!"

Kit.

They stared at each other for a long moment.

"What are you doing here?" she finally managed.

"Why do you always scream when you see me?" he asked.

Victoria smiled sheepishly, recalling the moment when he had discovered her in her secret room at Summerset Abbey in the middle of the night.

Victoria's lips quirked upward in spite of herself, but then she remembered her anger and pulled her mouth back down into a frown. "Because you always startle me. Or maybe it's your ugly mug that does it," she taunted.

"Really? You're the first woman who has ever disliked my face." His lips curled into a smile and Victoria wanted to slap him. Hard.

She tilted her nose in the air. "Maybe they were just being polite."

"Oh, I doubt that." His smile widened and the urge to hit him grew. Then she saw why his hand had looked so strange. It was covered in a cast from the midpoint of his palm to halfway up his forearm. "You're hurt," she cried, rushing over to him.

"I broke my wrist playing tennis," he said. "It's nothing

really. The doctor said he'll be able to remove the cast in about five weeks. Though it does make it difficult to eat or shave."

Victoria held the injured appendage in her hands and his fingers felt hot against hers. "What are you doing here? Shouldn't your mother be caring for you?"

"You've never met my mother," he said with a smile. "I obviously couldn't stay at my flat by myself, and besides, I'd already promised Sebastian a visit. I knew I would be well cared for here. I'll probably head home to let my mother fuss over me in a week or so."

She looked up into his face and saw a tightness around his mouth that hadn't been there before, and his skin was pale. The blue of his eyes burned brightly and she frowned. "You're in pain," she insisted, gently pushing him back into his chair. "Have you taken anything?"

She spied a brown bottle and a cup of tea next to him. The tea was cold and she wondered who was supposed to be looking after him.

"Now, don't be angry. All the maids are busy with the gossips downstairs or getting ready for supper. And no, I haven't taken anything. The doctor prescribed laudanum and I've seen what that can do."

"Don't be a juggins. It's meant to help. But I would be able to help you more if I had access to some herbs."

She snatched up a plaid throw and tucked it about his legs, then located and rang the bell for a maid. The maid was there in moments.

She found a piece of paper on the desk and, dipping a pen into an inkwell, wrote down some ingredients she thought the kitchen might have on hand. She wished she could go down and make the tea herself, but she didn't want to leave Kit, and besides, she had a feeling that would be frowned upon by both her aunt and Lady Billingsly. Victoria conferred with the maid at the door, keeping her voice low.

When the girl had left, Victoria went back to Kit, who had closed his eyes, though Victoria was reasonably sure he wasn't asleep. She laid a hand on his head. "You have a bit of a fever, I think."

"I think I got chilled the day I broke my hand. It was pouring that day and I got awfully wet."

"Why didn't you have your umbrella with you?"

"You know, you're being awfully nice," he said, his voice accusing. "I thought you hated me."

The tone of his voice was nonchalant, but it seemed to Victoria that there was a tone of uncertainty underneath. She pulled up a worn leather footstool and took his good hand in hers, giving in to her happiness at seeing him again. "Of course I hated you, but that doesn't mean I was going to hate you forever. I don't know why you had to stay away for so long."

He opened his eyes and looked at her. "How am I supposed to know that? Guess?"

"No. Just ask. I told you when we became friends that you needed to forget everything you thought you knew about women. If you want to know things, you have to ask me. I'll be only too willing to let you know. If I don't hate you that day." She smiled to show she was teasing and also to show that she really did want to put the past behind them. She was tired of missing him and wanted their friendship back.

He shook his head. "I don't know if I can survive all these ups and downs."

She frowned. "What do you mean? I thought you hated being bored. You can't say that friendship with me is ever boring."

He shook his head again and then winced. The maid came in just then, carrying a tea tray with two pots, followed by another maid with a white bowl, a pitcher of water, and a clean kitchen towel.

"Mrs. Billingsly was informed and she told me to tell you to call if you need anything else. She will be up to check on you before dinner," the first maid said.

Victoria nodded. "Did the cook have everything on my list?"

"Everything except the valerian root, miss. But the rest of it is in there." She pointed to the smaller of the two teapots.

"Thank you."

She poured herself a cup of tea from the big pot and took a sip. The tea in the second pot smelled strongly of mint. Victoria only hoped the cook had used the right amounts and that the mint would hide the bitterness of the other herbs and the laudanum. She took the brown bottle out of her pocket, where she had secreted it, and poured in what looked to be about a spoonful. Combined with the herbs, it should put him to sleep in no time.

She took his tea over to him and told him to drink it. "Miss Bossy," he complained, but the slight smile on his lips told her he liked being fussed over. But then again, what man didn't? She knew next to nothing about men, but she did know that.

She found a small pillow and put it behind his head, watching as he sipped his tea. He grimaced. "What the hell is this? Are you trying to poison me?"

"No! Trust me, if I wanted to poison you, you'd be good and poisoned already. Those are just some of Nanny Iris's herbs to help drive off a chill and dull the pain."

"Well, if they're Nanny Iris's . . ."

Victoria smiled. He had met Nanny Iris only once and even

though it had been the difficult night when Victoria had found out about Prudence's true parentage, he and Nanny Iris had gotten along like anything, which was odd when she thought about it. Why would Nanny Iris like a bored, cynical, rather lazy young man like Kit?

She poured some water into the bowl and dipped the towel into it. Then she sat back down on the footstool and began wiping his forehead.

He frowned at her. "I had no idea you had it in you to be so kind."

"That's not a very nice thing to say."

"I *know* I'm not nice."

"Drink your tea." She watched as he took another sip. "You can do better than that." He glared at her and then swallowed the contents of the cup. She relaxed. "Well, maybe I'm not nice either," she said, going back to their conversation.

"You certainly weren't last time I saw you."

His voice sounded accusing and she tamped down her irritation. Why couldn't he just leave it alone? "That will teach you to stand me up and then show up later completely blotto." She kept her voice mild and smiled deeply to reassure him.

His hand reached up and caught hers. "The problem is that I'm not sure I can say with any certainty that it won't happen again. I'm not much good, you know."

She looked into his eyes and her pulse raced at the flame she saw in their blue depths. "Then it's a good thing we're just friends, isn't it?" she asked. She tried to pull her arm away but he kept it, taking the cloth from her fingers.

"You have such tiny hands. I can cover your hands with mine. Look."

She relaxed. His lids were heavy and his speech was slower. He should be asleep in no time. "Oh, yes, you're a great big man and I'm a little weak woman," she teased.

He frowned at her as his eyelids kept trying to close. "Nanny Iris's tea made me sleepy. And no. You're not weak. You're strong. And pretty. Funny. I never thought about how pretty you were until after our fight." He leaned forward. "Another thing I didn't know."

"What's that?" Victoria asked, keeping her voice low and soothing.

"I never knew just how much I wanted to kiss you."

He let go of her hand and, reaching behind her head, gently pulled her head forward and pressed his lips against hers. For a moment, she was so startled she did nothing, but then she jerked back. His eyes were shut and a smile lingered on his lips. Her heart racing, she stood, staring at him in shock. When he didn't move, she resettled the pillow behind his head, her mind racing. Why had he done that?

With trembling hands, she put their tea things back on the tray. Kissing him had never crossed her mind and she'd assumed it hadn't crossed his either. They were just *friends*.

She pressed her fingers against her lips, which were still warm from her first kiss.

A smile curved her mouth that she was only half aware of. She could see why kissing was so highly thought of—it was really rather pleasant.

Too bad it mustn't ever happen again.

CHAPTER TWELVE

rudence strode back and forth on the platform, excitement warring with trepidation in her chest. She'd been excited about Susie coming to help out until she realized that Susie thought she lived in a luxurious flat with a full staff. How disappointed she would be when she discovered Prudence's lies. And then there was her conversation with Muriel, whose thin, expressive face showed marked concern. They had been making kidney pies for their respective families and happily gossiping about this and that until Prudence had brought up Susie.

"What?" Prudence had asked at the look on her friend's face.

Muriel, who had lived her life knowing when to keep her mouth shut, had just shaken her head.

"Oh, come on," Prudence had pleaded. "I know that there's something on your mind. Why don't you tell me what it is?"

Muriel sighed and wiped her hands on her apron. "Do you think it's wise to bring another person into your home, you being so recently married and all?"

Prudence kept rolling out the pie crust. "I don't know what you mean. I trust both Susie and Andrew and—"

"Oh, Lord, no!" Muriel shook her head. "I forget what a baby you are in spite of your age."

"I'm hardly a baby!"

"An innocent then. That isn't what I meant at all. What I meant is that you and your man are still learning how to be a married couple. Anyone can see you're as lonely as can be without your sisters. So instead of turning to your husband, who is, for all intents and purposes, a stranger to you, you bring your best friend for an extended visit. So now you're as happy as a clam, but guess who gets left out in the cold?"

Prudence stamped her feet to warm them in the freezing weather. She promised herself she would do everything she could to continue to tend the fragile intimacy that had sprung up between her and Andrew.

"Prudence!"

She whirled at the sound of her husband's voice. He hurried forward, a smile on his face. He wore a heavy wool overcoat, and a herringbone cap sat straight on his head.

"What are you doing here? I thought you were going to go work today?"

He took her hands in his and kissed her cheek. "I was walking down to the docks and then thought to myself, I should be with my pretty wife when she meets our guest and take them both out to lunch. How often do we have a houseguest?"

His hazel eyes smiled down at her and a lump rose in her throat. "I don't deserve you," Prudence said.

"Don't be a goose. It's a special occasion."

But he looked pleased at the success of his surprise.

Another train squealed into the station and Prudence hoped it was Susie's. She linked her arm in Andrew's. People began disembarking and Prudence craned her neck until she realized she was looking the wrong way. Susie wouldn't be on that part of the train. She would be on the common section.

"Oof!" She had barely turned around when Susie lunged at

her with a hug so fierce that it would have toppled her over if she hadn't been holding on to Andrew's arm.

"Oh, Lord, I am glad to see you! Is London always this brown? There was a foul-looking man on the train who kept smiling at me. Do you live very far away? Look at how pretty you are!" She turned to Andrew. "Thank you so much for letting me come visit!"

Prudence grabbed Susie's shoulders and pushed her away a bit. "Let me look at you!" The girl looked the same as always, small but sturdy, thin brown hair pulled back in a bun, and a wide smile with slightly crooked teeth. She wore a severe black shirt and a warm black overcoat that looked new, probably a last-minute purchase with her meager earnings. Only her eyes seemed different, as abnormally wide and excited as they were. Prudence folded Susie back in her arms. Susie had been the only servant to welcome her and help her in those dark, confusing months at Summerset when she was relegated to the downstairs. She didn't care about Muriel's warnings, or that she would soon be caught in a web of lies—she had never been so glad to see someone in her whole life.

After Andrew had checked to make sure Susie had all her luggage—one large carpetbag and a reticule—he led them both out of the station. Prudence kept one hand on Susie's arm, as much to see that she didn't wander out into traffic as to make sure her friend was really here.

Once they neared their flat, they ducked into a warm tea shop, where Andrew lavished them with a high tea fit for the Queen. He ordered a pot of tea, tea sandwiches, scones and clotted cream, jam, and, after a wink for Prudence, big slices of sponge cake for them to share.

Susie assumed a bored, haughty look, as if she did this sort of thing every day, and Prudence grinned, proud and overcome by her husband's sweet generosity to their friend.

She nodded toward Susie's bags. "You best put your bag under the table between our knees if you don't want to lose it."

Susie's eyes widened. "Would someone steal right here in front of God and everyone? My mum told me that's the way it is here in London."

Prudence shrugged. "I've never had a problem, but you can never be too safe." She knew her own prejudices about this part of the city had everything to do with being raised in Mayfair.

The waitress set their tea down and Prudence smiled her thanks.

"My sisters are so jealous. I think I'm the first person in my family to ever leave Summerset."

Humbled, Prudence poured more tea and spread a layer of clotted cream on her scone. All she had thought of was what Susie's visit would mean to her, not what it would mean to Susie. She looked up to find Susie smiling at her and stuffing sponge cake into her mouth. Prudence laughed.

"So tell me all the gossip back home." Prudence didn't really want to know what was going on at Summerset, a place where she had been miserable, but she knew Susie was chock-full of things she wanted to share, and Andrew was truly interested in all the happenings from back home.

Susie related all the news and Prudence listened as attentively as she could. The girl was a bit hard to follow and occasionally Prudence would have to stem the tide of words coming out of her mouth to ask who someone was, but she mostly kept up until Susie mentioned the wedding.

"Wait. What wedding do you mean? My wedding?" Very few people from Summerset had attended Prudence and Andrew's wedding, so Prudence could hardly see how it had entered the conversation.

"No, silly, the upcoming wedding, of course! The entire house is in an uproar and will be for months and the couple hasn't even set a date yet! Lord, am I glad to get a break of that mess. The kitchen is going to be a madhouse, that's what."

Prudence sat back in her chair, still puzzled. "Susie, I'm completely lost. What wedding are you talking about? Is Miss Elaine getting married?" That was the only person Prudence could think of whose nuptials would put the entire house in an uproar.

Susie's eyes grew even wider. "You don't know? How could you not know? Why, Miss Rowena's wedding, of course. Hers and Lord Billingsly's."

Prudence stilled. All around her the sounds of the café diminished and black spots floated in front of her eyes as dizziness overcame her. She gripped the fork in her hand and tried to steady herself.

"Prudence! Are you all right?"

Andrew's concerned voice called to her, and after a moment, the room righted itself again. She took a deep breath, ignoring the pain that stormed her heart. She gave him a wobbly smile. "I'm so sorry. I guess the shock of it . . ."

"And no wonder!" Susie said. "Her being your friend and all. I thought you knew."

Prudence shook her head and took a careful sip of her tea. Her pulse still raced wildly and jealousy gnawed at her stomach. So Rowena was going to marry Sebastian. How, how had this happened? "I didn't."

Andrew frowned at her, his eyes puzzled. "Are you sure you're all right? We could go home."

"I'm fine. Really I am." She gave her husband a bright smile even though she felt so brittle inside, she feared she would shatter.

* * *

Living in the Buxton mansion in Belgravia was not the same as living in the Buxton mansion in Mayfair, Victoria reflected as she hid from her aunt in one of the many tiny, useless rooms that lined the corridors.

For one thing, the house was deceptively big. It didn't seem much larger than the Mayfair home when viewed from the front, but it seemed to go inward forever, and though it had been refurbished since Aunt Charlotte had married into the family, it still seemed somewhat dated; its tiny, overaccessorized rooms seemed like relics of a different era, especially when compared to the spaciousness of Victoria's old home.

Victoria took a sip of the tea she had brought with her and put her tired feet up on an overplush, overtasseled footstool in front of her. The room smelled of fresh beeswax, and she wondered how many servants were kept on to make sure that every room in the house was ready for family at any given moment. She knew that her uncle and her cousin Colin often showed up without notice, and her aunt made the journey four or five times a year.

Victoria desperately needed to escape so she could check in with Martha and tell her how she was faring. Not too shabbily, really, considering how difficult it was to ask for funds without her aunt knowing what she was up to. It was an art, really, to shill her aunt's friends right in front of her. Victoria hoped Martha appreciated how much money she had been able to raise.

She'd even had to apologize to her sister and tell her all about her new cause, though she didn't tell her she was actually employed by the organization. Rowena wouldn't understand why Victoria felt such a strong need to do something useful and to be independent. Rowena had never felt that way. Perhaps she did now about flying, but who could be sure whether flying was Rowena's new passion or just a passing phase as golf and tennis had been?

Her cousin put her head in the door. "Mother is looking for you, but I won't tell her where you are if you don't tell on me."

Elaine quietly shut the door behind her. "I was about to thank you for this little impromptu trip to town until I spent all day at the dressmaker's with you. I already paid my dues last fall, thank you very much." She sat next to Victoria and put her feet up on the same footstool. "Couldn't you find a room with a fire in the fireplace? Or at least bring another cup of tea?"

"I didn't know you were coming, cousin dear. And I would have asked a servant to build a fire, but that would mean someone would know where I was. Now just hold your horses and learn."

Victoria got to her feet, wincing, wondering how many more fittings she was going to have to stand through. Kneeling down in front of the small, ornately carved marble fireplace, she quickly built a fire, much to her cousin's amazement.

"The things you know how to do!" Elaine said, shaking her head.

"My father taught me when I was a girl." She resumed her seat and, because talking about her father brought a lump to her throat, she changed the subject. "So tell me, cousin dear, how do you suggest I go about getting a few hours on my own here in the city?"

Elaine shrugged. "We could go for a walk. The weather is finally getting nicer, so that wouldn't be a stretch."

"I said on my own." She eyed Elaine meaningfully.

"Oh, alone, alone. What do you have, a secret lover no one knows about? Are you meeting Kit? Do tell, I can't seem to find a secret lover to save my life."

Victoria laughed. "You goose. No, there's no lover and, *once again*, Kit and I are just friends." She thought of the kiss they had shared and hid a smile. She hadn't seen Kit since then.

"Okay, then, why don't you tell me about your Suffragettes for Female Equality? I've been thinking I should join one group or another."

Victoria frowned, suspicious. If there was anything she'd learned about her cousin, it was that she wasn't nearly as silly or stupid as she acted. It was a defense against a mother who thought her useless. "You can join another group, then. The National Union of Women's Suffrage Societies is a much better fit for you anyway."

Elaine's blue eyes were bright with curiosity. "And yet, how much money have you collected for your cause?" Elaine waved her hand at Victoria's ferocious face. "Oh, don't bother. Keep your secrets. I just wanted you to know that you don't fool me."

The door opening made both girls jump. A parlormaid poked her head in the door. Relief crossed her face. "Oh, there you are. Her ladyship is looking for both of you."

"How much could we pay you to go away and pretend you never saw us?" Elaine wanted to know as Victoria got wearily to her feet.

The maid just shook her head. "You don't have enough, Lady Elaine."

"I was afraid you'd say that, Nora." Elaine groaned as Victoria pulled her to her feet. "A cozy fire gone completely to waste."

"Look on the bright side," Victoria told her as they followed the maid down the hall. "At least we'll get our tea."

The next morning, Victoria begged off more fittings by saying she'd made plans to visit Prudence. Aunt Charlotte's face carefully blanked at the mention of Prudence's name.

"Just don't forget we still need to shop for accessories," was all she said.

Victoria looked away, trying not to remember the terrible night when she had threatened her aunt and uncle with the knowledge of Prudence's parentage. Victoria had learned that night just how formidable her aunt really was and had promised herself she would never cross her again. She only invoked Prudence's name now to gain herself a day alone. Desperate times called for desperate measures.

Then she caught sight of the longing on Rowena's face. She knew that Ro missed Prudence. *I'll try to fix things between them as soon as I can*, she promised herself. In a way, she wished she really were seeing Prudence today. Not a day went by that she didn't miss her, too.

Elation buoyed her step when she finally made her escape from the house. How wonderful it would be to have her own little flat away from her family. To be able to come and go as she pleased. Martha had that luxury. Someday Victoria hoped she would, too.

Martha waved a hand when Victoria entered the building, as if she had only stepped out for lunch. At first Victoria felt a pang of hurt, and then she realized how sensible it was. Why waste time on ceremonial greetings when one had such important work to do?

Martha and Lottie stood with a group of women who

seemed to be arguing in a good-natured way that Victoria had noticed a few times before in the loft they affectionately called their headquarters.

Martha raised a finger when Victoria joined them. "Hold that thought, there's someone I want you to meet. Mary Richardson and Lilly Johansson, this is the woman I've been telling you about, Victoria Buxton. You'll see her story on the front page of the next edition of our newspaper. She is also the canvasser who has those nice little checks coming in."

All three women clapped and Victoria beamed. "I actually have a few more . . ."

"Wonderful," Lottie said. "This place eats up money like the giant ate Englishmen."

"Ha!" Martha said.

The other woman, Mary, watched them, her wide mouth unsmiling and her back ramrod stiff. Impatience poured off her in jittery waves. She obviously wanted to get back to their previous conversation. "Was I interrupting something?" Victoria asked.

"No," said Martha and Lottie simultaneously.

"Yes," said Mary. The woman raised an eyebrow and tapped her shoe. "My apologies if I seem rude, Miss Buxton. But as important as fund-raising is, it is worth nothing if you don't have action as well, don't you agree?"

"Of course," Victoria agreed, looking from Lottie to Martha for a clue as to what to do. They stayed silent and Victoria wondered whether this was some sort of test. Lilly, the quiet woman with soft gray hair, just sort of drifted away as if it was a discussion she didn't wish to become embroiled in.

"And do you think the action should be agreed upon by all the members of a particular group? Or perhaps just a select few?" Mary persisted.

Victoria swallowed. "Depends on whether the group is a democracy or a dictatorship. If it's a democracy, you need the consensus of the voting members. If a dictatorship, then you only need to get the permission of the dictator. Unless, of course, you are the dictator."

Mary Richardson's eyes widened. "Very well put, Miss Buxton." She turned to Martha and Lottie. "Not bad at all for your token aristocrat. What else can Miss Buxton do? Sit up and bark when asked?"

Lottie's mouth fell open and Martha hissed in outrage, but before either one of them could speak, Victoria laughed. "Actually, I can do a great many things. I'm a fairly decent writer, my memory is a steel trap for poetry and literature, I'm very talented at ferreting out secrets, and I can make an excellent pot of tea. Would you like a cup?"

For a moment no one spoke and then both Martha and Lottie erupted in laughter. Even Mary's mouth quirked upward. "Touché, Miss Buxton, touché. And I would very much like a pot of tea."

Victoria felt a moment of triumph as she made a pot of tea on the coal stove, but it didn't last long, as the three women retired to the corner of the room to wait for their tea. They resumed their previous conversation but didn't ask Victoria to be a part of it, and none of them said thank you when she brought them tea.

Annoyed, Victoria took a seat at an empty desk and pulled out the papers she had brought with her, including three checks from her aunt's friends. She had carefully typed several copies of her list containing every group in support of women she could find, and she placed one on each of the desks in the room.

She glanced back at the trio. From the gesticulations, it

looked as if it was heating up again. Finally, Mary stood up and shook hands with Martha and Lottie. She stopped at Victoria's desk as she left.

"Excuse my brusqueness, Miss Buxton. Sometimes my mind is so full of plans I forget what it's like to be polite. We are at war, whether or not people realize it. I just want all the leaders to accept that, and show it by their behavior." With a final glance at Lottie and Martha, who were still in earnest conversation in the corner, Mary gave a nod and left.

Was the suffragette cause really a war? Martha had given her the task of answering correspondence from women in any sort of crisis from all over London. Victoria was charged with the task of answering the letters, telling these women where, if anywhere, they could get help. She became more and more sober as she worked. Women were in trouble everywhere. One woman desperately needed a doctor, another needed food for her children. Women asked for jobs, food, rent money, someone to care for their baby or their mother—the list was endless.

A cheering startled her and she looked up to find that Martha had brought a basket of meat pies into the room. Victoria glanced at the clock. She had been working for three hours.

She asked Martha and the others about their thoughts as they ate.

"Of course it's a war," said one woman from East London. "In order to change society, we have to be able to vote for people who care about the things women care about."

"I dare you to find a man who does," Lottie put in.

"My father did," Victoria said. "Many of his friends do."

Lottie tossed her head. "No offense, Miss Buxton, but where are those friends now? The number of men who will actually go against their fellow men in our favor is almost nil. I'm sure they exist, but they are damned sure quiet about it."

"What we need is more women willing and able to do the hard work necessary to get their attention, if you know what I mean." The woman from East London gave a grim smile.

Victoria wondered what the woman meant as she made her way to her aunt's house. Emily Davison had given her life for the cause. Could Victoria ever go that far, be that committed, that selfless, for the cause? Or was she merely going through the motions, secure in the fact that she was a wealthy aristocrat with free time and connections to lend to the movement?

CHAPTER
THIRTEEN

How did this get so completely out of control? Rowena thought as Aunt Charlotte and Lady Edith launched into another round of bickering over wedding details. Rowena had never been more grateful for her relative independence than when Sebastian's mother joined them for their trip to London, purportedly to buy a few last-minute garments and accessories for the season. But Rowena suspected that she mostly wanted to ensure that no wedding decisions be made without her input.

Though Rowena and Sebastian had refused to give their families a firm wedding date—which they had assumed would keep the preparations to a minimum, allowing time to plot their eventual breakup—it seemed that nothing could stop this train now that it was in motion. Both she and Sebastian were trying to figure out a way to break off the engagement without creating a scandal, but so far both had come up empty-handed.

Now, as a tug-of-war over the event's location began anew, Rowena managed to slip away with the promise that she'd meet up with her aunt in time for supper.

The fact that she could escape at will was a wonderful luxury, especially considering the note she had received just that morning.

R,

   In town with D. Meet me at the needle at 2?

J

March had turned balmy and the sky gleamed blue above the Grosvenor Gardens as she walked to the Victoria Embankment.

Rowena wondered how Jon had talked Douglas into a London trip. She and Jon kept in touch through letters sent to his mother. If she thought it strange they didn't write to each other directly, she said nothing about it, and Cristobel was always delighted to see her when she dropped by to collect the newest message from her beloved. George, on the other hand, would skulk around, glowering until his mother ordered him off, apologizing for her eldest son's behavior. Sometimes Rowena wondered whether George was completely in his right mind.

She walked diagonally across the Cathedral Piazza, banishing George from her thoughts. She loved being back in London. Summerset was in her blood and she loved it there, but London was home. She had spent most of her life in the city with her father, Victoria, and, of course, Prudence. Her heart gave a funny little pang as it always did when she thought of her father or Prudence—two family members she had irrevocably lost. She wondered what Prudence was doing and whether she was happy. Victoria said she seemed happy when Victoria had seen her last, but Rowena wished she could see for herself. Could explain that everything had just gotten so out of control . . .

Rowena took a deep breath. She would not be unhappy today. She would not let the grayness of those lost months overcome her again. Not ever again.

Instead she forced herself to think of Jon. It had been almost three weeks since she had last been in his arms and almost four since the last exhilarating flying lesson—he had finally given her some control, allowing her to drive the plane all over the field. Her pulse kicked up a notch as she remembered the excitement of sitting in the pilot's seat. He had called her a natural.

Next time he was going to sit as her passenger. Then she would be able to fly on her own. Completely solo.

She smelled the river before she saw it, an odd combination of tar and rot. When she spotted the needle, she stopped the next man she saw with a watch chain draped across his waist-coat. "Excuse me, could you tell me the time, please?"

He took the watch out of his pocket and peered at it with the squint of the nearsighted. "Half past one, miss."

"Thank you."

She found a bench near the needle and sat, letting the sun warm her back. Pigeons cooed around her feet until they realized she had nothing to feed them and went off in search of greener fields. People crowded the square, taking advantage of the sun after a long winter—pale, squinting babies in severe black prams, equally pale children, unruly with unexpected freedom, and distinguished gentlemen taking an extralong lunch to enjoy the weather.

Her whole body crackled with excitement at the thought of seeing Jon. The last time she'd seen him, he'd kissed her behind the Martinsyde S.1 until she grew dizzy. Her eyes shut, remembering.

She swatted at a tickling feeling on the back of her neck, which quickly turned into the feeling of lips being pressed against the very top of her spine. She stopped swatting and shivered. "I certainly hope that's my Jon scandalizing the nannies," she said, leaning her head back.

"Who do you think?" he whispered in her ear, and she shivered again.

"Oh, Jon!" She stood as he leapt around the bench and took her into his arms.

He pressed his lips against hers until she broke away, gasping. "Stop! We're going to be arrested for such a public display."

"Not by any red-blooded bobby, I'll tell you that. They would all be too jealous of me to care."

His blue eyes twinkled and blazed at her all at the same time and she laughed out of sheer happiness. He sat with her then, one arm holding her close. Her pulse raced as the heat of his leg pressed against hers.

"I can't believe you're really here," she said, leaning close and rubbing her index finger against his jaw. "However did you talk Douglas into it?"

Jon caught her finger with his free hand. "I can't think when you do that." He grinned down at her. "Actually, I didn't have to. Douglas was called into meetings with some high-up muckety-mucks in the government who want to give us a contract for the Flying Alices."

"Oh, I knew she was a good one!" Rowena exclaimed.

He squeezed her fingers. "I did, too."

They sat in silence, their fingers intertwining over and over. She yearned toward him, wanting more than she even knew how to ask for. Her throat thickened with emotion and she could scarcely breathe for the wanting.

His fingers tightened around hers. "Douglas is in meetings for the rest of the day. We're staying at the Parkrose, a few blocks that way."

His blue eyes flickered over her and then away and she

caught his meaning immediately. Her chest grew tight. She could be alone with him . . . if she dared. "Is it a comfortable hotel?"

He grew still. "Comfortable enough, I believe."

Rowena's heart pounded and she drew even closer, and her cheeks heated with how brazenly she was behaving. "Hmm. Well, perhaps I should take a look myself. Just to make sure you're being well taken care of there."

He turned to her then, his eyes drinking her in. "Are you sure?" he asked, his voice husky. She wanted to run her hands through his long hair and pull him close. Her breath caught.

"I've never been so sure of anything in my entire life. Well," she amended, her lips curving. "Well, other than the moment when I told you I wanted to become a pilot."

He pulled her to her feet and pressed his lips against her cheek. Rowena knew it was a promise of things to come. He walked slowly, perhaps giving her the space to change her mind. But it wasn't necessary. The heat of his hand on her lower back took her breath away. She would never feel this way about anyone again. If she didn't spend this time with him now, she knew in her heart she would always regret it, no matter what might happen after.

Rowena would never remember whether they spoke or not. She couldn't even remember how they got into his room. Had they gone up in a lift? Had the concierge watched them go? These details were gone forever.

What she remembered was the clean scent of his skin. The softness of his hair beneath her fingers. She didn't remember the pain, but she would never forget the smoothness of the sheets as they wrapped around their legs or the roughness of his cheeks against her neck. Impressions that would last a lifetime, so vivid, all she had to do was close her eyes and the sensory memories would come flooding back, filling her with equal parts joy and pain.

"I love you," he told her after.

"I know," she told him. He hit her with a pillow and she collapsed, laughing, against his chest. *Who knew*, she thought as she pressed her lips in the location of his heart, *who knew that a man's chest would have hair and would be so delightful to lie against.* "No wonder people keep young women in the dark," she murmured. "We would all be doing this all the time if we knew."

"It's for your own good," he told her, his mouth against her hair. "You are supposed to wait for the right man."

She raised her head. "What about men?"

He snorted. "Imagine if neither party knew what they were doing."

She laid her head back down. "I don't know. I think we could have figured it out." She frowned, jealousy gnawing at her stomach. "Did the first woman you were with know what she was doing?"

"Yes. She was an older woman, a maid, actually."

Rowena shuddered, thinking about her lecherous grandfather, who never got over his desire for maids, and of Prudence's mother, who had to bear the burden of that lust.

"But"—he pulled her around to face him—"there has never been anyone in my heart but you."

She searched his eyes for a moment, trying to sort out her thoughts. "And my world was meaningless until I met you. I know that sounds dramatic and I don't mean to be, but it's

true. I didn't know what my purpose in life was until I went flying with you. I had given up on finding a passion . . . on finding
passion, even. I only ever felt half-alive."

His arm tightened around her and she laid her head back
down on his chest. His heartbeat sounded in her ear and she
could feel hers aligning with his.

"What are we going to do?" he asked quietly.

For the first time, real fear entered her heart. How could she
ever let him go? She couldn't. "We will just have to figure out
a way to tell them all," she said simply. "Your family loves me
now. Well, those who really know me, in spite of my surname,
so perhaps my family will accept you."

He stiffened. "That's just it," he said slowly. "I don't want
your family to accept me, because I will never be able to forgive
your uncle for what he did."

She sat up and held the sheet in front of her chest. "So my
family doesn't matter then?"

He sat up, too, and already she regretted the distance between them, which seemed so much more than just a few
inches. "If your father were alive, it would be different," he told
her. "I'm sure he probably knew nothing about what your uncle
was doing to my family."

"Of course he didn't!" she cried. "He wouldn't have done
anything like that."

"And of course, I won't mind meeting your sister, but I have
to draw the line there. In honor of my father, I draw the line
there."

She searched the hard planes of his face. She recognized the
truth when she heard it and gave him a nod. "I understand," she
said.

But as she got dressed, she had to wonder about her sacrifice. She would be giving up her aunt and uncle, her cousins, and Summerset. And what if her uncle disagreed with her choice? Would she be giving up her inheritance, as well? She would have to speak with her solicitor.

His arms suddenly slipped around her. "I'll make it up to you," he whispered, and she smiled, everything except the feeling of his lips against her neck forgotten.

"You already have," she whispered.

* * *

Kit was worried. Kit never worried. And, like everything else upside down, backward, and crazy in his life, it had everything to do with Victoria, that lovely, painful thorn in his side.

At least breakfast at his mother's house in London was hot, plentiful, and never too early. His mother had given up their country home when his father had died to live year-round in London. Personally, Kit wondered how his father had been able to talk his mother into going to the country as often as she did. In her younger days, his mother had been considered scandalous. As she grew older, she had turned into an eccentric. Though his parents had bought themselves into the right social circles, that didn't necessarily mean that either of them actually enjoyed it. As he grew, Kit often wondered why they bothered. He had been brought up to be a gentleman, as idle and useless as any of the real gentlemen who ran in his get. It only recently began to dawn on him that the only women who had ever remotely interested him sneered at such idleness and preferred men who were, as Victoria so maddeningly called it, industrious.

He speared a sausage savagely.

"Someone is in a bad mood," his mother said from behind him. She kissed the top of his head. "How's your arm this morning, darling?"

His eyes narrowed. "You're being nice. Why are you being nice?"

"I'm always nice," she said, her voice mild.

She moved to the ornate mahogany buffet and helped herself to a plate of eggs and ham, and a bowl of strawberries swimming in cream and sugar. Taking a seat across from him, she poured herself a cup of strong coffee, which she far preferred to tea.

His mother was wearing one of her Oriental morning dresses, as she called them, a gauzy, incredibly expensive dress made like a caftan, with a tie under her ample bosom. It showed off her assets, without showing off her equally ample waist.

"You're never nice, unless you want something," Kit said.

"See. I knew you were in a bad mood. A mother knows these things."

He stared as she took a bite of her eggs and she returned his look, her large, dark eyes giving away nothing. For a moment their eyes clashed and then she smiled. "Oh, fine. I'm simply waiting for you to tell me about Victoria."

"Aha!"

She shrugged. "Other mothers wouldn't have to stoop to such tactics to find out things."

He snorted. "I have the only mother in the kingdom to whom being nice to her child is considered a tactic."

"But other mothers are so boringly predictable. At least your mother isn't boring."

"True," he conceded.

"Now about the girl?" she wheedled.

"I don't know what you're talking about," he said, concentrating on his sausage. His mother always could read him like a book. But then again, men were her specialty. Secrecy was his only weapon against her.

"That's not what Colin said when he dropped by to see you yesterday. You were out somewhere, but he looked in need of nourishment."

Kit closed his eyes briefly. He could see it now. Colin would be putty in his mother's hands. Most men were. Even though the years had added bulk to his mother's already curvaceous figure, she still had an exotic air that most men found irresistible. Whether it was the straight, black hair cut in a slashing fringe on her forehead or the almond-shaped eyes that were more an accident of birth than a story about her background, men seemed to believe his mother far more exciting than she actually was. Colin would be no match for her years of experience.

"His young cousin, I believe? It's odd. I never saw you with a woman that young."

He snorted again.

"What?" she asked, her eyes wide.

He sighed. He might as well give in. God knew what she already got from Colin. "Victoria isn't young. I mean, she doesn't act young. Most of the time. She's . . ." He paused, searching for the right word. "Complicated."

His mother raised an eyebrow. "Complicated? How interesting."

"See, you don't mean that. You say you want to know about her, but then you act like that."

She sighed. "I'm sorry, darling, you're right. I just find other women's complications boring. Could you get me one of those pastries next to the sausage? And was your sausage good? Go ahead and bring me one of those, too. Thank you, darling. Now go ahead. I'll be good. I promise."

Kit brought her the food and took a couple more sausages for himself. Oddly, he found himself *wanting* to talk to his mother about Victoria, which just showed how truly upside down things were. He never wanted to talk to his mother about anything.

"What is she like? Colin said he guessed she was pretty."

He thought about it for a moment. "She isn't really pretty. *Pretty* is too conventional to describe Victoria. She's small and rather delicate and her face is rather the shape of a heart and her eyes are blue."

"Don't tell me you fell for a blue-eyed blonde? How common." His mother's lips curled and he glared. "Sorry, sorry."

"She's not like anyone else. She's tremendously smart and keeps me on my toes. And she's bold enough to say what everyone else merely thinks about saying. And we're just friends."

"Men and women can't be *just friends*," his mother said with a dismissive wave.

"That's what I told her, but I really think we are."

She shook her head. "No, because one of them always falls in love. If they are lucky, both of them do, but it's usually just one of them." She looked at him and Kit thought he saw sympathy in her dark eyes.

"And you think it's just me?" His voice came out more belligerent than he'd intended.

They ate in silence for several moments before he mused, "She has always said she never wanted to marry."

"Well, I suppose you will just have to change her mind and then marry her," his mother told him matter-of-factly.

He looked at her in astonishment. "Married? Who said anything about getting married?"

"Oh, my dear, stupid, boy," his mother said, shaking her head. "You've been talking of nothing else."

He stood. "Why do I even try to have a conversation with you? You're quite crazy, do you know that?"

His mother nodded and popped the last of her pastry into her mouth. "But I have never been as crazy in love as you are right now."

Kit left the room, the sound of his mother's laughter following him.

CHAPTER
FOURTEEN

Prudence looked at the silver fish with distaste. It stared back at her with one smoky eye. "I don't even like bloaters," she whined to Muriel and Susie, who were both busy getting other ingredients together. "Why do I have to know how to prepare them? Why can't we have lessons on how to prepare haddock or sturgeon?"

"Because bloaters are cheap," Muriel told her bluntly. "Sometimes the only meat a family can afford is bloaters, so you want to be able to prepare them in different ways."

Susie, pounding a horseradish root, ceased long enough to nod. "Plus, they can be good. I like them in a paste and spread on toast or Suffolk rusks."

Muriel smacked her lips. "I like them poached in milk. By lunch, you'll be a bloater expert."

Prudence wrinkled her nose. "I can hardly wait."

"Good. Then fill that pan about halfway up with water and put it on the stove. Bloaters have been lightly smoked and are kind of hard. You have to soften them first."

Susie had been there for several days and Prudence kept waiting for a confrontation regarding her tales of city glamour, but to her surprise, Susie said nothing. Suddenly it dawned on Prudence that Susie thought her flat lovely and her furniture from the Mayfair house quite fashionable. Still, Prudence had trouble brushing aside the shame she felt at lying—falsely boasting, even—to such a kind friend. Susie did, however, take Prudence to task over her lack of servants.

"Why don't your servants do the laundry?" she'd asked after her first trip down to the cellar.

"I don't have any servants," Prudence had confessed. "I made that up."

Susie's brown eyes widened. "Why on earth did you tell me you did if you didn't?"

Prudence shrugged helplessly because she wasn't sure about that herself. "I don't know. Maybe because I knew you would tell Vic and Ro what I wrote to you . . . and I wanted them to think I traded Summerset for some grand life in London . . . not for this." She swept a hand around her flat.

Susie's mouth turned down and she gave a disapproving sniff. "I'd say you were a bit spoiled if you don't think this is a fine life. You have beautiful clothes to wear, a lovely flat, and a good, smart man who loves you. You don't have to conjure up servants."

Prudence shook her head and smiled over at Susie, still pounding horseradish with ferocity. In many ways, Susie, who had spent only a few years in school before going out to work, was more knowledgeable than Prudence despite her years of education.

"Now you drop the fish in the hot water, take them off the heat, cover them, and let them soak for ten minutes," Muriel instructed.

Prudence did what she was told. "Now what?" she asked.

"Now the fish plump back up. Remember that bloaters still have their innards, which make them extra tasty."

Prudence pressed her lips together to keep from whimpering. *Tasty?*

A few hours later, after the bloaters had been prepared in several different ways, Prudence had to admit they weren't as bad as she thought they would be. She had a large jar of paste flavored with horseradish and cayenne pepper to take home for dinner and she was even feeling confident she could duplicate the Suffolk rusks, a sort of twice-baked scone Muriel had taught her to make. Andrew would be delighted.

Her favorite part of the lessons came after they had cleaned the mess in the kitchen and sat down for a cuppa before Prudence went home. It helped break up her lonely afternoons. Today she had the added bonus of Susie, who got along with Muriel, no doubt because they were cut from the same tough cloth. Prudence smiled as Muriel tried to persuade Susie to move to the city.

"But there are so many opportunities for girls such as yourself," Muriel said. "You don't have to waste your talents in the country anymore. The world is changing. You could work in a factory or take classes and get a job in an office, like my Katie did. Young women have many more choices these days. And when we get the vote . . ."

Susie scoffed. "As if that will ever happen!"

"Oh, it will, mark my words! One of the women renting a room from us is working for just such a thing."

"So is Victoria," Prudence said.

Muriel nodded. "I know. She works with Lottie."

So that was how Victoria found her job. "What's Lottie like?" Prudence asked, curious. She wanted to know about the life Victoria had made that no longer included her.

Muriel made a face. "I guess she's nice enough. I don't want to be uncharitable, but she's a bit too serious for my taste. Very committed to the cause, though. Of course, women with no prospects of a husband often are."

Susie laughed.

"Victoria seems very committed," Prudence said.

"That's different. Victoria is a saint. Lottie is just lonely."

Prudence thought about that later on her afternoon walk. Susie had begged off, wanting to write some letters, so Prudence had gone on her own. This time she had taken the Tube to her old neighborhood, a place she hadn't been to since she had picked up her furniture.

Prudence strolled along, swinging her reticule and umbrella, though she hadn't needed the umbrella in a week, as unseasonably warm weather had brought March in like the proverbial lamb. Walking the streets of her former neighborhood left her with a lonely, bittersweet feeling. No matter how things had turned out, she had been happy here. Everywhere she looked, memories played out behind her eyes. She spotted the small park where she, Rowena, and Victoria had taken their riding lessons. Three bright, mischievous girls dressed in severe riding habits, following the riding master on three fat, roly-poly ponies. Oftentimes it was just she and Rowena, if Victoria wasn't feeling well, and Prudence almost laughed out loud, remembering the time she and Rowena had taken off cantering when their master had dismounted to remove a rock from his horse's hoof. They hadn't gotten far, of course, they had nowhere to go, but the freedom had felt wonderful.

But as always, the depth of her antipathy toward Rowena colored her memory and she turned away from the park and hurried on. She stood for a moment in front of the Mayfair house, emotion constricting her throat. She wondered what her life would be like if Sir Philip hadn't died. She never would have met her husband.

Noting the menacing clouds gathering in the sky, she hurried down the street, hoping to make it to the Tube before the rain let loose. Prudence knew that Susie would have hot tea waiting for her when she got home and supper would be on the stove. Bringing Susie for a visit had been a stroke of genius on Victoria's part. Prudence loved Susie's company and would still be drowning in housework without her cheerful help, though with each passing day it felt as if her camaraderie with Susie was alienating Andrew more and more. She resolved to make it up to him. He'd been so very good to her.

The trees, which had just recently sprouted tender young leaves, whipped around in a frenzy, and a newspaper, having been freed from its confines, scattered and blew in the wind like dozens of kites. One hit Prudence in the face and wrapped itself around her head like an octopus. She grabbed at it, laughing, and tried to pull it off as another one curled around her ankles.

"I do believe you've been attacked by the news," a voice said.

Prudence froze, knowing the voice instantly. He plucked the newspaper from her eyes and halted the moment he recognized her. They stared, transfixed. Immobilized. It was like the first time they had spotted each other at Sir Philip's funeral and when they met again at Summerset. A complete annihilation of everything around them, as if nothing had existed before the moment they met and nothing would exist again after. She hadn't felt anything like it since the night she had fled from Summerset, alone and beaten by the knowledge of who she really was. Sebastian didn't know—and if she had her way, he would never know—just how stupid it had been to think even for a moment that they might have had a future together. They didn't then, and they most certainly didn't now. She was married. He was engaged to Rowena.

So why couldn't she will herself to break his gaze, to look away? Why did she want more than anything for him to take her into his arms?

"Thank you," she finally managed, casting her gaze downward.

He still held the offending newspaper in his hand. "Why did you leave so quickly? I thought we had an . . . understanding?" He blurted out the words as if they had been on his mind for months.

They probably had.

For a panicked moment, she wanted to deny she knew what he was talking about, but she felt enough shame at the way she had left without a word to him that she knew she owed him an explanation, or at least a response. If she could.

Droplets of rain started coming down and still they stood. Finally she said, "You know of the argument, correct? Of what Rowena did?"

"She didn't mean to—" he started, and she held up her hand.

"Don't defend her to me. I'm trying to answer you . . ."

He subsided.

"After the argument, I was taken upstairs to talk to Lady Summerset." She bit her lip as he waited. The rain came down harder, but neither of them wanted to move, afraid to break the fragile spell that bound them together. She fought with herself. His eyes were as dark as coal, and filled with more pain than she ever could have imagined. The sure knowledge that she was the cause of his pain lacerated her. She'd never meant to hurt him.

"I learned some things that made a—*friendship*—between us impossible."

He let go of the paper then, but the rain had taken away its ability to fly and it sank to the ground. He moved closer and she put her hands between them. He reached up and took hold of her elbows. She could feel the warmth of his fingers through the light wool of her coat.

"What things? What things did you find out, Prudence? Didn't you know I would have helped you? Stood by you?"

She shook her head, tears forming behind her eyes and spilling over. They were undetectable since the rain was already covering her face.

"If you want to know how impossible it was, ask your fiancée!" She spit the words out from the depth of her pain and his head snapped back as if he'd been slapped.

"Maybe I'll do that, *Mrs. Wilkes.*"

They stared at each other, and Prudence felt the chasm widening between them, and though she knew it was for the best, it still cut deeply, painfully, into the part of her that had been holding on to hope that maybe there would come a time when they could still be together.

And then he kissed her. His lips smashed against hers, hurting her at first, and she knew he meant to hurt, needed to hurt. Then he made a noise deep in his throat and everything changed, his lips changed, became gentle, kissing away the pain, and though she didn't want them to, her whole body and heart responded to him. She kissed him back in a way that she had never kissed anyone back.

Not even Andrew.

Gasping, she pulled away. They stared at each other, and his eyes were filled with things unsaid, things that could never be said, and Prudence turned and ran. She heard him call her name, but she couldn't turn back.

* * *

Victoria ran diagonally across Trafalgar Square to the National Gallery. It had taken her a little longer to reach the Gallery than she had anticipated and she saw Mary Richardson pacing at the top of the steps. The skies over the square were gray and ominous, as if they threatened a downpour at any moment.

She'd learned from Martha that Mary Richardson had been jailed several times in her zeal for women's suffrage and Victoria swelled with pride at the idea that this dedicated person wanted to meet with her.

"I'm sorry I'm late," Victoria said. "I didn't get your message and—"

"It's fine, it's fine, you're here now. I knew I could count on you. We only met that one time and all I could think of was that you were a young woman a person could count on."

Mary's pale skin was even paler than Victoria had remembered and her dark eyes seemed to look right through her. She seemed agitated, though Victoria couldn't think why. She wore a long, dark coat and held one of her arms so stiffly to her side that Victoria wondered whether she'd hurt it somehow. "What did you need to tell me?" Victoria asked.

"Not yet, let's go inside. You'll understand better then."

Because it was a free day, the Gallery was filled with people, and for a few minutes Mary and Victoria followed the crowd. Then they left the crowd and walked into a room filled with Dutch paintings.

Victoria tilted her head and regarded a small one by Godfried Schalcken titled *A Man Offering Gold and Coins to a Girl*. "I've never been much of a fan of the Dutch school of painting. The colors are so very depressing."

"Do you know what's depressing?" Mary said, continuing her walk around the room. She didn't seem to be looking at any of the paintings in front of her and Victoria wondered why she had chosen to meet at a museum if she didn't want to look at pictures.

"It's depressing that money is more valued than human rights. The government is filled with such hypocrisy. If men could figure out a way to profit from suffrage, women would have had the vote long ago."

Victoria nodded. "I agree. I—"

"You have heard of Emmeline Pankhurst, haven't you?" Mary went on as if Victoria hadn't spoken. "And her daughters? She is the head of the WSPU and such a sincere person. Absolutely tireless in her work for women."

Victoria nodded as Mary continued her aimless, unseeing walk through the Dutch Masters.

"She was taken last night from a train platform after a meeting in Glasgow. They treated a woman of such character as they would a common criminal."

Mary bristled like a dog, and it was on the tip of Victoria's tongue to ask whether she was all right, but clearly the woman was *not* all right. She wished Martha were there, or even Prudence, who had the ability to calm crying children, lovelorn girls, and even mad dogs. Surely she would know what to do with Mary Richardson, who seemed to grow more and more agitated as the minutes passed.

"They've taken Mrs. Pankhurst from us; now it's time to take something of value from them."

"What?"

Mary shook her head. "Never mind, never mind. Here, come

with me." Mary took her arm and they left the Dutch room and went through several other displays until they came to the Spanish room.

"Stand here. Pretend to be studying the Madonna. On my signal, create a diversion."

"What?" Victoria asked, confused, but Mary had already walked away from her side. Ice formed in the center of Victoria's stomach and she stood exactly as she had been instructed. What was Mary going to do? Part of Victoria wanted to run, but her limbs seemed frozen. She studied the Madonna as though her life depended on it. Out of the corner of her eye, she saw Mary take a sketch pad out of her reticule and begin sketching as she sauntered around the room. Not far from where Victoria stood, two guards sat, watching everyone who came into the room. At the door was another museum attendant, helping people find their way. Mary appeared to notice none of these things as she walked.

Victoria felt very conspicuous just standing in front of the painting, but fear kept her rooted. She frowned and squinted her eyes at the Madonna, as if studying the brushstrokes. Surely someone would notice that she wasn't moving? But no, this was what people did at museums.

Sweat beaded on Victoria's forehead and her muscles cramped from tension. It occurred to her that she could just walk away. No one would connect her with whatever Mary was about to do, with whatever act of protest she had planned. Mary's words ran through her mind, that Victoria seemed the kind of woman she could count on. Victoria's legs began to tremble and she felt her chest grow tight. *Oh, no. Please, no.*

Just then Mary gave her a nod and walked resolutely toward

a canvas. Victoria watched and it seemed as if Mary were walking in slow motion. At the same time, she pulled an ax out of the sleeve she had held so protectively against her side.

It was when she saw the ax that Victoria screamed. The detectives and the attendant turned toward her and the moment they did, the sound of shattering glass filled the air. The detectives looked up to the skylight in the center of the room, puzzled.

Still Victoria screamed. Behind the detective she saw Mary striking blows with the ax against a painting of the Venus.

The detectives and two attendants turned then and went after Mary. One of them slipped, while the other successfully grabbed her ax. It was then that Victoria turned to run. The attendant who had slipped tried to redeem himself by grabbing onto Victoria, but she eluded his grasp and made her way to the stairs. She could hear Mary screaming in the background. She nearly threw herself down the stairs and finally the front doors of the museum came into view. Her only hope was to get outside. Maybe she could blend in with the crowd.

But she couldn't breathe. She slowed, her legs shaking as she felt her lungs closing off.

She heard people yelling behind her and felt herself being grabbed from behind.

"That's her! They came in together!"

Victoria opened her mouth to tell them she hadn't meant for it to happen, that she had only screamed because she saw that Mary had an ax, but she couldn't speak. Black spots floated in front of her eyes and everything went black.

* * *

It was dim when Victoria opened her eyes. She lay on a bed of white sheets and blankets. The room was so small she could probably lie down and touch three of the walls at once. The scent of bleach and camphor couldn't overcome the smell of human urine.

She was definitely not at home. The door opened and she shut her eyes like a child afraid to look under the bed.

"She still hasn't come to yet," said a woman.

"She's very lucky. She might have died. I've never seen someone struggle so hard to breathe," a man's voice said. "There's nothing more we can do except alert the wardress when she has recovered."

Wardress?

"Yes, Doctor."

The door shut again and Victoria heard the unmistakable sound of a lock being shut. Her eyes flew open. She struggled to sit up before realizing that her arm was handcuffed to the top of the iron bed frame. She stared at the cuff for a moment before a scream rent her body.

The door opened. "What's wrong? What's wrong?" a woman with a starched cambric nurse's cap cried, hovering over Victoria. Victoria could see a man in a dirty white coat behind her.

"Shut her up. She may trigger another breathing attack," the doctor said.

The nurse slapped Victoria. Victoria stopped screaming and looked at the woman in horror. "You hit me."

"I did and if you scream again, I might do it again."

Defiance and fear took over and Victoria began screaming again. It was the doctor who moved in and hit her twice more as Victoria kicked her legs and screamed at the top of her lungs. The doctor made like he was going to hit her again, but the nurse who had disappeared after slapping Victoria the first time came back, holding a bottle and a rag.

"Hold her down!" she commanded.

Another young man crowded into the room and between him and the doctor they managed to hold Victoria still. The nurse put the rag over her nose and mouth and for the second time in a day everything went black.

CHAPTER
FIFTEEN

"Let me know as soon as she comes in," Rowena instructed the butler before going into dinner.

Rowena entered the dining room with a smile on her face, although the last thing she wanted to do right now was smile. She wanted to wring Victoria's neck. How dare she make her worry right now? It wasn't as though Rowena didn't have enough on her mind, especially now that pressure was mounting from both her family and Sebastian's to name a wedding date.

To make matters ever so much more complicated, Sebastian had informed her he bloody well wasn't ready to call off their engagement yet and further, as she had been the one to get them into this mess—and because he had so nicely gone along with it and saved her hide—she could put up with it a while longer. She conceded that this was only fair, but she wished she knew his plans. Why on earth would he not want to cancel the engagement? He had to be under as much pressure as she was to name the date.

And now Victoria was grievously late. She had gotten a note earlier and had left in a hurry, only saying she would be back before tea. Now it was suppertime and her aunt and their guests were wondering where Victoria was.

Sebastian stood as she entered the room. The dining room

here was far smaller than the formal one at Summerset, but just as elaborate, with a Chippendale dining room table and chairs for twenty as the centerpiece.

With an entire room watching them, Sebastian pulled out her chair for her. "Did you have a good day, my darling?" he asked as she took her seat. He briefly laid his hands on her shoulders before scooting in her chair.

Inside, Rowena winced at the endearment and the caress, but she managed a sweet smile. "Yes, thank you . . . darling."

"How sweet they are!" Kit's mother exclaimed from her seat toward the end of the table. "It almost restores my belief in true love." She beamed at them, but Rowena caught a wicked glint in her eye.

Was Mrs. Kittredge being sincere or facetious? With Kit's mother it was difficult to tell. Rowena shot Kit a questioning look. She knew that Sebastian had clued him in as to the reality of their engagement. Had he told his mother?

He shrugged his shoulders and shook his head.

"Any word from Victoria?" her aunt asked with a meaningful glance at the empty place at the table.

Rowena gave another smile, hoping her worry and irritation didn't show on her face. "I'm afraid her errand must have kept her late."

In fact, she remained so thoroughly committed to maintaining a smile throughout the dinner that her cheeks ached by the time they got to the third course. Under the eagle eye of both his mother and Aunt Charlotte, Sebastian played his role of attentive fiancé to the hilt and had Rowena blushing with his fulsome compliments.

"Isn't she lovely this evening? Of course, she's lovely every evening, but she's looking particularly beautiful tonight." Sebastian's voice sounded brittle and he kept his wineglass full.

Rowena vacillated between wanting to hit him and feeling concern over his behavior. Lately, he seemed to have an edge about him that wasn't there before and she wondered what had happened.

Aunt Charlotte had sat Kit's mother next to Victoria so she could get to know her. Now she had only a deaf general for company and her irritation could be felt all the way across the table. Kit looked as if he'd been struck by lightning. He kept gazing across the table as if he could conjure Victoria up with his eyes.

They had barely begun the fifth course, a flaky beef and burgundy pie, when Aunt Charlotte told everyone she had an announcement to make. Rowena looked up in surprise. Sebastian's mother gave her a tender look and, her heart pounding, she glanced at Sebastian, who kept his eyes on her aunt.

"As many of you know, Lady Billingsly and I are very good friends and we have made it no secret that we wish our families to be joined. Of course, we had always assumed that it would be Sebastian and Elaine who would make the match."

Alarmed, Rowena glanced at Elaine, who smiled weakly.

"But to my surprise, it was my darling niece who would be Sebastian's bride. It's also no secret that Edith and I did not want a long engagement, and to my joy, we were told by Sebastian that we would not have to wait. The happy couple finally set the date for August first."

Rowena made a noise of surprise and Sebastian put his hand over hers.

There was a murmur among the guests and her uncle stood.

"If my brother were here, he would do the honors, but in his stead, I am very proud to make the toast myself. To Rowena and Sebastian, may you continue to make each other happy."

Everyone drank from their glasses while Rowena sat in stunned silence. The dinner resumed and Rowena leaned over to Sebastian. "What on earth did you do that for?"

He whispered back, "Because it's far enough away that plans won't get too far out of hand and it gets them off my back. You should be happy, too. You can spend more time with Jon. Smile, people are watching."

But Rowena was tired of the entire game. She wanted to find a way to be with Jon, to marry Jon, not playact that she was engaged to Sebastian. And where was Victoria?

Her aunt asked her the same thing after the men had gone off for their cigars and claret.

"I think she is staying the night with Prudence," she answered, even though she had no idea whether that was true or not. It was instinctual to hide the truth from her aunt and she prayed that Victoria would be back soon.

At the mention of Prudence's name, her aunt called to Kit's mother across the room and left Rowena standing alone. Rowena sought out Elaine. "I have no idea where Victoria is," she said in a low voice. "Did she tell you where she was going?"

Elaine shook her head. "She doesn't tell me anything. Do you think she could be working?"

Rowena shrugged. She didn't even know where Prudence lived so she could go check on her, though the thought of seeing Prudence made her stomach knot. "I told your mother that she probably stayed the night with Prudence, but I don't know anything for sure. What should we do?"

"Is it a possibility she stayed with Prudence?"

Rowena frowned down at the tea she held in her hand and wished it were something stronger. "It's Victoria. Anything is a possibility."

"We need to tell the boys as soon as possible," Elaine said. "Kit is going to go crazy when he hears she's missing."

"She's not missing. She's just . . . absent." Even though Rowena was none too happy with Sebastian right now, she knew Elaine was right. They needed help.

When the two groups met in the game room, Elaine and Rowena pulled Colin, Kit, and Sebastian aside and filled them in. Kit glanced around the room wild-eyed, as if they were going to find her in a corner somewhere.

"I'm sure she is fine," Rowena told him, her voice firm. "This is Victoria after all. She is probably with Prudence."

She noticed Sebastian startle and her eyes narrowed.

Kit straightened. "I think I know how to find her." Then he reddened. "At least my driver does. He knows where her friend Katie lives. I know she's been there a couple of times at least."

"I'm going with you," Rowena said.

"How are you going to get out of the house?" Elaine asked.

"I'll tell Aunt Charlotte that I have a headache and am going to bed." She looked at Kit. "I will meet you out front."

Kit nodded. "Colin and I are heading to the club, aren't we, old mate? As long as Mother isn't ready to leave, we should be fine."

"Will she be?" Rowena asked, worried.

"Not while bridge is being played," he said, nodding toward where Aunt Charlotte had paired up with Kit's mother against Lord Summerset and the deaf general. "See you in a moment."

She told her aunt that she was retiring early and dutifully kissed Sebastian's mother's cheek before she made her way out of the game room and hurried to get her coat.

"Are you ready?" Kit asked a few minutes later.

She nodded and he helped her into the motorcar.

"I don't understand why she would do this," he muttered.

"It's Victoria. It's not like she has to have a reasonable explanation for everything she does. What do you know about this job she's taken with the Suffragettes for Female Equality? How did she even become involved in that?"

He shrugged. "That all fell into place after we had an argument . . . so I'm not sure. I know she was incredibly distraught over *The Botanist's Quarterly*."

"*The Botanist's Quarterly*? What do you mean?"

"She didn't tell you? The editor accepted one of her articles for publication and even sent a check. He was very appreciative of her talent, except of course, he didn't know that she was a woman. She never revealed her full name to him."

"Oh, no," Rowena said softly.

"Oh, yes. He was very surprised when Victoria showed up on his doorstep looking to meet her mentor and get more assignments. She must have gotten connected to the Suffragettes for Female Equality through the friends she stayed with that week."

"Prudence?" Rowena asked, confused.

"No. She stayed with Katie."

"So that week she said she was visiting with Prudence, she was actually meeting with the editor of *The Botanist's Quarterly*, staying with Katie, and getting a job with a women's suffragette group?"

Kit nodded.

"My God," Rowena said. "We better hope nothing has actually happened to her. Scotland Yard wouldn't know where to start."

"She is"—Kit paused and Rowena watched his face in the darkness—"rather independent."

Rowena snorted. "To put it mildly. But honestly, she is more spoiled and indulged than independent, and both Prudence and I are partially responsible. She was such a frail little thing and then before we knew it, she had grown into this monster."

"She's not a monster," Kit snapped. "She's mercurial and impulsive, but she's hardly a monster. Her intentions are good."

"Oh, Lord have mercy. You're in love with her," Rowena breathed.

Kit didn't deny it, and Rowena turned the thought over in her head. She had originally been suspicious of Kit's motivations regarding her sister, but had been too involved in her own drama to keep an eye on them. When had this turned from friendship into something more? She shivered, regret hollowing her chest. Was Victoria's behavior these past few weeks partially due to the fact that Rowena had just not been paying attention?

She sighed and then shook her head. None of that was important now. What was important was to find her sister and make sure she was all right. But Rowena promised herself she would change things. She had been too preoccupied, at first with the overwhelming sadness of her father's death, then with losing Prudence and her part in that, and then, of course, with flying and Jon. But none of it was more important than her baby sister, and Rowena resolved to keep that uppermost in her mind if they found Victoria. She shivered and then changed the wording in her mind. *When* they found Victoria.

It was late by the time they reached Katie's house. Rowena remembered Katie as the very sweet but shy kitchen maid when they lived in the Mayfair house. Trust Victoria to have made a friend of the maid. And Prudence had, too. The only person who didn't know her was Rowena. Maybe she had always been too preoccupied with her own thoughts, Rowena pondered ruefully as they knocked on Katie's door.

After a few moments, a thin, older woman opened the door a crack. She frowned when she saw Kit. "What are you doing here, you drunken sot?" Then she spotted Rowena and her eyes widened. She threw open the door. "Miss Rowena! What are you doing here?"

Rowena frowned, puzzled. "Do I know you?"

"Oh, no, miss. I'm sorry. I have seen you a few times from afar. I'm Katie's mother. Come in, come in."

Katie's mother ushered them inside, scowling at Kit. Rowena found herself in the front room with arched doors on either side. Katie stood in one of them in a wrapper, blinking away sleep.

Rowena didn't waste any time. "Has anyone seen Victoria today?"

Katie shook her head. "I haven't. She didn't come to the house, did she, Mum?"

Katie's mother also shook her head. "No, I haven't seen her for a week."

"Do you know where she might be?" Rowena asked, disappointed. "She ran out this morning after receiving a note and hasn't been seen since."

Katie turned her head. "Lottie," she called. "Was Victoria at the SFE today?"

"Not when I was there," came the response. A woman with a voluminous nightgown and a nightcap appeared in the doorway next to Katie. She reddened when she saw Kit and crossed her arms over her chest.

"Can I get the address of the building where she worked?" Rowena asked. If Victoria didn't show up tonight, that was going to be her first stop in the morning.

Katie's mother got a pencil and paper and the woman in the nightcap scribbled down the address, rather reluctantly, it seemed to Rowena.

"Do you know where Prudence lives?" Rowena asked Katie. "We're going to try there next."

"Sure. I'll give you the address."

"Thank you so much for your help," Rowena said as they prepared to take their leave. "If my sister does show up here, tell her that we are looking for her and are desperately worried."

They promised to keep an eye open, and Rowena and Kit hurried back to the motorcar.

"Did you find it odd that the woman in the nightdress was so reluctant to part with the address for the women's society?" Rowena asked once they got settled back in the car.

"I could only focus on the oddly shaped nightcap."

Rowena rolled her eyes in the dark. "Kit."

He shrugged. "No, you're right. She didn't seem too keen on giving us the address."

"Right. Victoria certainly has some questions to answer about this society when we find her," Rowena said.

"I know she was very happy working there, but I'm not exactly sure what she did," Kit said.

Rowena sighed as the motorcar came to a stop in front of a greengrocer. "Is this it?" Rowena asked. "There must be some mistake."

"I think the lady in question lives in a flat above the green-grocer," the driver said, his voice patronizing.

Rowena frowned. Prudence lives above a grocer? Rowena's heart ached. *Oh, Prudence*, she thought. *What have I done to you?*

* * *

"Is there anything you would like to tell me?"

Andrew's words stopped Prudence in her tracks. Her pulse raced and she swallowed, her mind going immediately to the kiss she shared with Sebastian. "I'm not sure what you're talking about."

She and Andrew were standing in their bedroom. He had worked a long day at the docks and was heading to bed early. Because Susie was still visiting, Prudence had taken to tucking her husband in so they could steal a few minutes alone. He stood with his back to her at the small dresser he used for his clothes, as hers took up their entire wardrobe.

Could he have found out about the kiss? Her face flushed with guilt. Prudence had managed to put Sebastian mostly out of her mind. Nothing would come of telling Andrew of it—it would only hurt him. And she knew that it never would, never *could* happen again. In her mind, it was simply the kiss she should have received on that long-ago afternoon, back when Sebastian had first hinted at his feelings for her.

Andrew turned, holding up a T-shirt, one brow raised. "I just noticed these T-shirts are not my type. Why did you buy me all new T-shirts? I didn't need them and we really can't afford them."

Relief weakened her knees and she stumbled to the bed and sat. Andrew came and sat next to her, the offending shirt in his hands. She leaned against him, sniffing deeply. He was wearing a nightshirt that was worn and soft and he smelled cleanly of fresh soap. Her eyes filled with tears. She didn't deserve this good man.

"I ruined your other shirts," she confessed. "I used too much bluing and ruined them. I didn't want you to know . . . especially after Victoria told you how incompetent I was at keeping house, so I went and bought some new shirts and new sheets."

"You ruined the sheets, too?"

She nodded, her cheek pressed against his chest. The tone of his voice sounded strangely strangled and she dared not risk looking up at him. *How could I have kissed Sebastian?* She only wanted to be a good wife to Andrew, but instead she ruined laundry, burnt meals, and kissed another man. *What kind of woman have I become?*

Suddenly Andrew erupted in laughter and Prudence pulled back, her eyes wide. "What?"

"Why didn't you tell me, you silly girl? Did you think I would be angry?"

Tears of both humiliation and relief spilled down her cheeks. "I just don't want you to be disappointed in me."

He drew her back in against her chest. "I could never be disappointed in you. Why do you think I married you, anyway? If I just wanted someone to keep house for me, there were plenty of maids at Summerset to choose from. But I didn't, did I? I chose you."

"But why?" she asked, her voice muffled against him.

He was silent for a moment. "Two reasons," he finally said. "You know I come from a poor farm family. They didn't put much value on book learning and I had to get my education after grammar school on the sly. I don't want my children to have to do that. I wanted something better. And then there you were—smart, well spoken, ladylike. The kind of woman I never thought to meet in a million years. The kind of woman I want rearing my children."

The emotion in Prudence's chest swelled. "What was your other reason? You said you had two."

"Your eyes," he said softly, his mouth against her hair. "They were so sad. I wanted to erase that sadness from your eyes and do everything I could to make sure it never came back."

Prudence pressed against him as his arms encircled her and she wished fervently that Susie wasn't just outside the door. Andrew chuckled as if sensing her wanton thoughts. "I love you," she said, her voice fierce.

"I love you, too."

For the next hour, Susie and Prudence stayed up, visiting and mending. Susie was teaching Prudence to darn socks and Andrew provided them with a never-ending supply.

This was the time when Susie's presence was most welcome. Prudence had never spent much time alone and the days Andrew was gone and the evenings he went to bed early were the loneliest for her. She could only read and visit with Muriel and Katie so often.

The knock on the door startled both of them. Prudence glanced at the bedroom, but the door remained shut and nothing stirred.

They both went to the door and Susie grabbed a heavy candlestick from the table at the last moment. Prudence tried to project a confidence she didn't feel and she eased the door open.

Her pulse skyrocketed the moment she saw Rowena's face. She would have slammed the door had she been able to move, but shock kept her still, her mouth agape.

Rowena gave Prudence a small, sad smile and her beautiful green eyes brimmed with tears. "Hello, Prudence."

Rowena's beautiful face had changed, Prudence realized. Whereas she always had been lovely, the firmness of her jaw showed a certain maturity that hadn't been there before, while a new softness in her features showed the telltale signs of a woman in love.

With Sebastian.

She tried to shut the door, but Rowena stuck her foot in the doorway. "Victoria is missing."

Prudence stilled, her heart in her throat. "What do you mean she's missing?"

"She got a note this morning and ran out of the house. She hasn't been seen since."

Prudence opened her mouth but Rowena forestalled her. "I've already been to Katie's. That's how I found you."

More than anything in the world, Prudence did not want to let Rowena in the house. Just the sound of her voice reminded Prudence of two of the most painful moments in her life, but Prudence had never let Victoria down when she needed her; she wasn't about to start now. She opened the door and stood to one side. "Come in," she said. She turned to Susie, who had replaced the candlestick. "Could you please make a pot of tea?"

Prudence tried not to look at the naked relief on Rowena's face. Her pain was still raw, and as far as she was concerned, this changed nothing between them.

Prudence lit a lamp and they sat at the table. Susie busied herself making tea and taking down cups, while the man Rowena was with stood awkwardly in the middle of the room.

Rowena introduced them without ceremony. "Prudence, this is Victoria's friend Kit. Kit, this is our sister, Prudence."

Kit's eyebrows rose. "I believe we've met, but it is nice to see you."

Prudence blushed. They had met before, briefly, but she had only had eyes for Sebastian. "Yes, and you as well."

The bedroom door opened and Andrew came out. To Prudence's relief, he had heard voices and came in fully dressed. She introduced Kit and Rowena quickly, although too late she remembered that he already knew Rowena, having served as a footman at Summerset.

"What can I do?" Andrew asked after hearing about Victoria. He stood behind Prudence's chair and she reached back and captured one of his hands. He was such a good man. Prudence didn't intend to ever forget that again.

"I'm not sure any of us can do anything tonight," Kit said. "Rowena and I are going to go to the Suffragettes for Female Equality in the morning and find out if they know anything."

"You have no idea who she was going to see?" Prudence's stomach clenched at the thought of Victoria out in the darkness, alone and hurt. *Where could she be?*

Rowena shook her head. "You know what Victoria is like. She kept everything a secret. But despite her fondness for being mysterious, I'd have thought that even Victoria would want to boast about her position as a suffragette, and yet she said nothing to anyone about it. Did she ever talk about it with you?"

"She told me when she got the job, of course, but she gave me few details, only that she was to be a spokeswoman for the group, which I thought strange for someone completely new to the organization."

Susie freshened their tea and Prudence took a sip. Making up her mind, she turned to Rowena. "I want to go with you in the morning."

Rowena put her hands in front of her face and Prudence saw her shoulders shake. She wanted to remind Rowena that she was doing this for Victoria, not for her, but kept silent. It wasn't the time.

Rowena and Kit left soon after, promising to let Prudence know if they heard any news. Andrew gathered Prudence in his arms after he shut the door.

"She'll be fine, Prudence," he said into her hair. "I'm sure she'll turn up safe and sound before breakfast."

But Prudence was watching Susie's face as Andrew made his assurances, and Susie seemed far from assured.

CHAPTER SIXTEEN

he next time Victoria opened her eyes, the light was on. She blinked a couple of times and was startled when a woman with a thick East End accent said, "You're awake now, so don't you be playing possum, and don't start your screaming or else the doctor will be sending you to the asylum, and trust me, darling, you would rather be here."

Victoria froze. The scent of bleach and urine still assaulted her nose. The one small window above her head let in no light and she could see bars at the top. Her heart pounded a little faster. "Tell me where I am!"

"You can say please, you know. Just because I'm a nurse and you're a suffragette doesn't mean you needn't use your manners."

Victoria tried to move and realized that not only was her arm chained but her leg was as well.

The woman laughed. "You'll not be kicking me again."

"I'm sorry," Victoria said earnestly. "Please. Where am I?"

The woman came closer. She wore a blue-and-white-striped shirt, a long skirt of cheap wincey, and a crisp white apron that covered her head to toe. A white linen cap covered her hair. She smelt strongly of lye soap, but it was infinitely better than the urine stench. Her eyes were a bright, saucy blue. "That's more like it. You're in Holloway Prison."

Victoria whimpered, her heartbeat accelerating and her chest tightening. She closed her eyes and counted, taking little breaths until the vise squeezing her chest eased. Once she could breathe easily again, she asked, "Why am I here?"

"You don't know?" The nurse sounded surprised. "That's a new one. Most of you suffragettes are proud of your exploits! Don't you remember?"

Victoria thought hard. She remembered being at the National Gallery with Mary and then Mary had . . . Memories came flooding back and Victoria groaned.

"I see you're remembering."

She struggled to sit again and then gave up, settling back against the mattress. The pillow under her neck scratched, and she prayed it was cheap linen rather than bugs. "Prison is different than I thought it would be."

The woman snorted. "This isn't prison, this is the clinic. You were almost dead when they brought you in. You have a breathing disorder?"

Victoria nodded. "Yes, I'm . . ." Victoria choked a bit on the word but used it anyway. It was what she was, no matter how much she denied it. "I'm an asthmatic."

The woman nodded and made a note on a chart. "That's what the doctor thought. And don't worry. You'll be seeing the inside of a prison cell soon enough, though you suffragettes usually rate one to yourselves. Just don't try to starve yourself. We *will* force-feed you, and it's the most God-awful thing I've ever seen or done." Her face wrinkled into a stern look as she took Victoria's pulse.

"Why wouldn't I eat?" Victoria asked. She'd heard of suffragettes going on hunger strikes, but she thought trying to kill oneself was a poor way to give to the cause.

224 ~ T. J. BROWN

"Why would any of them stop eating?" the nurse asked reasonably. "But I'm sure a young woman such as yourself, who has struggled for her very life's breath, would look at death a great deal differently than most idealists. You're very lucky to be alive, miss. I thought you were a goner. You were as blue as my shirt. Now, do you need to use the privy?" Victoria nodded and the woman indicated a bucket in the corner.

Victoria blanched.

"I know it's not fancy, but then, I suspect the wardens don't feel the need to roll out the fancy for those who break the law. Now, if you promise not to throw another fit, I'll let you loose long enough to do your business. Give me a single moment's worry and I'll call in Ed and you'll have to do whatever you need to do in front of him."

Horrified, Victoria promised. After the nurse had gotten her back into the bed, she told Victoria to try to sleep. "I won't cuff you, if you promise me no more trouble. If you do, it's my arse on the line and I'll have to truss you up like a Christmas goose." The woman rattled the cuffs for emphasis.

The blood drained out of Victoria's face. "I promise," she whispered. "Thank you."

The nurse got Victoria into bed and settled the covers over her. Victoria's bones ached, and even the roughness of the gray woolen blankets and the hard mattress felt wonderful. When the woman moved to leave, Victoria caught her arm. "Wait," she pleaded. It seemed as if this woman was the only person between Victoria and unknown terrors. "When will I see a judge? When can I see my family?"

The woman shook her head and flicked a switch off. The only light now came from the open door, and long shadows spilled over Victoria's bed. "I don't know. It's hard to tell."

"What's your name?" Victoria pleaded. Anything to keep the door from shutting.

"Eleanor. I'll check on you before my shift is up. Now try to get some sleep."

The light slivered and then was gone. The darkness, once the door had closed, was absolute, and Victoria trembled. She'd never liked being alone at night, and for years she had slept with Prudence to keep the nightmares away.

There was no one to keep the nightmares away now. Of course, how could anything her mind conjured be worse than her current reality?

Tears rose and fell down her cheeks in the darkness. How did she get here? Why hadn't she just ignored Mary's note? The woman was mad. Victoria wondered where she was and then realized that Mary was no doubt locked in a cell in this very prison.

She wiped the tears with her hands. Her uncle would get her out if he could. He was an important man and a rich one to boot. Surely he could do something.

With a sinking heart, she remembered some of the newspaper articles she'd read over the preceding months. Public opinion might be mixed on the suffragettes, but the justice system was not. Most judges had no sympathy whatsoever, and they had been known to throw a suffragette in jail and toss the key at the same time. And if they really thought she had plotted to destroy the painting . . . Victoria shuddered.

Something dropped outside the door and she stilled. She could hear muffled voices for a bit as the nurses and orderlies worked their way from room to room, checking on patients, and she listened intently. At least she knew there were people out there and she wasn't all alone. But the noises grew fainter and fainter and soon there was only the sound of her own ragged breathing. Then a soft moaning began and her heart leapt jaggedly in her chest. She screwed her eyes up tight against the darkness and began to recite:

> " 'Twas brillig, and the slithy toves
> Did gyre and gimble in the wabe;
> All mimsy were the borogoves,
> And the mome raths outgrabe . . ."

Victoria paused with a shudder. No. Lewis Carroll's "Jabberwocky" was much too frightening for this situation. Her father used to run his fingers through his hair and recite it while making the most horrible faces. *Father!* She swallowed and began again. This time choosing Rudyard Kipling's "The Bee Boy's Song."

> "BEES! BEES! Hark to your bees!
> 'Hide from your neighbors as much as you please,
> But all that has happened, to us you must tell,
> Or else we will give you no honey to sell!' "

She started softly and then grew louder and louder as the words chased the last of the shadows from her mind.

Her heartbeat and her breathing had both returned to normal, and she racked her brain for the vast reserves of Kipling poetry she had stored there. She wouldn't think about being alone in a dark place. Alone in a notorious prison where they sent murderers and robbers. Where women lived out their entire lives, forgotten by the world. Victoria whimpered and sank down further under the blankets.

Desperately she moved from poetry to stories: " 'This is the story of the great war that Rikki-tikki-tavi fought single-handed, through the bath-rooms of the big bungalow in Segowlee cantonment . . .' "

* * *

She must have dozed, but her sleep was marred by unremembered nightmares that woke her each time into an unrelenting reality. Hours later she was awoken by the sound of the bolts being thrown open. She concentrated on the door, praying it was Eleanor.

The light blinded her when it was flicked on and she heard Eleanor's voice. "I told you I would check on you again."

"Thank you." Victoria's eyes welled up with tears of gratitude.

"Oh, stop it now. I liked you better when you were rude."

Eleanor let her get up and use the bucket again and then took her pulse. "You're as fit as a fiddle as long as you're breathing," she said. "Now if you promise to be good, I'll just cuff your leg."

Victoria promised. Eleanor got her settled again. "I probably won't see you when I come back on this evening." She looked at her and shook her head. "Look at you. Your dress costs more than my entire month's paycheck and yet you weren't happy or satisfied. I want the vote every bit as badly as you do, but I won't risk everything I've worked so hard for to get it. Crazy girls."

Dim light shone in the window high above Victoria's bed and she watched it increase until the bolt was thrown and the door opened. A woman in a gray uniform walked in with another nurse wearing a uniform similar to the one Eleanor had worn.

"I told you she was ready to go," the nurse said after removing Victoria's cuffs and giving her a quick examination.

The other woman, who had a stern, unsmiling face, threw a black dress at Victoria. "Change into that and be quick about it." She turned to the nurse. "She may be ready to go, but I'm not sure where we are supposed to put her. The first-class cells are all taken."

Victoria tried to hurry, but her fingers were clumsy and she fumbled with the buttons. "If you don't have any room for me, you could always let me go," she quipped.

The woman in gray stopped talking and casually pulled up a billy club she had hanging from her belt. Victoria swallowed and began unbuttoning her dress with increased fervor.

When she had finished changing into the plain black wool dress, the woman took her by the arm and led her away. Victoria was almost sad to leave the horrid little room. She didn't know what awaited her as she was led down one windowless hall after another, and she ached for something familiar.

She was put into a small room about four feet by four feet that had one chair. The gray woman, as Victoria now thought of her, didn't say a word; she merely pointed at the chair. Victoria sat. And waited.

By the time someone came to get her, she was desperately hungry and thirsty, not to mention she had a serious need to find a WC. The woman who came wasn't the gray woman, but so much like her that she might as well have been.

"You missed breakfast?" The woman sounded accusing, as if Victoria had done it on purpose. "Oh, Lord. Why me?"

The woman brought her a cup of water and Victoria drank thirstily. "That will have to do you. I can't get you any extra food."

Victoria wanted to point out that since she hadn't had breakfast, it could hardly be called "extra" food, but she had already learned that lesson and kept her mouth closed.

She was taken down a long hall and into a wide room with a soaring ceiling that went up three stories. On each side of the room were rows of cells stacked vertically, one on top of the other, like children's blocks. When Victoria looked again, she realized that they were on different floors. They walked through the cavernous space and into another hallway. The walls were mostly stone and brick. At least she wouldn't have to worry about being trapped in a fire. Holloway castle, as all of London called it, wasn't going to burn down anytime soon.

They stopped at a locked closet on the way, and the woman handed Victoria two gray woolen blankets, a counterpane, and a white towel. The woman grabbed a large tin pitcher and filled it at a nearby spigot. By the time they finally reached Victoria's cell, her foot, the one that had been cuffed most of the night, was swollen and sore. She didn't dare complain, though. Just looking at the billy club caused ripples of fear to crawl up and down her spine. Victoria had never been struck before last night, and she couldn't believe that she could now be hit for any given reason at any time, and there was nothing she could do about it.

The cell was about ten feet long and five feet wide and the walls were painted cement blocks. Against the back wall of the cell a large barred window overlooked God knew what. In the back corner of the room stood a cot and mattress folded in half, a metal washbasin, a towel, several tin buckets, and a wooden stool. A bare lightbulb hung from the center of the ceiling.

"Make up your bed with your clean blankets and then shut it again."

When Victoria turned to the bed, trembling, the woman

set the pitcher on the stool and left the room without saying a word. The sound of a lock clicking into place struck terror in her heart, but she clapped her hand over her mouth to stop the cry. She didn't want to be taken to an asylum, though how it could be worse than this she didn't know. But if Eleanor said she didn't want to be there, then Victoria believed her.

Victoria rushed to the window and saw lines of women walking a gravel path around a yard. Around and around they went, with pairs of guards, all dressed in gray, on each corner. The prisoners were all dressed in the same uniform Victoria now wore.

Remembering what the guard had said, she opened the bed and made it up. It took her a minute to figure out how to fold it back up, and by the time she had it latched, she felt a strange sense of accomplishment. Then she sat on the stool and waited.

She wouldn't send word to her uncle first, Victoria decided. No, if this could be handled by Martha, she would just as soon spare her family the embarrassment. She hadn't done anything wrong. She hadn't had any idea whatsoever what Mary had planned. She had screamed, not to draw attention away from Mary but because she realized Mary had an ax. Wouldn't anyone scream if she saw a menacing woman with an ax? They would believe her and let her go. They had to. She wasn't a criminal like Mary. She had never been to prison before. No. She would send word to Martha. Martha had probably handled things like this quite often.

Resolve and hope buoyed her for the next couple of hours. The women disappeared from the yard and Victoria was certain that it was lunchtime, but no one came. More hours passed and still no one came. Had they forgotten her completely? Was this how all suffragettes were treated? Was it a punishment?

She had no way to tell the time, except for the shadows

outside that crept longer and longer eastward. Victoria finally pulled apart her bed again and lay on it for something to do. She counted the stones in the ceiling, anything to keep from thinking about her stomach. She drank more water but didn't want to drink it all in case they really had forgotten her. She wrapped her blanket around herself to fight off the damp chill that was so pervasive she could feel it all the way to her bones.

When had she last eaten? What was it? Breakfast yesterday, she realized. Kippers, eggs, berries in cream. A scone. Her mouth watered. A good breakfast. She always ate a good breakfast. Without warning, the tears came and this time she couldn't stifle the sobs that wracked her body until, exhausted, she finally let sleep overcome her.

When she awoke it was dark out again and still no one came. She used one of the buckets as a toilet and dipped the corner of her towel in her precious water to wipe her face and hands. The cell smelled strongly of urine and mildew.

It wasn't until the light clicked off that she knew that she was in very real danger. The entire day had gone by without anyone even checking on her, let alone bringing her food. If suffragettes were going on food strikes, that meant they were being fed, so this couldn't be a punishment.

They must have forgotten her.

Knowing it would be useless to scream at night in a room made of stone, she felt her way to her bed and crawled back under the coverlet. She would begin her campaign in the morning, trying to get someone's attention. For now all she could do was rest.

Except that she had slept most of the afternoon and her terror of the dark kept her eyes open and staring into the oppressive blackness that engulfed her. The window, her only source of light during the day, had transformed into an object of terror, opening into a dangerous, shadowy world. Her imagination ran wild to Dracula and Frankenstein and she felt her chest tighten. No. She couldn't have an attack. She would die. So she counted and breathed until the tightness lessened. She kept counting until her eyes grew heavy.

She must have fallen asleep again, because by the time she opened her eyes, the sky outside was lighter, though there was no evidence that the sun had actually risen. She waited in bed until the overhead light flicked on. They probably had a schedule and would be taking food around at a set time.

She waited for as long as she dared and then, overwhelmed by hunger, started banging a bucket against the cell door. Every once in a while she would trade that racket with some yelling, but she began growing light-headed from the effort. She banged until her arms ached. Her ears were still ringing when she quit pounding and curled back up on her bed into a ball.

* * *

Rowena looked with horror at the building where the car had stopped. She looked at the address again. "Are you sure this is the right address?" she asked the driver.

Kit made a noise deep in his throat. "How often did you say she came here?" he asked Prudence, who sat across from them in his motorcar.

Prudence shrugged and reached for the door handle. "A couple of times a week. And what did you expect? This isn't the National Union of Suffrage Societies. They can't afford a nice building. They are probably spending all their money on the cause."

Rowena felt the sting of Prudence's retort and held her tongue. This wasn't about her and Prudence, this was about

Victoria. She followed Prudence out the door and up the stairs, with Kit close on her heels.

Rowena thought Prudence might knock on the door, but she walked right in and stopped still. A small, dark-haired woman stood in the center of the room, packing things into a box. She startled as Rowena crowded her way past Prudence. The woman blinked. "May I help you?"

"Yes," Rowena said. "Is this the Suffragettes for Female Equality?"

The woman hesitated and then nodded. Her eyes kept darting over to Kit, as if she was concerned with his presence.

"I'm looking for my sister, Victoria Buxton. Have you seen her in the last two days?"

"Victoria?" The woman's voice went up in surprise. "No, I haven't seen her in quite some time, actually. I thought she had quit. Some women are just dilettantes, you know."

Prudence shook her head. "That isn't like Victoria. I was under the impression she was working quite a bit for you."

The woman's eyes kept darting over to Kit, who was moving around the room and looking around. "May I help you?" she finally snapped.

Kit shook his head. "Just looking around."

"Well, don't." The woman tried to soften her words with a smile, but it was obvious to Rowena that she was uncomfortable with Kit's presence. She turned back to Rowena.

"Well, I'm not sure what she told you, but she didn't work with us for very long. We liked her just fine, but like I said, she just wasn't dedicated."

"Dedicated to the Suffragettes for Female Equality or the Women's Equality League?" Kit held up a paper and raised an eyebrow in inquiry.

The woman gave him a tight smile. "Either."

"Why do you have two names?"

Rowena's neck prickled. Something about this wasn't right.

The woman smiled again, a public smile meant to soothe. "I'm sorry for not introducing myself, my name is Martha Long. And we have two names because both organizations have very different goals. Two names keep them from being confused. But none of that has anything to do with Victoria."

"Are you moving?" Rowena asked, nodding her head toward the boxes.

"Just cleaning up," Martha said. "I hope you find Victoria. She was a very nice girl. Please send word when you do. Now I really should get back to work."

Tears of desperation filled Rowena's eyes. In this short conversation she had lost all hope that Victoria would be found quickly. And more than that, she realized that she finally needed to tell her aunt and uncle.

"Were there any protests planned for yesterday?" Prudence asked before they turned to the door.

"Not that I know of." Martha smiled again. She was altogether too cheerful for someone who should be concerned about a missing worker. "But then again, we don't know about all the protests every suffragette group has planned. Now if you will excuse me?"

Her meaning was plain and there was nothing left for them to do. Clearly, Victoria wasn't there.

By the time Rowena made it downstairs, Prudence was speaking to a young boy. Rowena saw Prudence hand the boy a coin.

"What was that all about?" she asked when Prudence rejoined her and Kit.

"Something was off about that whole situation. I don't know if it had anything to do with Victoria or not, but I thought we could use some information on where Martha Long goes after she's done here. I gave him a shilling and told him there would be more if he brought me the information tonight."

Prudence waved a hand at where the boy had taken up watch on the other side of the street and then climbed into the car.

Rowena just shook her head and followed her.

"What now?" Kit asked when they were all in the car.

Rowena shook her head. "I shall go to my aunt and uncle. No one knows where she is and we need help in finding her."

After dropping Prudence off, Kit had his driver take them back to Belgravia.

"You know, this isn't going to be easy," Kit said as they got out of the motorcar.

"That's an understatement," Rowena said. Sebastian was waiting outside for them as they walked up the steps.

He took one look at Rowena's face and wrapped his arms around her. Colin opened the door behind them and Kit shook his head and went inside. Rowena stood for a moment in Sebastian's arms.

"I'm so sorry," he said.

She lifted her tearstained face and he kissed her gently on the cheek. "Come on." He jerked his head toward the house. "I'll go with you."

Telling her aunt and uncle turned out to be as terrible as Rowena had feared it would be.

"Are you telling us that you knew she wasn't with Prudence last night and you didn't tell us?" Her uncle's look of disappointment and disapproval crushed her.

Her stomach sank as she realized that, once again, her inability to take action had let everyone down. She could only manage a nod.

He shook his head and rose. "I'm going to the office to telephone the authorities."

His wife put a restraining hand on his elbow. "Wait a moment. She rang a bell and the butler appeared. "Cairns, could you please take one of the maids and search Miss Victoria's room? Look for any papers in the dustbins. If someone has already cleaned in that room, please look through the garbage. We are looking for a note that someone delivered yesterday. Thank you." Lady Summerset looked at Rowena. "I'm disappointed. While I understand your desire to protect your sister from your aunt and uncle, I think in retrospect it seems rather unwise, doesn't it?"

Uncle Conrad turned to his wife. "I really think we should notify the authorities."

She nodded. "Of course. I just thought we might want to do some investigating first. If the girl ran off on her own, I would just as soon protect the reputation she and her sister seem to have so little regard for. Plus, her sister has already waited eight hours to inform us, with little regard for her sister's safety, so I don't think a few more minutes will hurt."

Rowena lowered her eyes. While her aunt's words were harsh, she deserved and expected little else. She had gambled on her sister's safety and this was the result. She just hoped Victoria wasn't paying for her stupidity right now.

Aunt Charlotte rang the bell again and a maid stepped into the room. "We need several pots of tea made, please, and we could use some sandwiches as well."

She looked at Colin, Kit, and Sebastian, who flanked Rowena. "If we do have to send out searchers, they will need to be fed. I suppose you three have friends capable of searching for a young girl?"

Relieved, Rowena sat back and closed her eyes as her aunt took over. Why hadn't she just taken the whole mess to her aunt earlier?

"Now, Rowena. You can still redeem yourself. We need as much information as you can give us about your sister's activities. Did she have a young man?"

Next to her Kit stiffened and without meaning to her eyes went to him. Her aunt must have caught the look because she raised her brows in comprehension.

Rowena shook her head. "No."

Her aunt continued. "Why don't you tell me exactly what her position with the Suffragettes for Female Equality is?" Rowena's mouth dropped open and Aunt Charlotte shook her head impatiently. "Of course I know. She didn't think she could canvass my friends for money and not one of them would mention it to me, did she? I shudder to think how much money they forked out on such an unseemly enterprise. She must have been very persuasive."

Rowena nodded. "Victoria can be very persuasive if she chooses to be, though I had no idea she was asking for money. I knew she had taken a position, but not exactly what it entailed. Victoria is not a very forthright person. She never got over her childish love for secrets."

Kit interrupted them. "You say she was canvassing for money? Were they giving the money to her or just sending to the society?"

"Both, I believe," Aunt Charlotte said.

"I wish I had known about such goings-on," Uncle Conrad said with a sniff. "I would have put a stop to this nonsense. If

Victoria needed an outlet for her energies, there are other, more respectable charities she could work for."

Cairns came in holding a small blue piece of paper. He handed it to Aunt Charlotte, who read it and handed it to her husband.

"Do you know of anyone named Mary?" Aunt Charlotte asked while her husband read the note.

Rowena shook her head.

Uncle Conrad ran his hand over his face. "Oh, dear Lord. Cairns, please go to my office and bring me this morning's newspaper."

He sank into a chair with his hand over his eyes. Aunt Charlotte moved swiftly to his side. "Conrad! You're scaring me. What is it?"

"I think I know where she is."

Kit stood, his hands clenched by his side. "Then let's go get her!"

Uncle Conrad shook his head. "I'm afraid it may not be that easy."

Kit snatched the paper out of Uncle Conrad's fingers and Rowena stood up to read the note with him.

Dear Victoria,
  Here is a chance to prove yourself. Please meet me at the National Gallery at two this afternoon. Tell no one.
  Mary

Rowena's stomach clenched, more from her uncle's reaction to the note than the note itself. "I don't understand. The National Gallery? What does that have to do with anything?"

Cairns reentered the room holding the newspaper. Her uncle

glanced at the front page and then held it up to show the rest of them. Rowena read the headline.

" 'Suffragettes Attack the *Rokeby Venus* at the National Gallery.' "

Rowena would have fallen to her knees if Kit hadn't caught her. Sebastian came up next to her and supported her while he read the next line.

" 'Mary Richardson, a notoriously hard-line suffragette, and an unidentified woman slashed Velázquez's masterpiece *Venus at Her Mirror* yesterday afternoon at the National Gallery.' "

Rowena shook her head. "No. Victoria wouldn't do that. She's foolish, but she wouldn't attack a priceless masterpiece. She had too much respect for the arts to do something like that."

Her uncle looked at the note again. "I hope you're right. But still . . . if she was in any way involved in this, I've no doubt she's been taken to prison."

CHAPTER
SEVENTEEN

ictoria must have finally fallen asleep once more, for when she awoke, sunlight was streaming in through her small window. She looked out the window and her heart sank at the sight of the empty yard. Once again, there was no one to hear her screams.

She was going to die here. Cold waves of helplessness flooded over her. All of her work, her attempt to become an independent woman, to make a difference . . . it was all for nothing. She would die here without ever having made an impact, without ever having left her mark. Her family would never know what had happened to her and she was so, so sorry. Why had she kept so much from them? Maybe she was just as childish as everyone thought her to be after all.

Just then a click in the door made Victoria sit up in alarm. The door opened and she stared at it in disbelief.

A guard in gray stood there, her hand on another woman's arm. The guard looked confused.

"What are you doing in here? This room is supposed to be empty."

Victoria's throat still ached from screaming. "They . . . forgot me," she managed to croak.

"I'll say. Hold on a minute. There must be some kind of mix-up."

The guard shut and locked the door before Victoria could beg her not to leave her alone again. *Please, God, don't leave me alone.*

Victoria wrapped the blanket around herself and stared at the door fixedly. When it opened, Eleanor stood before her with the guard.

Upon seeing a familiar face, Victoria burst into tears. Eleanor immediately wrapped her arms around the girl. "Good God. What kind of muck-up was this?" She turned to the guard. "I can't trust you with any of my patients, can I?"

"It wasn't my muddle," the guard muttered.

"Make yourself useful and get her some food."

"But—"

"Now!" Eleanor let go of Victoria and brought her the white towel. "Make yourself presentable. We're going to go see someone as soon as you eat."

Victoria did as she was told, her hands trembling. Eleanor took her pulse and felt her forehead. "How long have you been in here?" she asked.

"Since shortly after you left. They didn't seem to know where to put me."

Eleanor shook her head. "That would be my fault, I'm afraid. I talked the doctor into requesting a private cell for you because of your medical condition. I was afraid the shock of being in the general prison population might trigger another breathing attack. Probably one wasn't open and they brought you down here. We don't often use these cells except for patients with consumption."

The woman came in with a small loaf of rough brown bread and another pitcher of water. Victoria tried not to stuff her mouth the moment the food was in her hands. "Why did you come back?"

"I was asked to work the morning shift and I was curious about you. We didn't have your name because you came in so sick. When I tried to find out where Jane Johnson was placed—that's what we call no-namers—no one remembered. After a bit more digging, I realized that no one had any idea where you were, so I put out an alert. Of course, if the guard hadn't tried to put someone in here, I don't know how long it might have been before we found you. No one was much interested in finding a no-namer who seemed to have disappeared."

"So why were you?" Victoria asked with her mouth full.

Eleanor shrugged. "I don't know, if the truth be told. Perhaps because I heard you reciting such lovely verses to yourself to chase the bogeyman away. Stuck with me, I guess. At any rate you've been found. Now I'm going to take you to the wardress. You haven't even been properly processed yet. Have you seen the judge or the magistrate yet?"

Victoria shook her head.

"What is your name, anyway?" Eleanor asked.

"Victoria Buxton."

Eleanor led Victoria down a long hallway. She felt her body warming with each step she took away from her cell. Then they entered what looked to be the administration part of the prison, as it had offices on either side of the hall. Eleanor had an officer watch Victoria while she slipped into one of the offices to speak with the wardress.

Unlike in the actual prison or the clinics, the doors were not soundproof and Victoria heard Eleanor's raised voice: "I can tell she's posh just by the sound of her! Someone is going to be very angry when they find out how she's been treated. She hadn't even seen the judge yet!"

A few moments later, after a small, mousy woman came rushing out on an errand of great import, Victoria was escorted into a rather worn office consisting of two desks and rows of filing cabinets. The woman behind the desk intimidated by sheer size, not to mention the steel-framed spectacles she wore over a disdainful nose and stern mouth.

She stood when Victoria came in. Eleanor shook Victoria's hand. "I may not see you again, Victoria, if you don't have another breathing episode. It was nice to meet you."

Victoria resisted the urge to beg her to stay. As soon as Eleanor left, the wardress bade her to sit. "My name is Mrs. Liddell and I am the wardress of Holloway Prison. It is my understanding that a mistake was made and you spent a number of hours alone with no food or basic care. But while I feel badly for that, as we do not make it a habit to lose prisoners, I do not apologize. I did not make the choices that led you to this situation."

The mousy woman who had rushed out earlier returned and handed Mrs. Liddell a sheaf of papers. She then took a seat at the other desk and began typing. Mrs. Liddell leaned back in her chair and began reading the papers. Ignored, Victoria watched the small woman typing with a speed that made her ache with jealousy. She would never be able to type that fast.

Mrs. Liddell cleared her throat and Victoria jumped to attention.

"Your accomplice, Mary Richardson, received six months for her crime against property owned by the Commonwealth."

Victoria whimpered, and the wardress shook her head. "No. As you did not directly destroy property or wield a weapon, I doubt your sentence will be as harsh. And this wasn't Mary's first dance with us. It doesn't look as if you have been in trouble before. Is that so, Miss Buxton?"

Victoria shook her head. "No. Never."

"You will be seen by the magistrate first thing in the morning. Now, do you want to send word to your family?"

Victoria thought briefly of Uncle Conrad, then shook her head. "No. But I would like to send word to my supervisor."

Mrs. Liddell pursed her lips. "Your family would be in a better position to help you, but if you insist. Give Miss Lark her information. She will finish processing you and send your note. Good day, Miss Buxton."

Victoria knew she was dismissed and went to the mousy woman's desk. After answering countless questions, she sent a note off addressed to Martha.

The guard took Victoria back to her cell. Even though fear practically paralyzed her, she felt a bit of hope. Only one more night. She could do that. She was sure Martha would meet her in the morning and let the judge know that Victoria couldn't possibly have been involved. She wouldn't have to stay here much longer.

But Martha never showed up.

In a daze, Victoria went through the process of her hearing alone. She tried to tell the judge and the officials that she didn't have anything to do with the Venus, but after admitting to knowing Mary and being asked to create a diversion, the judge seemed disinclined to believe that her scream had been out of true shock and not a ruse to distract.

"Three months at Holloway."

Three months.

The words echoed through Victoria's mind and her knees

buckled. On the way back to the prison she had another breathing attack and ended up in the clinic. Eleanor wasn't there but they had a nebulizer for her and, after her breathing had returned to normal, they took her back to her cell.

And so her bleak, monotonous days in prison began in earnest.

The nights were the worst for Victoria. The lights went out at eight o'clock each evening and ten excruciating hours would pass before they came back on. Victoria spent the time staring blindly in the dark, reciting every poem she knew until sleep finally came in the wee hours of the morning.

At seven in the morning, the dirty water was emptied and a light breakfast of brown bread and a pint of tea were delivered, along with a large pitcher of water that was meant to last the day. At eight, the doors were opened and the women were taken in long lines to chapel. They weren't supposed to talk and Victoria was amazed at how much communication the women managed without the guards' knowledge.

Victoria had a hard time believing that each of these women had done something that warranted imprisonment. So many of them looked like doting mothers.

They probably were.

She saw Mary only once during chapel, and Victoria felt sick to her stomach. She was thankful that Mary passed without noticing her in return. Victoria never wanted to see her again.

After chapel, they were taken back to their cells, where they were visited by a doctor, if needed, or the governor of the prison if they had any urgent needs. Eleanor had come once with the doctor to check on Victoria, and her relief at seeing a familiar face, no matter how stern, was overwhelming.

At ten the women were taken outside, regardless of the

weather, to exercise. This was optional for Victoria because of her condition, though she went every day, grateful for the brief reprieve from her cell.

After exercise they were led back to their cells, where they could read or sew. Victoria discovered she was allowed to borrow two books a week from the rolling cart a volunteer manned each Thursday. The first week, Victoria chose *Jane Eyre* and *Robinson Crusoe*. She'd read both books before, of course, but felt that now she could properly sympathize with the isolation of the stories' narrators. One day a week, she was given a newspaper. She'd never paid much attention to the news before, but she did now, aching for word of the outside world.

The food was abominable, though Victoria realized that women who were not accustomed to three good meals every day would likely be satisfied with what little they were given. The small loaf of brown bread they received for breakfast was also present for dinner and Victoria wondered how many thousands of loaves were baked each week. Dinner was their largest meal and eaten in a communal dining room. On one day, she ate beans and potatoes, on another, suet pudding and potatoes, and on another pressed meat and potatoes. Like the brown bread, potatoes were ever present.

By the end of that first week, Victoria was surprised by another visit from Eleanor and the doctor. After the doctor pronounced her sound, he left the room, giving Victoria a few moments alone with Eleanor.

"I sent word to my employers about my whereabouts and asked them to send word to my family, but I've heard nothing. Is that . . . normal?"

Eleanor tilted her head to one side. "For a prisoner in the regular population I would say yes. But you first-class suffragettes get better treatment than most. Have you heard anything from your family? They can't visit, but you can get letters. Why didn't you send word straight to them instead of to your employers?"

Victoria shrugged. "I worked for the Suffragettes for Female Equality. I suppose I thought they would know best how to go about this." It slowly dawned on Victoria that maybe her loyalty to the society didn't necessarily guarantee their loyalty to her. She felt her lungs begin to constrict once again. "Could you get word to my family?" she managed.

Eleanor looked at the door and nodded. "Hurry, though. I have to catch up with the doctor."

She gave Eleanor Prudence's address. Victoria knew that Prudence would go directly to Rowena. She could only hope that they would be able to look beyond their differences and come together to help her. Victoria wanted nothing more than to get word from her family right now . . . and that included Prudence.

Prudence blinked at the plainly dressed woman at the door. "Excuse me?" Prudence's sleep had been haunted by nightmares since Rowena had sent word about Victoria's imprisonment, and she found it difficult to function. Apparently, the family was trying to help her but as of yet had been having a difficult time even getting a confirmation of her presence in Holloway.

"Are you Prudence Wilkes?" the woman asked.

Prudence nodded.

"My name is Eleanor James. I work at Holloway Prison?" The woman seemed to want confirmation that Prudence knew what she was about.

Prudence's heart skipped a beat and she nodded. "Come in."

Susie was out marketing and Andrew had already left for his tutoring session, so Prudence gave Eleanor the best chair and nervously asked whether she would like a cup of tea.

"That would be wonderful," Eleanor said. "I came here straight after work."

Prudence put the water on for tea and then turned to her guest, unable to wait any longer. "How is Victoria?"

The woman smiled. "She's an intrepid young woman, isn't she? She is fine now."

"Now?" Prudence asked.

"When they brought her in, she was completely blue and scarcely breathing."

Prudence put a hand over her mouth. One of her nightmares was Victoria having a breathing attack without her nebulizer.

"She's fine now," Eleanor reminded her quickly.

"Thank you." Prudence finished making the tea and sat at the table across from her guest.

Eleanor frowned and looked at Prudence. "When Victoria asked me to notify her family of her whereabouts, I have to admit, I didn't think I would be sitting in a flat in Camden Town."

"She and I were brought up as sisters. I expect she was concerned that if her family was notified, they wouldn't fill me in, whereas she knows I will run the news over to them immediately after you leave."

Eleanor nodded. "Fair enough. Victoria's situation is a bit odd. She wasn't properly processed and the warden is loath to reveal that a mistake has been made. I feel that's one of the reasons any inquiries about her may not have been immediately addressed."

She took a sip of her tea while Prudence leaned forward, tense and waiting.

"This is good, thank you."

Prudence nodded and refrained from telling her to just get on with it.

"Victoria has been sentenced for three months, half of what her compatriot must serve, because Victoria wasn't actually holding the chopper. But Victoria ran, which angered the judge. The other woman, Mary, did not."

Prudence snorted. "Maybe that's because Victoria didn't know what this Mary was going to do?"

Eleanor gave her a sharp look. "That's what I thought. Victoria sent word when she was finally processed, but apparently she sent it to her employers and not her family. The prison authorities have heard nothing from them."

"Can I go visit her?" Prudence asked.

Eleanor shook her head. "No, I'm afraid you can't. She can receive visits from the volunteer visiting committee and her solicitor, but no friends or family."

Eleanor rose to leave. "Thank you so much for the tea, miss. It right hit the spot."

Prudence placed an arm on Eleanor's elbow. "Why are you doing this? You must treat hundreds of prisoners. Why are you going out of your way for Victoria?"

"Just because I don't believe in the methods used by the militant suffragettes doesn't mean I'm not a sympathizer, miss. I want the vote and a say in how my country is run as much as the next woman. So I do what I can and consider it my contribution to the cause. And Victoria is little more than a girl. I had a hard time believing that anyone who could recite the best of

Rudyard Kipling could possibly be in cahoots to ruin a fine piece of art."

Prudence thanked her and pondered Eleanor's words after she'd left. No, she didn't think Victoria was capable of conspiring to ruin art of any kind, no matter what the cause. She'd been following Mary Richardson's story in the newspapers. There were sensationalized pictures and stories of Mary's former exploits, such as the time she rushed the King's carriage to hand him a petition. *How on earth did Victoria get tangled up with someone like that?* she wondered as she put on her coat.

She took the Tube to Belgravia to save time, her stomach in knots. She hadn't seen anyone from the Buxton family aside from Rowena and Vic since she had left on that horrible night when she learned the truth about her father. Perhaps all of these drastic upheavals were inevitable the moment that Sir Philip—her protector—passed away.

Prudence stood irresolutely before the front steps of the stately London manor and tilted her chin. No, she was not going to go through the servants' entrance. She was no longer a servant and she now knew that she was as much of a Buxton as the rest of them were, regardless of the scandal surrounding her link to that lineage.

She rang the bell and waited, her heart in her throat, for Cairns to open the door. When he did, he frowned at her, disapproval emanating from him in waves. "I'm here to see Rowena and Lord Summerset," she told him clearly. "It concerns Victoria."

Cairns's mouth tightened. He had no choice but to let her in, show her into the drawing room, and announce her presence. She faltered when she realized that the room full of people included Sebastian. Of course Sebastian would be here. He and Rowena were to be married. Pain rippled throughout her chest.

Rowena stood and greeted her with her hands outstretched and Prudence felt she had no other choice but to greet her in kind, though her resentment and anger at Rowena still simmered. She kept her gaze resolutely away from Sebastian.

"What is it?" Rowena asked after kissing her on the cheek.

Prudence turned to Lord Summerset, also avoiding eye contact with her former tormentor, Lady Charlotte. "I had a visit from a nurse from Holloway this afternoon. She brought me word from Victoria."

The party erupted and Lord Summerset closed his eyes briefly. It was the first flicker of emotion besides annoyance that Prudence had ever seen cross his face.

Kit leapt to his feet and grabbed her hand. "How is she? Is she all right?"

Prudence stared up at him, taken aback by his outburst. "She is as well as can be expected. When they took her to Holloway, she went directly to the prison clinic because she was having an attack. Apparently, they didn't process her correctly and weren't even sure of her whereabouts for almost a day. The prison officials are reluctant to admit this, which the nurse thinks might be one of the reasons that you're having trouble tracking her down."

Lord Summerset nodded. "Has she seen the magistrate? Has she been sentenced?"

Prudence took a deep breath. "Three months."

Rowena swayed on her feet and Sebastian caught her elbow to steady her. Then he encircled her with his arm, lending her his support. Prudence stared, unable to look away. She hugged her own arms to her chest, protecting herself from the onslaught of anger and loss reverberating through her body.

Lord Summerset shook his head. "This is not right. Why didn't she contact us? She needs a solicitor."

She tore her eyes away from Sebastian's arm and faced Lord Summerset. "She thought her former employers would have more experience dealing with her legal issues, but of course, she hasn't heard from them."

"They've dissolved, haven't they? That suffragette group?" Kit asked.

Prudence nodded. "How did you know?"

He shrugged. "I did a little checking. Asked one of the workers. No one has seen either Martha or Lottie for several days. Lottie has moved out of Katie's lock, stock, and barrel. The place is abandoned now."

"So she was packing," Rowena exclaimed.

Kit nodded. "Looks like it."

Lady Summerset stood. "Perhaps Victoria's fund-raising had something to do with their sudden departure. Or perhaps they simply wanted to distance themselves from Mary Richardson's heinous act. There has been such backlash against the suffragettes because of what she did."

Prudence pressed her hands together and took a deep breath. *Oh, Vic. What have you done?*

"That's probably why they hired Victoria," Sebastian said. "For her connections."

The sound of his voice sent another wave of hurt through her and she stole a look at him from under her lashes. His face was tight and his mouth drawn, but he kept his arm around Rowena, more as if she was holding him up than the other way around.

Prudence swallowed. She had to get out of here. "I should be going. That was really all the nurse told me."

Lady Summerset inclined her head. "Thank you so much for coming over straightaway."

"Of course. I want Victoria out of there as soon as possible. The best chance of that is through her family."

"Yes, thank you," Lord Summerset added, standing. "Please allow us to send you home in the car."

"Oh, no. Don't trouble yourself."

"It's no trouble," Lady Summerset said. "It's the least we can do."

Prudence stiffened her back. She didn't need this family's charity.

Kit must have sensed something in her face because he jumped in smoothly. "I have my car. I will take her home."

Rowena clutched Prudence's hand. "Thank you so much for telling us." Her green eyes searched Prudence's and Prudence felt a pang of loss. But Sebastian's hand still affectionately held on to Rowena's elbow and with the memory of his kiss still tingling Prudence's lips, the gesture was agonizing. She managed a nod and turned away.

"Thank you for coming so quickly," Kit said once they were in his motorcar. "I've never in my life felt so helpless. Perhaps her uncle will be able to do something. Three months is ridiculous."

Prudence twisted around at the pain in Kit's voice. "And what is your stake in all this, Mr. Kittredge?"

Kit was silent as the motorcar moved slowly through the twilight. Finally he said, "She's my friend."

"It sounds a bit more than that."

Kit laughed without amusement. "I don't know what it is, really. It snuck up on me."

He paused and Prudence could barely see his profile across the expanse of the seat. "If I can talk her into it, I'll be the first of the Coterie to get married," he confessed.

"Married?" Prudence shook her head. "Victoria had always said she wouldn't marry. And I believe her."

Kit nodded. "I know. I have my work cut out for me."

"Good luck. Perhaps you and Victoria can have a double wedding with Rowena and Sebastian."

Kit snorted. "Hardly. Those two will never get married."

Prudence straightened. "Why do you say that? They're engaged, aren't they?"

He shrugged. "It's a ruse. Rowena is in love with someone her family wouldn't approve of. Sebastian fessed up to it."

Prudence's heart stopped cold. She wanted to barrage him with questions, but at the same time she longed for him to take it back so she never had to think about Sebastian again. Why hadn't she left well enough alone? It wounded her to think of Sebastian with Rowena, but at least then she had closure, and, more important, she took comfort in knowing that she wasn't responsible for his loneliness. That he loved again as she did—because she did love Andrew. Maybe not in the same way that she loved Sebastian, but she loved Andrew's kind soul, his steadfast loyalty, and his quiet strength. And she needed, no, she *wanted*, to stay true to him no matter the cost.

Even if it broke her heart.

CHAPTER
EIGHTEEN

owena galloped up to the front of the Wells Manor, her heart soaring. Last time she'd seen Jon, he told her he would be home this week and—if she could manage to make it back to Summerset—she would finally get her solo flight. She thought they would be back much sooner, but that was before Victoria went missing. But now . . . delight bubbled up from deep within and she laughed as she reined in her horse. Part of her felt guilty for her happiness, like she shouldn't feel this way with her little sister still in prison, but she couldn't help it. The thought of flying with Jon filled her with such joy that it could only escape in laughter.

She'd told her aunt she wanted to go home to Summerset to make sure everything was ready for Victoria's arrival. There was little for her to do in London, after all. Uncle Conrad and his solicitor had finally obtained a meeting with the governor of the prison and succeeded in getting Victoria's sentence reduced to eight weeks. Eight weeks was still horrific, but Victoria had a cell of her own and was, for the most part, kept separate from the rest of the prison population except during chapel and exercise. She just had to endure.

Rowena dismounted from her horse and was about to tie him up when a voice sounded behind her.

"You're not welcome here anymore, Miss Buxton, so just get back up on your horse and leave."

She turned to find George with his arms crossed, staring at her. The gloating smile on his face unnerved her.

"I'm not here to see you, George, I'm looking for Jon. He said he would be here this week."

"He already left."

Her stomach twisted at the satisfaction in his voice. Something was radically wrong. She wrapped the reins around the pole and went to move past him. "I'll just go see your mother and Cristobel, then."

He grabbed her arm and shoved her back toward the horse. "I said you weren't welcome here."

Rowena froze for a moment. "How dare you handle me like that? How dare you touch me?" Her voice sounded shriller than she meant it to, but alarm had her pulse racing.

"Why? Am I not blue-blooded enough to touch you like your fiancé? Jon told me what he saw and said that he was done with you."

Her heart began to pound. "Where is he?"

"I wouldn't tell you anything. All I know is that you broke his heart just like I knew you would. Buxtons are good for nothing else. Now get back on your horse. You aren't welcome here."

He leaned forward and she stepped back against her horse. She didn't want to turn her back on George, but she unwrapped the reins and mounted her sidestepping animal, who was just as unnerved by George as Rowena was.

She started to canter away when she heard her name being called. Cristobel came running out of the garden, her hair whipping around her face.

"Rowena!" the girl cried again. Rowena rode up to her. "Jon is at the airstrip. Go find him and make things right."

Rowena leaned low on her horse's neck and touched the girl's cheek. "Thank you."

"Cristobel!" George screamed from behind them. "Get into the house!"

"I should go," Cristobel said, backing away.

Rowena nodded. "Don't worry. Everything will be fine."

She wondered about that as she galloped her horse past George and down the road. To spare her horse she interspersed walking with cantering all the way to the barn where the planes were held, even though her heart pulsed with apprehension. George might not have known that her engagement was fake, but Jon certainly did. What could Jon have seen that would have possessed him to tell his brother that he was done with her? There were several motors in front of the barn when she rode up. She tied her horse to the back of the barn, away from the planes, and hurried around to the front. She spotted Mr. Dirkes standing near one of the motorcars, watching as a plane disappeared over the horizon.

"Mr. Dirkes! Where's Jon?"

He turned to her, his red drooping mustache as sad as his eyes. "He just took the plane up. He's in a foul mood, missy. I didn't want him to fly."

"I need to talk to him. He doesn't understand . . ." She stopped, unable to explain something she didn't know, but if it made Jon this angry, then it had to be a misunderstanding of some sort.

He nodded.

Rowena scanned the sky, thankful for the temperate March

weather that left them clear. She didn't know when he would be back. Probably not until he ran out of fuel.

Mr. Dirkes excused himself to go talk to one of the men and Rowena nodded. Her limbs were trembling. What if she didn't get a chance to explain away whatever it was that made him so angry? She would just chalk it up to George's machinations, but Cristobel had known something was wrong, as well. The thought that he was angry with her made her feel sick. She needed to see him.

Making a snap decision, she backed up until she was in the barn. She went up to the Flying Alice and surreptitiously checked to make sure it was fueled up. Not enough.

Biting her lip, she glanced back toward the door where they kept tanks of fuel. Quietly, keeping to the side of the barn, she grabbed the tank and moved back to the plane. She'd seen the aeroplanes fueled several times and poured the liquid slowly into the tank.

It took her several tries to screw the cap onto the tank, as her fingers kept fumbling. After replacing the container of fuel, she paused in front of the propeller. She could still change her mind. Her heart felt as if it were ricocheting around her chest. No. She was done with being passive and apathetic. Wasn't that what Victoria always said about her? Well, now it was time to act. She loved Jon and she was going after him.

She found a leather helmet on the workbench where Mr. Dirkes kept some extra tools. Taking off her hat, she put on the helmet and tucked her hair back as best she could.

Then, glancing back at the wide-open door one more time, she turned the propellers of the aeroplane, then climbed into the cockpit. Taking a deep breath, she reached forward and turned the booster mag hand crank. Then she waited until the men came in to see what was going on. They rarely started the aeroplanes in the barn. As long as it wasn't Mr. Dirkes. She wasn't sure whether she could con him. One of the men came back and gave her a puzzled look.

"I'm practicing driving the aeroplane around. Can you help me get out onto the field?" She smiled at him, hoping that he couldn't see the sweat beading at her hairline. He nodded, ran to the front of the barn, and called for backup. Another man came in and she sighed in relief when she saw it wasn't Mr. Dirkes.

She buckled herself in as the aeroplane was pushed out of the barn and onto the field. Mr. Dirkes stared across the field and she veered away from him as the aeroplane gathered speed. Seconds later, he was waving his arms but it was too late. She turned from him and studied the instruments in front of her. Oil pressure gauge, speedometer, and fuel pressure. She noted the red tick marks on the speedometer, the higher mark indicating maximum speed for structural integrity and the lower mark indicating the stall speed.

Her heart in her throat, she placed her feet on the rudder pedals and pulled back on the yoke.

A strange calm spread through her and stayed with her as the nose of the aeroplane lifted up off the ground, as light as dandelion seed.

"That's a good Alice, my dear," Rowena murmured. When the entire aeroplane lifted, her heart lifted with it and for a moment she forgot her mission. She was flying. She was airborne. And she was completely solo. The wind whipping past froze her cheeks, but her eyes, protected by the goggles, were clear. Keeping one eye on her instruments, she kept climbing until she reached altitude, and then turned to the west where she had last seen Jon.

260 ~o T. J. BROWN

He is going to be so angry.

But then, he was already angry. And deep down she knew she didn't care whether he might be angry about the aeroplane. He had been training her, she knew what she was doing, and—most important—she knew this was something she needed to do. A gust of wind hit the plane and it shuddered, but she automatically adjusted for it.

This was what she was meant to do. She saw a spot to her left and swung the aeroplane that way. Alice balked a bit in the wind, but Rowena held firm and the plane turned obediently. She grinned. Almost like a balky horse. She flew directly toward Jon, who must've been heading back toward the field.

Careful to keep her distance, she got close enough to see the shock and anger spreading across his face before she made a wide circle. He slowed his speed and beckoned her to follow him. She approached him from the left and then, flying slightly behind and above him, followed him back to the field.

She inched the yoke down as they approached and tried to remember everything he'd told her about landings. She did know that takeoffs and landings were the most dangerous times of a flight. She held her breath as Jon landed his plane. It was her turn. She circled the field again and saw Jon jump out of his aeroplane and yank off his helmet.

She made another circle, inching the aeroplane down little by little before turning straight. Taking a deep breath, she pushed the yoke down, further and further.

The touchdown rattled her teeth and her hand jerked on the yoke. The aeroplane veered right and came to a shuddering stop.

She sat with her hands on the controls, her heart beating wildly in her ears. It wasn't as pretty as she would have liked, but she had done it—her first solo flight.

She unbuckled her harness and stood, her legs quaking. One of the men reached her before Jon did and helped her out of the aeroplane. She pulled off her goggles and unbuttoned her helmet.

Suddenly someone grabbed her arm and whirled her around. "What the hell were you thinking?"

Rowena yanked her arm out of Jon's grip. "What do you think? I was going after you!"

The light in his blue eyes grew dark. "If I didn't know better, I would think you were trying to kill yourself."

"Don't be daft. I was perfectly fine, Jon. I knew what I was doing and you know it."

"You have been up in a plane, what? A half a dozen times and have been training three times? How does that make you a pilot? How does that make you think you can risk an expensive machine that doesn't belong to you, not to mention your own life?"

They glared at each other, unwilling to fight as the men wheeled the aeroplane back toward the barn. Rowena jerked her gloves off and shoved them into her pocket, then advanced on him, her mouth tight. "And why would you care about my life? Your brother informed me in no uncertain terms that you were done with me and I was no longer welcome at the house. Look, I have the marks to prove it."

She pulled up her sleeve where George had gripped her arm to shove her back toward her horse. Delicate bruises in the form of fingertips were already forming.

The marks took the top off Jon's anger. She could see it in the horrified expression on his face. He reached out and ran his fingers gently down the marks on her arm. "I'll kill him for that," he said, choking on his anger.

She snatched her arm away from him. "That's not what

I want. What I want to know is what you saw that would make you tell him that we were finished? And why on earth would you choose to have that conversation with him, someone who hates me, before you would even have it with me?"

Hurt, angry tears formed and rolled down her cheeks.

His lip curled. "You act so innocent, but I saw you. I went to your aunt's house to try to get your attention. All I could think of was how happy I was that Dirkes had returned to the city so I could see you. And can you imagine what I saw when I arrived?"

Rowena shook her head, bewildered.

"You and your *fake* fiancé, rubbing all over each other out in front of your aunt's house like you had no shame. His lips on your cheek, whispering things against your hair, and you clinging to him like he was the last man on the earth, as though I was nothing, the farthest thing from your mind!"

Rowena reeled at his accusations. What was he talking about? She racked her mind but came up with nothing. "And when did you supposedly see me with Sebastian?"

"A couple of weeks ago. You got out of a motorcar with some man and then Sebastian came out and you practically ran into his arms." Jon spat the words at her, as if daring her to deny them.

"I don't know what you are talking about," she flashed. "I . . . I've never . . ." Comprehension dawned and he saw it in her face.

"Now try calling me a liar!" Jon stepped closer to her, his face twisted, and she took a step back. "Why couldn't you just break it off with me? Or did you want the forbidden excitement of a love affair with someone below your social status? Is that what I was? An experiment?"

Pain radiated throughout her entire body. She trembled as it moved from her heart to every limb, organ, and muscle. "Apparently, what we shared and what we had was not enough for you to give me the benefit of the doubt. You sound just like George. Victoria went missing that day. I had no idea what happened to her. Eventually we learned she is in prison for something she couldn't possibly have done. So what you saw was Sebastian comforting me because I thought my sister was *dead*!"

They stared at each other. Jon was breathing hard, but she spotted the moment shame crept into his face. He realized she was telling the truth. "How is your sister?" he finally asked.

"As far as I know, she's fine. There was nothing I could do in London so I came here because you told me you would be here. I arrived late last night and rode to your house first thing this morning." She paused, tears swelling her throat and making it hard to speak. "How could you think . . . and how could you tell George . . . was it really so easy for you to believe that I could just . . ." She stopped, too choked up to speak further.

He took her elbow and led her farther away from the men working on the aeroplanes. The dampness of the field tugged at Rowena's shoes and a slight breeze dried the tears on her face. "When I saw you in his arms . . . I don't know . . . I went a bit mad. All the warnings my brother had been whispering in my ear came to mind . . . I was jealous. And so hurt."

She pulled her arm out of his. "How could you not trust me? After everything."

Jon turned away and looked at the horizon. "Maybe this entire incident just reveals a basic problem between us, Rowena." He cast his eyes downward. "For me, the name Buxton will always mean deceit, duplicity, and betrayal."

The punch to her stomach almost doubled her over. "What

does that mean for us, then? That you are just going to let me go because my name happens to be Buxton?"

He didn't answer and alarms started at the base of her neck and ran through her entire body. She wanted to throw herself in his arms and beg him not to do this. She wanted to put her hands over her ears and run away so she wouldn't have to listen to the words she knew were coming.

"Perhaps the implications of your name, your heritage, everything your family stands for is something I can't get over. You love your family. Can you really walk away from them for me? My God, Rowena, you just lost your father, how could you stand losing everyone else, as well?"

She felt as if a crater had been blown into her chest. "So that's it. You're not even going to fight for me. For *us*. You're just . . . just going to walk away?"

"Rowena, I love you, but I think we're both being naïve to think this is something we can just overlook."

She turned to face him. She saw pain in his eyes but it wasn't enough, not nearly enough. "You didn't seem to have a difficult time overlooking my surname when you took me to bed, did you?" She slammed her fists against his chest. "No, you certainly didn't care that I was a Buxton then, did you?" She hit him in the chest again and he reached up and grabbed her hands.

"It wasn't like that, and you know it."

"I don't know what it was like. I thought I did, but now I don't because the man I made love to would have fought for me and you're just walking away."

She was breathing heavily, panic unraveling in the back of her mind.

"I know to quit when something isn't working. It's how I stay alive. You're an aristocrat; I'm not and never will be. Hell,

Rowena, your hats cost more than I make in a month! I don't have the kind of money . . ."

She wrenched her hands out of his. "I have my own money. I don't need a man for money."

"I should live off my wife's money then?" His voice was indignant and Rowena closed her eyes for a moment.

"You don't love me enough," she finally said, her voice soft. "I thought you did, but you don't. Not nearly enough."

She turned then and walked toward the barn, her entire being hoping and praying that he would stop her, but knowing that he wouldn't. *Coward,* she thought as she walked away. *Bloody coward.*

CHAPTER
NINETEEN

Endurance. Every day became an exercise in endurance for Victoria, who, like Robinson Crusoe, kept a tally of days hidden behind her cot. She would scratch out a vertical line with a hairpin she'd found in the chapel one morning and every Sunday she would scratch one diagonally across the six scratches to mark a week. It was her afternoon activity after her eyes finally gave out from reading.

Because she could only check out two books a week, she read them over and over, committing long passages to memory. Anything by Charles Dickens or Jane Austen was a treat, though she adored the newer books by E. M. Forster as well. Eleanor came to visit twice a week, ostensibly to give her a checkup, but mostly to give her news from her family and to relay news back.

Through Eleanor's urging and patronage, Victoria was able to volunteer for a program educating inmates. Twice a week, a guard led her to the cafeteria, where they were supplied with old schoolbooks, papers, and pencils. She had three students that she tutored diligently, good girls, whose only crime was doing what they had to in order to survive abject poverty. Penelope was a former prostitute; Camilla stole food from the restaurant she worked in, food that was earmarked to be thrown away; and though Ann never mentioned why she was in prison, Victoria couldn't imagine such a sweet girl doing anything illegal. The simple act of teaching these young women to read and write fulfilled her in ways she had never dreamed of, and she knew it was something she wanted to continue doing.

"There's such a need," Victoria told Eleanor, who had come by to give her a checkup.

Eleanor nodded. "In my neighborhood alone, the number of uneducated women is astonishing. I do what I can, but I am so busy giving medical checkups, I don't have time for anything else."

"What do you mean, medical checkups?" Victoria was curious. It seemed to her that Eleanor was always at the prison. How did she have time for anything else?

"There's a settlement house in an old abandoned building down the block from me. Once a week, I give checkups and such. I beg, borrow, and do everything but steal medicine to hand out to those who can't afford it."

Victoria was intrigued. "What else do you do there?"

"Me? Oh, I don't do anything else there, except attend when they have a speaker come in."

"What kind of speakers?"

"Oh, no one well-known. Just people trying to help." Eleanor pronounced her in good health and began putting her tools away.

"Maybe I could help once in a while," Victoria suggested.

"Perhaps," was all Eleanor said, and Victoria saw the wisdom in that. Hadn't nearly all of Victoria's own problems come from being too impetuous, allowing herself to be seduced by a cause—and a woman—she truly knew so little about? Not gaining counsel from those who had the wisdom to guide her?

Victoria saw all too clearly that her own quest for independence had been more childish rebellion than a sign of any true maturity on her part. She vowed that when she finally got out, things were going to be different. Her father had worked quietly and diligently to right the wrongs he saw in the world—not through splashy gestures, but instead by giving money and time to causes he thought appropriate and, she now realized, by educating his daughters, including Prudence, in a way that prepared them for the modern world.

She'd been so blind not to have seen all of this before.

After Eleanor had gone, she scratched another line into the whitewash covering the block walls. "Two more weeks," she told herself. "Two more weeks."

Nerves fought in her stomach with excitement. What would it be like to be out in the real world again? She had almost forgotten what it was like to turn on and off the lights at will.

She already knew what she wanted. She didn't want to stay in London at all; she wanted to go directly to Summerset and spend the rest of the spring and summer there. She needed to spend time with her beloved nanny Iris and with Rowena. And she would think about her future.

She had sent word to Kit regarding her plans because she knew he would help her make it happen—no matter what the family said.

And Kit. What would she do with Kit? Did he love her? Or was his behavior merely the attitude of a protective best friend?

And more important, what would she do with his love if he offered it?

* * *

Prudence put the finishing touches on the cream cake she had made and decorated for Andrew's party. Susie had gone back to

Summerset earlier in the week, so Prudence had baked the cake herself under Muriel's strict tutelage. It looked perfect, but the taste testing would have to wait.

Andrew had spent the last three days in Glasgow, sitting the examinations that would either place him in the Royal Veterinary College or show him what he was lacking and make him wait five months to try again.

Prudence didn't know how he would handle failure. They had made friends from the college, a young couple who were sipping tea with Katie in the sitting room. The husband had to take the examination twice, but his family came from money and were able to fund an extra five months of study until he passed the exams. Prudence knew they could make it, too, but wasn't sure how her husband would feel about living off his wife for even longer, especially after such an initial failure.

She closed her eyes and thought back on their conversation at the train station earlier that week, a conversation that had been a revelation for her. With her emotional turmoil over Rowena and Sebastian still roiling in her stomach, she had kissed her husband on the cheek and wished him well, but that hadn't been enough for him. He'd taken her hands into his and bent his head down. His eyes had looked like green grass that morning and the quiet love she saw in them took her breath away.

"I know we didn't get married under the best of circumstances and I don't even know if I would have been your first choice." She'd started to hush him but he stopped her with his finger. "No. Let me say this." He took in a deep breath. "But that doesn't matter to me. I'll spend the rest of my life trying to make you happy. No matter what happens at the examination, I will always be grateful to the beautiful woman who gave me a chance, who believed in me like my own family never did." He bent his head and kissed her gloved fingertips. Tenderness filled her heart, leaving no more room for guilt. Yes, she loved Sebastian. Part of her would always love Sebastian, but for the first time, she knew without a doubt that her choice had been the right one. She trusted her future in the strong, capable hands of this good, good man.

He'd sent a telegram saying he would meet her not at the train station but at home. He didn't say whether he had passed the exams or not, and Prudence worried about her impromptu party. How would he feel if he didn't pass? Would he appreciate that his wife believed in him no matter what, or would he be humiliated to have his failure paraded in front of their friends?

She glanced at the clock on the mantel behind the stove and hurried to the window. Mr. and Mrs. Cash stood talking with Katie and sipping their tea. Mr. Cash was finishing up his first year of veterinary school while Mrs. Cash minded babies for a small weekly stipend. "The less money we have to get from my in-laws the better," she once said with a toss of her blonde head. Apparently they had not approved of their son's wife.

"There he is!" Katie said, pointing.

Prudence followed her pointing finger and spotted him about a block away. His steps were slow and uncertain, and fear clutched at her heart. He did not look like someone with anything to celebrate.

It's going to be fine, she told herself, though inside she was cursing herself for her spontaneous welcome-home party. She just wanted to show him how much she loved him. That even if she had had doubts in the past, she had pushed them aside. Andrew was her husband now. Not only was she building a happy life with him, but she was going to build a family with him as well. He deserved nothing less than her whole heart.

But nerves propelled her down the stairs and street. At least she would be able to warn him about the party.

He spotted her halfway down the block. She tried to gauge his success or failure by his face, but his hat shaded his eyes. He shook his head slowly and her heart plummeted. *Oh, why, Lord? Why couldn't you just let him pass? He is such a wonderful man.*

She launched herself at him down the street, not caring what she looked like. He caught her in his arms. "Oh, my darling, I am so sorry. Next time. You will get it next time, right, but I have to tell you, I did something . . ,"

She paused and he looked down at her, his eyes grave. "What did you do? Buy a piano in place of a bed? Adopt a pet hippopotamus from the zoo? Tell me, love, what mischief have you been up to?"

She grabbed him by the lapels and shook him a bit. "No, of course not. I'm being serious." She looked down at the ground. "I was so sure that you were going to pass your exams that I baked a cake and invited some friends over."

There was a moment's silence and then he put a finger under her chin and lifted her face to meet his gaze. "You mean you threw me a celebration party before you even knew for sure that I would pass?"

She nodded. To her surprise, tears welled up in his eyes. "I'm so lucky to have you, but you're even luckier," he said.

"Why is that?" she asked.

"Because I passed."

Her heart thudded against her rib cage. "You passed?"

He nodded and she leapt into his arms for a moment before turning to their building and lifting a victorious fist.

Then she turned to him and hit him in the chest. "You're horrible! I can't believe you did that to me."

272 ~◦ T. J. BROWN

He grinned, his green eyes laughing at her. "Just imagine. After four long years, I'll be a veterinarian. Can you wait that long
for a real home of your own?"

She nodded, more sure than she had ever been of her decisions. "Wherever you are will be our home," she told him.
Smiling, he took her hand and they headed to their flat.

* * *

Rowena sat in the conservatory and watched through the windows as Victoria and Kit strolled through the rose garden. The
roses were just beginning to bloom, that moment when every
blossom was precious and new, unlike later in June when the
garden would be a riot of colors and scents.

Victoria had been home for almost two weeks. When
Rowena had first seen her, she had broken down and cried at the
number of delicate bones that stuck so prominently out of Victoria's parchment paper–thin skin. She looked as if a stiff breeze
would blow her away to a place where no one would ever be able
to reach her again.

She even moved slowly, as if her bones were brittle and she
were afraid of breaking. Not like her old self at all. Even Aunt
Charlotte had cried, though she tried to hide it behind a handkerchief. Now she and Cook devoted hours planning food to
put flesh on Victoria's fragile frame. The family had never been
privy to so many cream soups and rich desserts.

Rowena wondered what kind of changes had been wrought
in Victoria that were unseen.

"Do you think he's going to ask her to marry him?"

Rowena jumped as Sebastian came up behind her. She smiled
and indicated the chair next to her. "I'm not sure. I think he
would be wise to wait. She needs time."

"She certainly seems changed, but how long do you think it will last?"

Rowena shrugged. "We can only guess at her experience and how it affected her. I know she's a lot quieter and much more serious than she used to be."

"Does she know about Martha and Lottie?"

Rowena took a deep, shuddering breath, tears at the edge of her voice. "I think she took their treatment of her worse than the prison sentence. They knew she was in prison but did nothing. They used her to get money for the cause and then disappeared when she needed them. She is such a trusting person. Or was."

They sat in silence, watching as Victoria threw back her head and laughed at something Kit said. "You know I was really concerned when those two became friends. He's such a cynical bastard. I was afraid he would hurt her."

Sebastian snorted. "Now I'm rather worried it will be the other way around. He's so smitten with her he can't even see straight."

"She always said she would never marry," Rowena mused.

"If anyone will change her mind, it'll be Kit. He has a silver tongue."

Sebastian put his hand over hers and she looked up in surprise. "What about you, Rowena? What are you going to do?"

She laughed, though tears slipped down her cheeks. "Is it that obvious?"

"It's hard to hide a broken heart." He looked back out the window, though his eyes seemed blind to the beauty outside. "Trust me, I know."

She turned her hand in his and gave it a warm squeeze. "We never did break off our engagement."

He laughed softly. "No. Between Victoria and everything else, there just never seemed to be a good time."

She nodded. "Well, no need to hurry on my account." Bitterness laced her words. "It seems as if Jon can't possibly get over the fact that I'm a Buxton." She shrugged, her eyes welling with tears. After spending the last few weeks crying over a man who wouldn't answer her letters, she had decided that she would no longer cry for him. He didn't love her as much as she did him and that was that. She was just lucky their lovemaking hadn't resulted in a child.

Sebastian said nothing, so she continued. "My family hurt his family, so apparently, we're not allowed to be together, even though I told him I would walk away from my family for him." She shrugged again and watched as Victoria and Kit disappeared behind a hedge of boxwoods.

Sebastian's laugh echoed the bitterness in her voice. "Prudence wouldn't trust me because of my position and wealth. Jon wouldn't marry you or trust you because of your wealth, position, and name. Who would have thought that being rich and titled would cost us both the people we love?"

She shook her head. "Who indeed?"

"There's no need to hurry on my account either. Prudence has been married for months now. There's no going back."

"No, there's no going back," Rowena said, though her heart ached at the thought of it.

"So we can just stay engaged, then?" His voice sounded casual, but there was something in it that caught her attention. She turned her head to see his face better. He stared toward the rose garden, his face still.

"What do you mean?" she finally asked.

"I think we make a good pair, Rowena. We have both been in love and have both had our hearts broken because of it, through no fault of our own. As an engaged couple, we'll get a lot less harassment from our families, which I'm sure you'll agree is a bonus."

He turned to her then. "Right now, I can't imagine ever feeling about someone the way I felt about Prudence, and I saw you with Jon. Can you ever love someone the way you loved him?"

Her breath caught and she shook her head.

"Do you want to end up alone?"

Again she shook her head.

"Neither do I. I think we could build a good marriage. A good life. Just think about it, Rowena, that's all I ask."

She nodded, her throat constricting at his kindness. No wonder Prudence loved him. What had she been thinking when she walked away from someone who loved her so much? Or perhaps she'd never known the extent of his love for her. Rowena prayed that Andrew would make Prudence as happy as Sebastian would have. "I will," she managed as soon as she could find the voice to speak.

He squeezed her fingers and they sat in silence until she heard footsteps behind her.

"I thought I would find you two out here," her uncle Conrad said. "Would you mind if I joined you?"

He pulled up a wicker chair and looked out over the gardens. "Your father redesigned the rose garden when he was just sixteen," he said after a moment. "Our father didn't want to make any changes to the estate, but Mother saw Philip's vision and insisted. And it turned out far more beautiful than it had been."

He was quiet as a maid brought them a silver tray with a pot of tea and cups. Rowena smiled her thanks as the maid handed her a cup. When she had gone, her uncle turned to her. "I fear I've rather neglected my duty as your uncle these past few months." Rowena tried to interrupt, but he held up a hand.

"No, I know it's true. I've been occupied with business and distracted by my own grief. I know you think I'm a hard man and in many ways I am, but I do love my family and try to do what is right by them."

He paused and Rowena's eyes widened. Could this be her staid, traditional uncle speaking this way? She turned to Sebastian but he shook his head, as bewildered as she was.

"You have spent most of the winter desperately unhappy and don't think I don't understand the part I played in your unhappiness."

Rowena's pulse raced. Prudence. He was talking about Prudence. Would he say her name?

"But I rarely waste time regretting my behavior, far preferring to make amends."

So no. Even now, after Prudence was so helpful with Victoria's internment, he couldn't bring himself to say her name.

"I don't understand, Uncle Conrad."

He smiled at them both. "I cannot describe how happy I was to find that you two had made the match." He nodded at Sebastian. "You and Elaine both know your mothers have been plotting your marriage for years, but I feel that you and Rowena are far better suited to each other. You are both far more thoughtful than my frivolous girl and I think you will take your roles seriously, within your modern sensitivities, of course."

Rowena shifted in her seat. She wasn't even sure she was going to accept Sebastian's proposal that they make their engagement real.

"I'd like to think my brother would be happy as well." He looked at the rose garden, a small smile playing over his lips. "I remember telling you once that your father and I frequently butted heads. Over almost everything, actually, even in how he brought up his children. But I have come to realize that he wasn't bringing you up to fit into our world; he was educating you to fit into the modern world. I've watched the past few months as both you and Victoria have bashed about, trying to fit into a world that you were never meant to inhabit."

Tears filled Rowena's eyes. Her uncle understood far more than she had ever imagined.

"So I spoke to your intended to get an idea of what you might like for an engagement gift, what might make you even just a bit like the happy, cheerful girl who used to spend every summer here. What he told me, young lady, shocked me to my very soul, but in my eagerness to become a part of the new century, I followed his advice."

She frowned, glancing at Sebastian, who was trying to hide a smile.

"You didn't have to get us anything, Uncle," she said uncomfortably.

"Not get my own niece an engagement present? I think not."

Rowena watched him suspiciously. She'd never seen her uncle show this kind of suppressed emotion before, as if he had a secret he was dying to share.

Uncle Conrad pulled a couple of slender cigars out of his pocket and handed one to Sebastian. After he lit his, he handed his lighter to Sebastian, who did the same.

"Besides, it's too late. Your very own Vickers biplane will be delivered to Brooklands Aero Club in Surrey in about a month. They have an aeronautic school there that actually admits women. In fact, Hilda Hewlett was one of the founders, as well as becoming the first woman to be granted a pilot's license."

Rowena put a hand over her mouth. "How did you know? Why would you do that for me?"

Her uncle picked up her hand and gave her fingers a squeeze. "After talking with Sebastian, I contacted Mr. Dirkes and he told me that you had been spending a great deal of time at the airfield and that you wished to get your pilot's license. Then he gave me a ten-minute lecture on how the times are changing. I don't truly subscribe to his motto of adapt or die, but I think I am adapting just a bit." Her uncle looked smug at his own growth.

"I still can't believe you're doing this for me," she said. She wanted to accept. God knew she wanted to accept. She would be one of how many civilians to own her own aeroplane? One hundred in all of Britain? And surely the only woman!

But though her uncle didn't know it, accepting the aeroplane meant accepting Sebastian's suggestion that they make their engagement real, and she wasn't sure she could do that. Wouldn't that be the same as admitting that things with Jon were truly finished forever?

She drummed her fingers on the arm of her chair. But in reality, wasn't that the truth? Could she ever forgive him for walking away from her? For refusing to fight for their love?

She turned to him suddenly, a smile lighting up her face. "Uncle, I thank you so much for your kindness. I can't even imagine what it must have taken for you to allow your niece to become a pilot."

"I'm not nearly as backward as you think I am. Mr. Dirkes was doing his best to talk me into it and then I thought about your father and how proud of you he would have been."

Her throat tightened. "Do you really think so?"

He nodded. "Yes, I think he would have been."

Her chest tightened with too many emotions too express.

Excitement, regret, anticipation, and loss fought for supremacy in her heart. "Thank you, Uncle Conrad." A tear slipped down her cheek and she leaned forward and threw her arms around her uncle's neck.

He patted her shoulder in that awkward way he had before moving away from her.

"No tears, Rowena. The time for tears is over. Look how lovely the weather is. Spring has come and it's time for things to begin anew."

* * *

Victoria leaned on Kit's arm far more than a stroll through the gardens would necessitate. But then, her confinement, poor prison food, and lack of exercise had weakened her already frail body. Cook had taken to whipping up new culinary creations for her to try and Nanny Iris brought a new kind of tea or medicine almost every day. Everyone, it seemed, was concerned about getting some "flesh on her bones."

Victoria had spent the recent weeks of her freedom thinking about what she had done that led to her downfall. For it was a downfall. She wasn't proud of her prison sentence as so many other suffragettes were. She knew the truth. She was only there because she had been so easily duped. Instead of seeing a serious woman with valuable skills, Martha, Lottie, and Mary had seen a child so eager to prove herself that she wouldn't stop to think about what she was doing. Her uncle had done some checking and was fairly certain Martha and Lottie hadn't disappeared for nefarious purposes, but rather had simply been fearful of being implicated in the *Rokeby Venus* scandal and had closed down the London offices and opened up shop in Liverpool. Victoria hoped that, if nothing else, the money she raised was doing some good for women who needed it.

Her pace slowed and Kit bent his head, concern in his keen blue eyes. "Are you all right? Would you like to go in?"

"Oh, stop fussing so. You're getting to be such an old woman. Just find me a bench, would you?"

Without warning, he picked her up and tossed her over his shoulder. His long legs meandered this way and that while she pounded on his back, laughing. Lord, she had missed him. But after her release, she immediately noticed that the tenor of their relationship had changed. Now she proceeded carefully, hoping that he wouldn't be so bold as to put voice to the feelings she read on his face.

Didn't he know that would ruin everything?

He settled her down onto a bench and sat next to her. She turned her face up to the last rays of the sun. She'd missed the sun while she'd been in her cell. She'd missed so much.

"Are you sure you feel all right?" he asked.

She detected the worry in his voice. "I'll tell you when I don't."

"So I've been wondering about something," he said, his tone so casual that she immediately put her guard up. "Could you explain to me exactly what your problem with marriage is? It's an institution that has survived thousands of years."

"And it will go on to survive a thousand more without my help. Honestly, did you never listen when I told you I didn't want to get married?"

He snorted. "Trust me. I am well aware. I just want to know why."

She sighed. Obviously, she was going to have to explain

herself over and over until he understood. "I am only nineteen, for one thing. I want to live my life the way I want to without worrying about what my husband will or won't let me do. Why is marriage supposed to be the height of my ambition when clearly it isn't yours, considering you've reached the ripe old age of twenty-five without succumbing? Besides, I have everything figured out."

"Of course you do," he said drily. "When have you not?"

"No, listen. I've been talking to my uncle and he has given me some very good ideas. I am going to move to London and work. Real work, like teaching impoverished women to read and write. I've never dedicated myself to such a fulfilling pursuit as when I taught in . . . in prison."

"Your uncle would never agree to that," Kit scoffed.

"That shows how much you know! He's the one who suggested it. I plan on spending the rest of the summer here to recuperate and then move in with Eleanor. He's fond of Eleanor, and she is a nurse, so I will be well looked after."

"You promised me you were going to look after your health. How are you going to do that living and working in the bowels of London?"

"I won't be living in the bowels of London. I will get a flat in a fashionable part of London, perhaps Kensington or St. James. Uncle will probably insist on giving me a car and driver, so I won't even be out in the cold. Now stop being such a grump."

Kit sighed, and she could see that there was still more he wanted to say. But she was grateful that, for now, he was leaving it unsaid.

She smiled, looking out at the beautiful rose garden her father had designed. Then she quoted:

"They are not long, the days of wine and roses,
Out of a misty dream
Our path emerges for a while, then closes
Within a dream."

"I always thought Dowson was a rather lonely chap," Kit mused.

"Mm-hmm." Victoria stood and held out her hand. "Come, my dearest friend. Let's walk through the roses and watch them bloom."

AUTHOR'S NOTE

As an author, I have always dreamed of living in a foreign country to write and do research. I can envision myself wandering the streets of Rome, Paris, or London, taking pictures, making notes and breathing in the atmosphere to help create the perfect setting within my books. But I realized something as I began doing research for the Summerset series—1914 London does not exist.

Even if I were to hop on a plane and wing my way across the Atlantic, the London I lived and breathed for months would not be waiting for me. So authors of historical novels have a unique disadvantage when compared with our contemporaries who write more modern fare—the worlds we are writing about have passed away and can only be discovered in photographs, paintings and drawings, literature, history books, and newspapers.

In truth, historical authors are much like detectives trying to put together the pieces to make a coherent whole. Most of the time we accomplish this beautifully. We wouldn't be writing historical fiction if we didn't love and appreciate history. Historical authors think research is fun and many of us would give an eyetooth to be able to go back and experience the time period we're writing about firsthand.

The following are just a few of the many Internet resources

I used in assembling the world of Summerset Abbey. As always, any inaccuracies in the book are mine and not the fault of the resources I used, nor of my fabulous research assistant and Edwardian expert, Evangeline Holland: www.edwardian promenade.com

WEBSITES
The British Newspaper Archive: www.britishnewspaper
   archive.co.uk
David Cohen Fine Art (Art of World War I):
   www.davidcohenfineart.com
BBC Learning Zone (A sound recording of a suffragette):
   http://www.bbc.co.uk/learningzone/clips/a-suffragette
   -describes-her-actions/9877.html
Manor House: http://www.pbs.org/manorhouse/edwardian
   life/introduction.html

BOOKS
The Perfect Summer: England 1911, Before the War, by Juliet
   Nicolson
*Consuelo and Alva Vanderbilt: The Story of a Mother and
   Daughter in the Gilded Age,* by Amanda Mackenzie Stewart

SUMMERSET ABBEY: A BLOOM IN WINTER
T. J. BROWN

After Prudence's desperate marriage and move to London, sisters Rowena and Victoria fear they have lost their beloved friend forever. Guilt-ridden and remorseful, Rowena seeks comfort from a daring flyboy and suddenly finds herself embracing the most dangerous activity the world has ever seen. Her younger sister Victoria, in a desperate attempt to prove herself, defies her family and her illness to make her own dream occupation as a botanist come true . . . but she instead finds herself lured into a dangerous and controversial society dedicated to the fight for women's suffrage.

As England and the world step closer to conflict, the three young women flout their family, their upbringing and their heritage to seize a modern future of their own making.

QUESTIONS AND TOPICS FOR DISCUSSION

1. *Summerset Abbey: A Bloom in Winter* picks up a few months after the final scene of *Summerset Abbey*. In the opening chapters, we are swiftly updated on the lives of our three heroines: Victoria is more determined than ever to prove that she's no longer a child as she follows in her father's footsteps to pursue a career as a botanist; Rowena seems as gloomy and listless as the gray winter skies, given that she

hasn't seen Jon since they shared a passionate kiss at the end of *Summerset Abbey;* and Prudence is living in squalor, trying to find a way to love her husband as much as he loves her. How does each of the circumstances illustrated in the early pages of the novel correspond to your expectations for how these women's lives would be impacted by the surprising turn of events at the end of *Summerset Abbey*?

2. Victoria claims that she signed her article for *The Botanist's Quarterly* as "V. Buxton" rather than "Victoria" because she wants to be known for her own merits rather than those of her father, and because it sounds more "impressive" (p. 11). Were you surprised that Victoria never actually intended to mask her gender behind her pseudonym? Is Victoria too optimistic about the state of gender equality—perhaps due to her liberal upbringing—or is she just too naïve?

3. Aunt Charlotte can be considered the villain of *Summerset Abbey,* and yet she's a much softer character in this second novel in the series now that Prudence has been cast out of Summerset. Did you anticipate this change in Lady Summerset, or did you expect her to be just as conniving in *Summerset Abbey: A Bloom in Winter*? Or do you feel that she's just as manipulative as she was in *Summerset Abbey,* but in a subtler way?

4. Did you expect Prudence's life with Andrew to be so squalid, especially following the letter that Susie describes in the opening chapter, or did you see through her Prudence's lies from the outset? Can you relate to Prudence's desire to paint a completely different picture of her life to her friends rather than revealing the truth?

5. Consider Mr. Herbert's argument as to why he refuses to hire a woman to write for *The Botanist's Quarterly*. Each of

his arguments represents a widespread belief held by many at the time. Which of these arguments would most enrage you were it used against you or someone you know today?

6. Rowena's family history proves a major obstacle in her quest for happiness with Jon. Considering George's position in the Wells family in the wake of his father's death, as well as the rigid division of social classes at the time, do you find George's unwavering resentment of Rowena due to the actions of her uncle extreme, or do you understand his reasons for wanting to keep her away from Jon?

7. Victoria's illness clearly affects the way others view and treat her. Consider how both Victoria's asthma and her position as the youngest sister in her family motivate her decisions in this novel. When she can't help but shed tears following her rejection by the editor of *The Botanist's Quarterly,* she wonders how she can expect anyone to "take her seriously" if she keeps "acting like a child" (p. 67). Do you see her illness and her role in her family as main motivations behind her desire to become involved in the women's suffrage movement, given her pressing desire to prove that she's an independent adult?

8. Muriel calls the housekeeping lessons that she gives Prudence "lessons in slavery and servitude" (p. 69). Did this statement surprise you? Do you find it to be indicative of the changing attitudes toward women's rights at the time, or do you think that this attitude is specific to the particularly sharp-tongued Muriel?

9. Describe Martha as she's reflected in Victoria's awestruck and impressionable gaze, and then describe her objectively. Do you find her manipulative, or simply misguided by her overzealous passion for women's rights? Do you think that

Prudence's desire to become involved in the movement is driven in some way by her desire to be more like Martha, who seems so bold, confident, and in control of her life?

10. Consider Kit's reaction to the announcement of the (faux) engagement between Sebastian and Rowena. "Shall I never see a bachelor of three score again?" he laments (p. 146). Were you surprised by his outrage, or, given Kit's own muddled romantic status, does his anger at the prospect of losing one of his best friends to an institution he claims to despise ring true? Can you relate to Kit's fear of losing a friendship over a relationship?

11. Rowena's affection for Jon seems inextricably intertwined with her passion for flying. Do you think that Rowena would have the same feelings for Jon if he wasn't also her gateway to flying planes?

12. Additionally, what is it about piloting airplanes that has Rowena so enamored, and how are those reasons different from or similar to Victoria's own passion for the women's suffrage movement? In what way are these women's passions—and the reasons behind them—indicative of the limitations placed on them by their social statuses, and by society at large?

13. Were you shocked by the severity of Victoria's sentence given her role in Mary's crime? How did Victoria evolve while serving her sentence? Do you see this experience as formative as it was traumatizing for Victoria? In what way?

14. Additionally, how do you feel about Martha's abandonment of Victoria in the wake of the crime? Did this color your impression of Martha, or is this in line with the type of behavior that you'd expect from her? Why?

15. Given the tenor of Kit and Victoria's friendship in *Summerset Abbey*, did you expect romantic feelings to ever develop between them? Are you excited for the possibility of a romantic rapport between the two of them, or would you prefer that their relationship remain platonic? Why?

16. *Summerset Abbey: Spring Awakening* is the third and final installment in the *Summerset Abbey* trilogy. Speculate on what the future holds for our three heroines, as well as the male leads. What do you anticipate will likely happen in the final tome? If you could write *Summerset Abbey: Spring Awakening*, how would you conclude these women's stories?

ENHANCE YOUR BOOK CLUB

1. T. J. Brown drew quite a bit of inspiration for the scenes in which Victoria languishes in prison from personal accounts of suffragettes who were imprisoned (sometimes more than once!) for the cause. Visit the website http://www.alicesuf fragette.co.uk/audio.html#prisonnotes to listen to recordings of suffragette Alice Hawkins's own letters and notes from prison.

2. Prudence's storyline centers on her struggle to settle into her new life as a homemaker and wife to an aspiring veterinarian, and one of her biggest obstacles is cooking. Create a dish like one Prudence would have had to learn from Muriel to serve to your book group, like meat pies or scones. Do you relate to her struggles in the kitchen after attempting these recipes?

3. Host a viewing party of the PBS series *Downton Abbey* or a similar series such as *Upstairs Downstairs*. If the *Summerset*

Abbey novels were made into a film or television series, who would you cast, and why? Which role would you most like to play?

4. Learn more about author T. J. Brown and the women of Summerset by visiting her website: http://www.tjbrown books.com